JIHADI
APPRENTICE

DAVID BRUNS
AND J.R. OLSON

JIHADI
APPRENTICE

THANKS TO ALL OUR SUPPORTERS

This paperback edition of *Jihadi Apprentice* would not have been possible without the generous support of our Kickstarter backers. Our sponsors are listed below in the order in which they backed the campaign.

Colleen & Tim Herold
Holly Holdgraf Baker
LtCol Alex Plechash, USMC (ret.)
Pam Olson
Dave Priddy, USNA '80
CAPT Chip Sharratt, US Navy, USNA '74
Chris Pourteau
Preston Leigh of The Leighgendarium
Jon Redmond, USMA – Beat Navy!
Carolyn, Chris, Zac & Tristan Johnson
Jay Bentivolio, USN
Frances Rowat
Cody Bruns
Dick and Regina Bruns
Kelly Pickens
James Fenhouse
Glenn Dyer
Jason Feipel, USNA '08
Alex Cabrera
Steve, Tara, and Ella Hanson
Jeff Hohn
Eric and Jennifer Schumacher
Jerry Witowski
John Davis
Jessica Wyn Miller
Rich Goodheart
David Ratte
Edward Braun

Joe Symeonides
Natalie
Reggie Bowerman
Jim Conn
Henry and Doris Schumacher
Captain Mark J. Salmen, USN (Ret.)
Chris and Duncan Hart
Shemi Hart
Keith & Davis Meyer and James Bauman
James Densley
Roderick Davidson
Ardy Johnson
Chris Bentley, USNA '79
Bill Sykes
Brett Seiling, USAFA '94, Beat Navy!
Stephanie Johnson
Michael Light
Shannon Fouts
Doug Baden
Tim and Sue Kennedy
Espen Sae-Tang Ottersen
Sarah Kolb-Williams
Michael Farley
Megan Bartell
Marit Brock
Tony Bradshaw
Tom Wiesen
Ed Wallin

For Larry Olson,
decimated by Alzheimer's

You may never be able to read this book,
but I know you support everything I do.

Love, JR

CHAPTER 1

Minneapolis, Minnesota
18 November 2016 — 2120 local

The headscarf itched. *Hijab*, Liz reminded herself.

She drew the indigo-blue material tighter against her neck as she weaved through the knots of people, food trucks, and craft tables outside the Cedar Cultural Center in downtown Minneapolis. The crowd attending the Muslim-American Arts Festival seemed on the youngish side—Liz guessed most were in their late teens and early twenties—and much more diverse than your average Minnesota crowd. She heard mostly English, peppered liberally with Somali and some Arabic. She even picked up a distant side conversation in her family's native Farsi, but didn't dare show any interest.

Liz caught sight of her mark entering the theater: Zacharia Ismail, Somali-American, twenty years old, and hopefully their path to capturing Hamza, one of the FBI's most wanted al-Shabab operatives. Hamza had grown up in the Minneapolis

Somali community. Eighteen months ago, without telling a soul, he boarded a flight for Mogadishu and joined al-Shabab. Hamza had stayed in touch with his friends in Minneapolis, using social media to recruit new members to his cause—six in the last twelve months.

According to their sources, Hamza was back, rumored to be in Minneapolis on a recruiting trip.

Not for the first time, Liz reflected on how normal Zacharia seemed. When they observed him, listened to his phone calls, read his email and texts, he seemed like a normal young American. Good-looking, too. With close-cropped hair, broad shoulders, and a ready smile, Zacharia Ismail looked more like a starting quarterback on the football team than a potential terrorist. But then again, those were the best kind of terrorists—the ones that hide in plain sight.

Don't get ahead of yourself, girl. One step at a time.

She slipped her ticket out of her hip pocket. "*Soo dhowow.* Welcome." The attendant scanned her ticket, then held onto it when she tried to take it back. "I like your *hijab*," he said with a wide smile. "Very pretty."

Liz tugged firmly on the ticket and it came free. "Thank you." She did not return the smile.

The dark blue material woven with a silvery thread was beautiful, but Liz wondered if maybe she'd overdone it on style. At the pre-mission briefing, it had frustrated her to no end how much time the men—and they were nearly all men—devoted to whether or not FBI Special Agent Elizabeth Soroush was or was not going to cover her hair.

We're trying to catch a freaking terrorist, she wanted to scream at them, *and all you can talk about is what I'm going to wear.*

"I'll do it," she finally said. "It'll cover my earpiece, anyway."

2

But I'm wearing Western clothes—and no more discussion on the matter." Her outfit for the evening was dress jeans, her favorite pair of ankle-high boots, and a white silk blouse. Her short leather jacket concealed the shoulder holster containing her service weapon, a Sig Sauer P320.

She stepped into the theater, a cinder block–walled room about the size of a high school gymnasium. In fact, with its high ceilings and wooden floor, it looked *exactly* like a high school gymnasium. On the far wall, a small stage rose a few feet above the floor with an array of dimmed lights hanging above it.

Liz found a spot against the wall where she could observe Zacharia. "I'm in," she whispered. "I have the target in sight."

"Roger that, Liz." The deep voice of Tom Trask sounded in her earpiece. "Any sign of our suspect?"

"Negative, but our guy's head is on a swivel." Zacharia had met up with a group of friends and greeted them with a combination of fist bumps and elaborate handshakes, but his eyes traveled across the room as if he were seeking someone in the crowd.

"This is Rambo. I concur. He's looking for someone." They'd had to go outside the Minneapolis field office to find "culturally appropriate" agents for this op. Martin Ramboni was of Ethiopian-Italian descent. As Trask had told her in an unguarded moment, Martin got his looks from his Ethiopian mother and his attitude from his Italian father. For God's sake, the man insisted on being called "Rambo."

"Heads up, people, we've got incoming," said their third agent, Gus Vallens. Gus was from somewhere in Latin America, but had the kind of multicultural face that seemed to blend into any setting. A good agent, too. She'd take Gus over Rambo any day of the week.

Liz pushed herself off the wall, sidling closer to Zacharia

and his friends. A pair of young women had approached the Somali boys. The shorter of the two harangued Zacharia while the other hung back and smiled at him shyly. Both of the girls wore long, loose robes and tight-fitting headscarves that draped over their shoulders and upper torsos. If this was a meet, the body language was all wrong. The girl talking acted too familiar with Zacharia, too open for this to be a clandestine connection. Liz angled her approach so she could get a glimpse of the shorter girl's face.

"Relax, everyone, it's the sister," she said. Liz could not recall the sister's name. She was a high school senior, average grades, with a round, unremarkable face. Her presence on social media was similarly bland. Nothing to worry about there.

The hall was more than three-quarters full now with plenty more people pouring in. Must be a pretty popular warm-up act. The overhead lights dimmed as Liz squinted at her ticket.

Imaan. The Arabic word for "faith."

A lone female voice soared out of the darkness. It was a pure tone, without accompaniment, both soulful and hopeful at the same time, husky with promise. Liz caught her breath, turning toward the sound. It had been a long time since any music had affected her like that.

Zacharia and his mates, along with everyone else in the audience, moved closer to the stage. The silhouetted singer raised her arms, swaying with the music, as her band started to underpin her voice with a soft beat and a bass line that settled in Liz's gut. The singer started into a melody and Liz caught the Somali words for "home" and "mother." The people around her swayed and mouthed the lyrics.

In the dark and the crush of bodies around her, Liz lost sight of Zacharia. "I've lost visual contact," she whispered. A girl next to her glared at her for making noise.

"Rambo and Gus, do you have him in sight?" Trask's voice was tight with tension.

"Negative," Rambo replied.

"No—wait," Gus said. "I see Hamza! I'm moving in."

Gus was stationed to her left. Liz shouldered her way into the crowd, heedless of the angry spectators who hissed at her along the way. The crowd thinned on the margins and Liz pushed herself to go faster.

As the ethereal music of Imaan floated through the theater, Liz broke into an open area. Hamza was there, wearing the same lop-sided grin and shaggy Afro as in his high school yearbook picture they'd used to identify him. The al-Shabab fighter looked more like a kid out on a Friday night than a terrorist recruiter. He raised his hand to someone in the crowd, but the smile froze on his face.

"FBI—freeze!" Gus entered the space, badge hanging from his neck, weapon drawn.

A blur of shadow flashed in Liz's peripheral vision and Zacharia tackled Gus. Gus's weapon boomed, freezing the entire room. The beautiful music was buried under the screams of a panicked crowd. Hamza dove into the wall of milling people.

"He's running!" Liz shouted. "Rambo, cover the front exit. I've got Hamza." She whipped out her weapon and plunged after him.

They had all the external exits covered, but Hamza had somehow gotten in here undetected, so Liz was taking no chances. She caught a glimpse of him fighting his way through the crowd, but there was no way to get off a clean shot with all these people around.

He's headed for the stage. He's going to go out through the backstage.

Liz shouldered aside another man and she had a clear view of her target. "Freeze, Hamza! FBI!" He threw a look over his shoulder but didn't slow down as he ducked behind the stage.

"No you don't!" Liz ripped off the headscarf and sprinted after him down the narrow corridor. If he managed to reach the double doors and get backstage, who knew how many hiding places or hostages he'd have access to.

She was gaining on him. Liz dove, stretching out her fingers as far as she could reach. She snagged a loose shoelace and held on. The nylon cord ripped into her skin, but she managed to hold onto a shred of plastic encasing the end of the shoelace. Liz pulled as hard as she could.

Hamza lost his balance and sprawled out. His head slammed into the metal doorframe and he lay still. Liz scrambled to her feet, training her gun on the prone form. The young man's dirty jeans and T-shirt hung loosely on his thin frame. Liz couldn't see a weapon.

"Hands where I can see them, Hamza!" she yelled.

The terrorist didn't reply.

"Do it now!" Liz advanced and kicked him in the leg.

No movement.

Liz stepped around him until she could see his face. His eyes were open, his neck at an odd angle.

"Shit." Liz knelt next to him and placed two fingers on his carotid. No pulse. "Team leader, I'm at the backstage entrance. Suspect is down. I don't want to move him. I think his neck is broken. Send an EMT team now."

Liz stepped back and blew out a long breath as FBI agents and paramedics swarmed around her.

Liz watched the paramedics place Hamza's corpse into a black body bag and lift it onto a gurney. After the EMTs pronounced him deceased, she'd been allowed to search his body. She'd found nothing, not even a burner phone, on his person. How did he get from Somalia back to Minneapolis? Who were his local contacts? Hamza went to his death with all that intel.

They were back at square one.

"It's not your fault, Liz," came Trask's voice from behind her. He placed a comforting hand on her shoulder. "He ran. Sometimes bad things happen to bad people. Mr. Hamza's number was up."

Liz shook off his hand. "What about the kid who tackled Gus? Zacharia?"

"Rambo's talking to him now. We're taking him into custody, but he claims he never saw Gus's badge, only the gun. He reacted to a threat, he says. Saving innocent lives—that's his story."

A Minneapolis cop broke in to ask Trask about questioning the rest of the audience. It was going to be a long night. Liz spun on her heel.

"Watch out for the sister," Trask called. "Name's Ayana. She's a firecracker, that one."

In Liz's estimation, Zacharia's sister was about thirty seconds away from being arrested for obstructing justice. The girl's *hijab* was askew, probably from the way she was waving her arms as she screeched at Rambo.

"My brother has done nothing wrong! You cannot come into our community with your guns and your badges and arrest people. He was only trying to protect innocent people from getting hurt."

Liz inserted herself between the girl and Rambo. "Can I help you, miss?"

The young woman shut up and took a step back as the FBI

agent invaded her personal space. Liz studied her face. The eyes beneath the black *hijab* were large and brown, flared with anger. She had a squat nose and narrow mouth that turned down at the corners. Her round face was devoid of makeup.

One of the local officers handed Liz her blue and silver headscarf. The girl's eyes widened and she looked as if she might spit at Liz.

"You! It was you! Where is my cousin? Hamza? What have you done with him?"

If she was upset before, the girl seemed positively thermonuclear now. Liz took a step back. This was about to get ugly.

"Perhaps I can help, officer?" The silky voice was like a bucket of cold water on the flames of the confrontation. The Somali girl pulled up short, her mouth agape.

"Imaan," she whispered.

"Yes, my child, it'll be alright." The woman slipped her arm around the girl and faced Liz. Maybe it was the contrast with the dowdy young woman, or maybe the lighting, but Imaan was . . . *mesmerizing* was the only word that came to Liz's mind.

Tall and willowy, she stood more than a head above her young charge. She wore a beautiful pink and blue headscarf over a Western hairstyle that allowed glossy dark hair to spill over her shoulders. A dark blue sheath dress clung to her curves, and she finished the outfit with a pair of black Manolo Blahniks that Liz knew cost at least a thousand dollars.

The singer extended her hand to Liz. "I'm Imaan, the singer whose concert you interrupted." Her ringed fingers were cool to the touch and a jumble of golden bangles tumbled down her slender wrist. Liz found herself blushing.

"We're—um, we're sorry about that, ma'am—Imaan. We were after a fugitive—"

"What will happen to Ayana's brother?" Imaan squeezed the girl's shoulders in a gentle hug. Ayana seemed to have forgotten all about her brother. She stared intently up at the singer.

Liz hardened her tone. "We'll be taking Zacharia in for questioning—"

"How long can you hold him, officer . . . ?"

"Agent, actually. FBI Special Agent Elizabeth Soroush. We can hold Zacharia for up to twenty-four hours unless—"

"Then we'll expect to see him released tomorrow."

Imaan steered the girl toward the exit.

21 Sep 2016

MEMORANDUM

FROM: Commander, Naval Special Warfare
        Development Group

TO: Secretary of Defense

VIA: Commander, Joint Special Operations Command
        Chairman, Joint Chiefs of Staff

SUBJ: AFTER ACTION REPORT – RAID ON AL-SHABAB
        COMPOUND

Executive Overview

Mission: To capture or kill the leader of the al-Shabab terrorist organization, Abdulkadir Mohamed Abdulkadir, also known by the nom-de-guerre Ikrima, as well as any other high-ranking al-Shabab militants near the town of Baraawe, Somalia.

Mission Date/Time: 15 September 2016, 0000Z – 0305Z (time ashore)

Mission Outcome: Raid failed due to early discovery by guard forces protecting Ikrima and his leadership circle; overwhelming and reinforced enemy defense precipitated withdrawal by raid force.

It is believed Ikrima and most/all of his top echelon leaders escaped and remain alive. Further post-raid analysis indicates a much higher level of readiness and area coordination than believed possible from autonomous al-Shabab units.

Based on follow-on communications, it is possible that Ikrima may have established a working relationship with Daesh.

Casualties: Minor injuries to four assault force commandos; numerous al-Shabab fighters killed or wounded. Casualty figures among non-combatants are unknown.

<u>Mission Summary</u> – See Attachment A

<u>Recommendations</u>

Raid force commander recommends dedicated reconnaissance element be used prior to any future assault. While excellent coverage is provided by REAPER UAV, patterns of movement are best assessed by special operations forces with expertise in reconnaissance missions.

Recommend larger raid force with dedicated close air support provided by AC-130 SPECTRE if future assault is ordered. Precision close air support from SPECTRE gunship would have alleviated numerical advantage by al-Shabab fighters in the compound and the reinforcements which arrived shortly after the firefight began.

Recommend additional intel assets establish or disprove possible linkages between Ikrima and Daesh.

Classified By: Commander, Joint Special Operations Command
Declassify On: Manual Review

Copy To:
Secretary of State
National Security Advisor
Commander, US Africa Command
Commander, US Special Operations Command
Director of National Intelligence (copy to: Director, National Counterterrorism Center)
Chief of Naval Operations (copy to: OPNAV N3, OPNAV N2/N6)
Director, Central Intelligence Agency (copy to: Deputy Director for National Clandestine Service)
Director, National Security Agency
Director, Defense Intelligence Agency
Director, National Geospatial Intelligence Agency
Director, Federal Bureau of Investigation (copy to: National Security Branch, CT Operations)

CHAPTER 2

The president-elect flipped over the last page of the report. She let the page rest for a long moment before she turned back to the beginning and its blaring red classification header. She put it on top of the other intel summary reports in the stack.

She'd known al-Shabab was active, but not to this extent. While Islamic State or Daesh had grabbed all the headlines, al-Shabab was creating chaos in Kenya, Somalia, and the rest of Eastern Africa. If these reports were right, al-Shabab under the leadership of Ikrima was directly responsible for the deaths of over two hundred people in the last year alone—a fact barely mentioned in the Western press. A US drone strike in March 2016 had set them back, but with this Ikrima character still on the loose, al-Shabab was back in business within weeks.

"That's quite a story, Jack," she said. "It's a wonder we've been able to keep it out of the news this long." The report she'd just read was a wake-up call to the world she was about to face as president. While the 2016 election was coming down to the wire, her predecessor had tried a more direct approach to take out Ikrima. The SEAL raid on the al-Shabab compound not only failed, they'd pretty much gotten their asses handed to them. Four casualties, but no one killed, thank God.

"Yes, ma'am." He'd sat there still as a piece of furniture for the last thirty minutes while she read the entire file. Thirty precious minutes in her transition team's schedule was like a week in real life. Tomorrow was Thanksgiving and all she had off was an hour for dinner with her family.

This was the problem with actually winning an election. You never really knew for sure what you'd gotten yourself into until after you'd gotten yourself into it.

And those who wanted to do damage to America didn't take time off for elections—or Thanksgiving.

A tension headache was building in that familiar spot at the base of her skull. She resisted the urge to close her eyes. No time for that now.

"So how about you tell me what's not in the report, Jack?"

"Ma'am?" Retired Vice Admiral Jack Daugherty seemed genuinely surprised. He shifted in his chair, careful to keep the expensive charcoal-gray suit from hunching up around his shoulders.

He wears the suit like a uniform, she thought.

The president-elect placed her palms flat on the table and stared into Daugherty's eyes. "We need to establish some ground rules, Jack. As my Director of National Intelligence, I need you to help me keep this country safe. Anybody can read a report. I need someone who can turn that report into action steps." She paused and stood, waving for Daugherty to remain seated. Her back was killing her. She walked stiffly to the window where a bitter November rain streaked the glass. Low fog clung to the South Lawn of the White House.

"The challenges are overwhelming right now. We've got Putin mucking around in Ukraine, the Chinese are building islands in the South China Sea, Turkey is on the verge of collapse, and God knows if Iran will behave under the new nuclear agreement—at least that one's up to them. Daesh or ISIS or whatever we're calling them this week is making hay while the sun shines in Iraq and Syria. The one bright spot in all this mess was that we had al-Qaeda on the run . . . now you're telling me that al-Shabab in Somalia is dropping al-Qaeda to form an alliance with Daesh? How many Somalis do we have in this country?"

"Approximately a hundred thousand, ma'am, but the majority have no connection with Somalia today—more than half of them were born here."

"I'm sure Fox News and the Freedom Caucus in the House will share your confidence about our immigrant population, Jack. You and I know it only takes one bad actor—what do you guys call them?"

"HVEs—homegrown violent extremists."

The president-elect returned to her chair. "So what's it going to be, Jack? Do you have what it takes to be my DNI?"

"Yes, ma'am."

She studied him again and noted that he met her gaze without hesitation. He would do nicely. Far better than that snake the party wanted her to appoint for Secretary of Defense.

"Good. Then let's have a real conversation, shall we? Let's start with this report." She picked it up and let it fall to the table with a slap. "What's the moral of the story?"

"Application of force, ma'am," the admiral replied. "We tried to do this op with the bare minimum of assets, relying on the element of surprise."

"So what would you have recommended, Jack?"

"Overwhelming force. JSOC, air assault, recon teams in place prior, the full monty. If it's worth doing, it's worth doing it all the way, no pussyfooting around."

She nodded. "I agree. What about this al-Shabab situation? Where's the largest Somali population in this country?"

"Minneapolis, ma'am." He hesitated. "That was also the site of the failed terrorist bombing in September, if you recall."

Recall? How could she forget? A nuclear weapon on US soil. If that bomb had gone off, she probably wouldn't be sitting in this chair right now. Thank God *that* never made the news cycle.

"Alright, Minneapolis and al-Shabab is as good a place as any to start." She glanced at her watch. "You've got another ten minutes. Tell me what you want to do in the great American Midwest."

CHAPTER 3

Most of Aya's friends stayed after sunset prayers this evening. Her true friends, anyway. She knew that a few of them had families that actually celebrated the American holiday of Thanksgiving. A few even prepared turkeys.

Not her parents. They observed the Muslim holy days exclusively. The rest of the holidays were for infidels.

Although she would never admit it, Aya secretly wished her parents would try to fit in more, try to be more American. Her father rambled on about the good old days in Mogadishu, but he was never going back. He could barely finish a shift in his taxi without Zacharia taking over—his back was that bad. To make ends meet, her mother ran a small coffee shop in the Karmel Mall, the local marketplace for the Somali community. She pretended the earnings from the shop were actually her husband's wages from driving the taxi. They all pretended, for her father's sake.

"Aya, how's Zacharia doing?" asked her friend, Caaliyah. "How is he handling Hamza's death?"

They all wanted to know about her handsome brother, but no one asked about her. Inside she still seethed from that night.

"Death?" she spat back. "You mean Hamza's murder? When Imaan took me away I was on the verge of being arrested—" She stopped when she saw the other girls exchange glances. They didn't believe that she'd actually met Imaan. After a few days, even Aya had started to doubt her own memory of that evening.

Caaliyah looked toward the door and gasped.

"It's good to see you again, Ayana." Imaan herself entered the women's prayer room and strode straight up to Aya. The singer kissed the girl on both cheeks. Not a stiff embrace, but a warm hug, like between friends. Her hand lingered protectively on Aya's shoulder.

"I'm leaving tomorrow for Europe, but I wanted to see how you were doing before I left." Imaan's voice was rich and warm, making Aya blush. Her friends gaped at the international superstar—and Aya's friend. Imaan's hand tightened on her shoulder. "Maybe you could introduce me to your friends?"

"This is Caaliyah, Yasmin, and Leylo," Aya said. "The rest of them went home for the American holiday."

"But you all keep the old ways," Imaan said, her eyes connecting with each girl. Every movement Imaan made seemed deliberate, elegant. "That is good. The Americans claim to separate politics and religion, but can you believe a country that puts 'in God we trust' on their money? Their Christian God is not ours, my Muslim sisters."

The girls exchanged glances. A few even looked around to make sure Imam Nabil wasn't listening. No one talked like that in this mosque. Aya felt a thrill of danger run up her spine.

"May I speak with you, Aya?" Imaan asked with a sidelong glance at the rest of the girls. "Privately?"

Aya's heart nearly leapt out of her chest. "Of course, Imaan!"

The older woman raised her eyebrow. "Is there somewhere we can go that's close by? Maybe a little more comfortable?"

"My mother runs a coffee shop. It's only two blocks away . . ." Aya let her voice trail off.

"That sounds perfect." She slid her arm into Aya's. "Shall we, sister? It was a pleasure meeting you all." Her voice left no doubt that they were not invited.

A chill November wind met them at the door of the mosque, but Aya didn't mind—the cold made Imaan huddle closer to her as they walked. A bell tinkled overhead when they entered her mother's coffee shop. Aya's mother rushed from behind the counter to greet her important guest, her face flushed and sweaty under her *hijab*. Next to Imaan, her mother seemed old and dowdy, a peasant next to a royal. But Imaan seemed not to notice, greeting the older woman with a warm kiss on each cheek.

The shop was mostly empty and they settled into armchairs next to the gas fireplace. Aya's mother bustled out with two cups of *kahawa*, her mother's specialty coffee made with cardamom and ginger. Imaan smiled at her and thanked her in Somali.

"Your mother's lovely," Imaan said after a tiny sip of her drink.

"No, she's not. She's old and stuck in her ways—she supports our family mostly. My father often can't work." It was so easy to talk to this woman. Aya found herself telling Imaan all kinds of family details that even her closest friends didn't know about her.

"You're a brave spirit, Ayana. I saw the way you stood up to those FBI agents when your brother was arrested."

Aya blushed. "I—I just felt such a rage at everything.

Hamza—that's my cousin, the one they killed—was a good boy, a good man. And then they put handcuffs on Zacharia . . . I just—"

"It's okay." Imaan slipped her elegant hand over Aya's. Jeweled rings glinted on her fingers and her long nails were painted a dark red. "It's not your fault. Your parents brought you to this country, but America failed you. They call this the land of opportunity, but only if you're white and Christian. If you're brown and Muslim, there's nothing here for you. Only lies." Her voice still held its warmth, but it was now edged with a tone of insistence.

"I know you see this, Aya. I travel the world and every time I come to America, I see it more and more."

"But what can we do?" Without thinking, Aya slipped her fingers into Imaan's and received a reassuring grip in return.

Imaan inclined her head toward the counter where Aya's mother was fixing another cup of coffee. "You just told me your mother provides for your family, right?"

Aya nodded.

"Does she take credit for that act of generosity?" Imaan paused, her gaze intent on Aya. "No, she does not. Yet without her intervention, your family would starve."

She raised Aya's fingers to her lips and kissed them gently. "Sometimes women are called to take action, to sacrifice for the good of their family, their culture, their religious beliefs. I think you, Ayana Ismail, are one of those women."

Aya's heart was beating so loudly in her ears she could barely hear her own response. "I am, Imaan, I am. What do you want me to do?"

Imaan smiled at her, a radiant baring of beautiful white teeth, a smile full of promise, just like on the cover of her last album.

"Gather friends of like mind and study the words of Allah. I'll be back in a few weeks." Imaan stood, and her expensive clothes seemed to flow over her lithe figure. Every movement dripped with grace and ease.

"I have high hopes for you, Ayana."

CHAPTER 4

FBI Field Office, Brooklyn Park, Minnesota
28 November 2016 — 1030 local

If Liz had learned anything as a US Marine, it was that you faced trouble head-on. And while you were at it, make sure you look good.

As per department policy, she'd been placed on administrative leave following the death of Hamza Abdul. The internal review should have taken a full week, possibly two, but the week after the Hamza incident was shortened due to the Thanksgiving holiday. Liz was surprised when Trask sent her an email on the Friday after Thanksgiving.

Pls come see me on Monday at 1030 in my office.

Typically Trask in its bluntness, the single line gave her pause. It was unlikely that the FBI had managed to conduct the full review of Hamza's death in just three workdays, so was there a problem? Liz put aside the piece of pumpkin pie she had been eating and studied the neatly laid-out papers that covered her dining room table. She'd managed to get a copy of every scrap of evidence from the Hamza takedown and done her own review of the situation. She was in the clear—unless there was something she didn't know about.

She shook her head. Not possible. It was a clean bust. She'd been aggressive in the chase, but she hadn't even fired her weapon.

Liz looked at the email again. Yet Trask wanted to see her at least a week ahead of schedule. Something was not right. She toyed with the idea of calling Trask, but dismissed it. He'd said what he wanted to say.

She took another bite of pie, then threw the rest in the trash.

Liz clutched the thick file in one hand and knocked on the doorjamb with the other. Special Agent in Charge Tom Trask, head of the FBI Field Office, looked up. He smiled.

"C'mon in, Liz."

She held the file folder in front of her like a shield as she tried to read his expression.

Her eyes swept over the framed photos of Trask in various stages of his career: Naval Academy midshipman, Marine second lieutenant graduating from The Basic School in Quantico, wife and three kids, FBI induction, and finally the newest picture of her, Brendan, and Don Riley all grouped with him at the White House when she'd received the FBI Medal of Valor from the president last month. There had been no press coverage at that ceremony—the public never even knew about the rogue nuclear weapon outside the Vikings stadium—but that didn't diminish the moment for her.

Brendan's smiling face looked out at her from the photograph and Liz wished more than anything that he was here with her right now. She'd declined the invitation from his parents to spend Thanksgiving with them, preferring to work through the evidence in the Hamza investigation. She knew every detail backwards and forwards. Of that, she was confident. But this meeting . . . something was up.

In between reviewing the Hamza evidence, she'd gotten a haircut, bought a new suit, and had her nails done. If things went sideways for some reason, at least she'd look good.

"Everything okay, Liz?"

She realized she'd been staring at the photo of her and Brendan. Her eyes slid to his desk where a closed folder lay. Even from this distance she could read her name on the tab.

"Yes, sir. I'm fine." She hefted her own folder a little higher on her chest.

"Sit, please." He motioned to the chair in front of his desk, then sprang to his feet to shut the door to his office. "We've got a lot to talk about this morning, Liz."

He took his time reseating himself at his desk and folding his hands in front of him. His lips curled into a noncommittal smile that told her nothing about why he'd asked her to this meeting.

"Let's start with the elephant in the room, shall we?" he said finally. "You've been cleared of any responsibility in the death of Hamza Abdul."

Liz did her best to keep a passive expression, but she felt her shoulders sag a bit as she processed the welcome feeling of relief. She lowered the file folder to her lap. "Thank you, sir."

Trask laughed. "Don't thank me. It was an open-and-shut case, a clean takedown. You never even discharged your weapon. Like I told you: when bad guys run, bad things happen. You knew that, right?"

"Sure, of course. Thanks all the same." Liz did her best to sit up straight in her chair, but with all the tension gone she felt like a rag doll.

"That's not why I asked to see you this morning."

"Oh?" The tension crept back into her frame. "There's something else?"

Trask was smiling again. "You could say that. Your work in this office has been exemplary by any standard, so I'm recommending you for an even bigger job. DC wants to get ahead of this Daesh recruiting problem that we have here in the Twin Cities. The incoming administration has asked me to form a new Joint Terrorism Task Force to focus on the situation. They were going to wait until after they took office in January, but this latest Hamza business has everyone in DC in a lather. They want to launch it now."

Liz nodded. "And you want me to be on the new JTTF?"

"No, Liz, we want you to lead it." Trask stood and extended his hand. "I'm here to tell you that you've been promoted to Supervisory Special Agent in Charge of the new JTTF on Homegrown Recruitment."

Liz stood and took his hand. "Sir, I don't want to sound ungrateful, but aren't I a little junior for that job?" Leading a task force of this magnitude was a job for an agent with at least five more years' experience than she—and there were three she knew of in the bull pen office right outside Trask's door. And they were all men, too.

Trask must have seen the look on her face. "Sit down, Liz."

She sank back into the comfort of the chair. This was happening way too fast for her to process. She'd come into Trask's office prepared to fight for her job and ended up getting a promotion. Her head was still spinning.

"Look, Tom, I'm sorry—"

He held up his hand. "I've watched you since you came into this office, Liz. You're a good agent—scratch that, you're a *great* agent. I've seen you follow your instincts and stop a terrorist attack when no one else even believed the threat was real. You work harder, run faster, and shoot straighter than anybody in this office—and we've got some damn fine agents in this office." He paused and laced his fingers together.

"We have intel that says these al-Shabab characters are aligning themselves with Daesh. And this business with Hamza shows that they know how to get back into the US. That's trouble with a capital T from where I'm sitting. When DC calls me and says they want my best agent on this, I gave them your name without a moment's hesitation. So, I have only one question for you, Special Agent Elizabeth Soroush. Your country needs you—are you in or not?"

Over Trask's shoulder, Liz could see Brendan's face in the photo.

"I'm in, sir."

CHAPTER 5

USS *Arrogant*, Christmas Island, Indian Ocean
30 November 2016 — 1030 local

Brendan put his feet up and reveled in the sheer joy of being alone for the first time in three weeks.

It's not that he didn't like his crewmates on the *Arrogant*, but five people on a fifty-four-foot sailboat was a little close for comfort. To make matters worse, the trip up from Perth to their patrol zone on the southern coast of Indonesia had been rough weather, which meant even more time belowdecks in close quarters. Togetherness—not all it was cracked up to be.

He'd volunteered to take the first watch onboard so the rest of the crew could blow off some steam in town. From what he could see of the town of Flying Fish Cove from this vantage point, they'd be back before too long.

In the shelter of the cove, where the seas were gentle and the sun warm, Brendan was tempted to take a nap. Forcing himself to his feet, he slipped into the gloom belowdecks to retrieve his unclassified laptop. He tried to do the math for the time zone difference between Christmas Island and Minneapolis and gave up. Better to just check Skype and see if Liz was online.

He missed talking to his girlfriend. They'd only been an official couple since September, thrown together by their involvement in foiling the terrorist attack on the Vikings stadium in Minneapolis, but in a way they'd been together for as long as he could remember.

While in port in Perth, they'd managed to squeeze in a few minutes on Skype every day, but once Brendan put to sea, mission parameters forbade the use of unclassified comms except to maintain their cover as a boat owned by a rich software engineer–playboy. That did not include talking to your FBI agent girlfriend in Minneapolis.

Skype took forever to boot up and even longer to link up with the local Wi-Fi signal. Three bars. It would have to do. Liz's screen name appeared in his online contacts. Brendan's heart beat faster as he clicked on the video call icon.

The call rang once, twice, three times. He started to think about leaving a video message for her when Liz's face filled the screen.

"Bren, is that you?" Her hair was mussed as if she'd just woken up and she rubbed her eyes with the heel of her hand. The room behind her was dark.

"It's me, babe. Did I wake you up?"

"Yeah. I'm glad I caught you, though." Liz's voice broke— or was it the connection? "It's been a rough few weeks . . . I've missed you."

Brendan squinted at the screen. Was she crying?

"Hey, what's going on? You seem upset." Brendan kicked himself mentally. *You seem upset? That's what you lead with?*

She smiled weakly. "You caught me at a bad time. I was involved in a takedown of a terrorist suspect and he died. It was an accident, but that doesn't make it any easier. He was just a kid. Then I got a promotion at work—task force on homegrown recruiting. There were at least three more senior agents in line for this job—all men, of course—and they picked me. You can imagine the office politics—"

"Wait a minute, Liz," Brendan cut into her rambling. "You killed a guy and they promoted you? How do I get that job?" He laughed.

"It's not funny, Bren!" Liz's face twisted in anger, then softened. "I'm sorry. This is the first time we get to talk in almost a month—"

"Three weeks."

Liz closed her eyes for a second. "Okay, three weeks, and I dump all this on you . . . but I just miss you. We spent so many years apart and just when I get you back you're gone again. It's not fair."

Brendan sat up straighter in his seat. "Look, Liz, we can get through this together. Whatever the problem is, I can help you solve it. We're a team—"

"I don't want you to solve anything, Brendan, I just want you to listen to me!"

"Okay, I'm sorry, I thought you . . ." He let his voice trail off. The local Wi-Fi was barely able to support video, but he didn't want to lose the picture. He tried standing up so the laptop was closer to the signal. "Liz?"

"I'm sorry, Bren. I finally hear from you and all I do is mess it up."

"I have some news that might cheer you up, babe."

Liz made an attempt at a smile—at least that's what it looked like in the heavily pixelated screen. "Oh yeah? Spill it, McHugh. I could use some good news for a change."

"I got a message from Baxter yesterday. He says he's transferring me back to the States in the next few months to take the job of Program Deputy Director at ONI." He smiled widely. If anything would make her happy, that would. Regular office hours and Baxter was obviously grooming him to move up the ladder at the Office of Naval Intelligence.

"ONI is in Maryland, right?"

"Liz, c'mon, you know where ONI is located."

"So that means you're not coming back to Minneapolis." She didn't ask it like a question.

"Well, no, but we'll be only one time zone apart. The flight from DC to Minneapolis is what, two and a half hours? I'll be home every weekend."

"So, more long distance—do you ever get tired of it, Bren?" She held up her hands to the screen. "You know what? I'm sorry. I'm in a terrible frame of mind and I never should have picked up the call. It's a snowy, cold, wet mess here and I'm lonely."

Brendan could hear the laughter of his approaching crew. He cleared his throat. "Hey, Lizzie, I'm going to lose this line in a minute. Can I call you later?"

"Hey, skipper, we got some awesome pastries!"

Liz grimaced at the camera. "Sounds like your friends are back."

"Yeah," he said in a tone that came out sharper than he'd intended. "The people that I work with are back. They also happen to be my friends."

"Whatever. Let's talk another time when I'm in a better mood."

"I love you, Liz."

But the line was already dead.

CHAPTER 6

Roosevelt High School, Minneapolis, Minnesota
01 December 2016 — 1600 local

Aya named their club the Muslim-American Women's Studies Club. By signing up through the school, she was able to hold meetings in the school classrooms. The only tricky part was finding a faculty advisor who would sponsor the club—but not come to any meetings.

She settled on Mr. Olafson, her English teacher, who always wrote things like "you show a lot of promise" on her papers. Aya filled in the rest mentally: "for a girl wearing a *hijab*."

Imaan had opened Aya's eyes to the slights and the slurs of everyday life as a Muslim woman in America. The insults were everywhere if you knew where to look. She'd been born in this country, just like them, but they treated her like a second-class citizen. Their eyes would take in her *hijab* and her robes, and in that instant she saw what they really thought of her. Pity that this poor girl didn't wear makeup and blue jeans. Pity that her religion didn't allow her to "party" with them—not that she'd want to even if she could. Pity that her brother, the Roosevelt soccer star, was now driving a cab like his father.

Imaan had changed all that. Imaan showed her how Muslim women are strong, how they wield influence in subtle ways. "You are destined for great things, my little flower," Imaan would say in their weekly telephone calls. "Great things. You will change the world, I am sure of it."

With each interaction, she felt the will of Allah come to her through Imaan's voice, strengthening her resolve. Hardening her will to act out against the unfairness of the world in which she lived.

Aya had managed to recruit five members to her new club. Imaan taught her how to evaluate each one, what questions to ask to weed out the ones who were just there to hear Imaan's voice, to find the ones with a core of iron like her.

Even though school had just let out for the day, this time of year it was already growing dark when they met in the empty classroom. The room was filled with vintage 1970s school desks, all-in-one constructions of metal with wooden desktops covered in graffiti from long-ago students. Aya had the girls arrange the desks into a circle in the center of the room so they could see each other. She placed her mobile phone in the pencil groove at the front of her desk under the carved name of "Robbie" scratched into the wooden surface.

Aware that the rest of the girls were watching her, Aya tried to appear calm, as if the most popular Somali singer in the world called her cell phone every afternoon. She checked the time on the phone. Three minutes left.

"We're all clear on the rules?" she asked.

The other girls, all outfitted in dark-colored *hijabs*, nodded.

"How much longer?" asked Caaliyah. "I can hardly wait."

"Be patient," snapped Aya.

The phone rang, the pop beat sounding out of place in the classroom. Aya let it ring one full cycle.

"Answer it!" hissed Yasmin.

Ayana touched the screen. "Hello?"

"Ayana, peace be upon you." Imaan's voice even sounded magical over the tiny mobile phone speaker.

"And you, Imaan." Aya's mouth went dry and she tried to still the ferocious beating in her chest. It was like this every time they spoke. The bottom dropped out of her stomach, her heart hammered away like a scared rabbit. If it was possible to love a woman, she loved Imaan.

"Did you bring friends today?"

Aya nodded then realized Imaan couldn't see her. "Yes," she choked out.

One by one, the girls introduced themselves. Imaan had a question and a compliment for each one. She asked how many brothers they each had and the role their mother played in the family. As the call went on, Aya had to tamp down a surge of jealousy. Imaan was hers.

But still, she began to see a pattern to the girls in the room that had escaped her before. All of their fathers were either gone or in some sort of reduced role in the family. Their mothers were all strong women who supported the family. And they all had older brothers, most of them either in gangs or working in low-wage jobs.

"And now we come back to Ayana, my little flower," said Imaan. Aya felt a rush of heat in her face as the older woman used her pet name. "You have done well to gather so many strong women to our cause."

"What is our cause?" asked Madino. She was the only one

Aya was unsure about. Madino was a tall, solidly built girl, with a permanent scowl on her face and a scar on her chin. She'd dated a member of the St. Paul Pistol Boys, a Somali gang across town. Madino always seemed to be in a hurry, always wanted to push a little harder than Aya was comfortable with.

"Madino," she said. "When it is—"

Imaan interrupted her with a musical laugh. "My sister, you are strong women of Islam living in a land of infidels. You are surrounded, outnumbered, but you will be called to change the world."

"So our cause is changing the world?" asked Hodan. Her delicate brow wrinkled under the strain of Imaan's words. She was Aya's closest friend and had a massive crush on Aya's brother, Zacharia.

Imaan's voice lowered as if she was telling them a secret. "Tell me this: if your mother and father have an argument, who wins?"

"My father," said Hodan. "He's the head of the household."

"Does he really? Think about it again, Hodan. Maybe your father has a way to claim victory and stamp around like an elephant, but how often does his decision remain in place?"

Aya thought about her own parents and their charade about the family finances. Her father barely worked more than two days a week anymore, but everyone acted as if he was the sole breadwinner in the family. Meanwhile, her mother worked twelve-hour days at the coffee shop. On the rare occasions when money was discussed openly in the family, her mother always deferred to whatever her father wanted.

The girls looked at one another, each seemingly reviewing their own family situations. Aya saw some nods around the circle.

"We live in a patriarchal society," Imaan continued. Aya loved to listen to the singer's voice. The rich tones settled in her consciousness, soothing her senses.

"We live in a world constructed by men, but we hold the real power—the power of influence. When we disagree with men, we do not strike them down with violence. No, we agree with them, we build up their egos—and then we do whatever we want behind their backs."

The circle of girls leaned forward, straining to catch every syllable of Imaan's words. Aya felt nervous energy tickle her spine. Seeing the intent looks on the faces of her friends—including Madino—she suddenly wanted to laugh out loud to release the tension.

"We are strong women who will change the world," Imaan said, her voice low and intense. "We are soldiers in the fight for our rights as Muslim citizens of the West. Practice your powers of influence, my sisters, and remember that one day we will be called to show the world what the women of Islam are made of."

Aya realized she was holding her breath.

"Stay together. Tell no one of our cause. Remain absolutely loyal to one another. Allah has a plan for us. I know it."

The phone went dead.

Aya let out a long breath. When she looked around the circle, three of the girls were crying. The rest, like her, sat in stunned silence.

CHAPTER 7

FBI Field Office, Brooklyn Park, Minnesota
01 December 2016 — 1300 local

Liz picked an invisible piece of lint from the knee of her navy blue pants, took a deep breath, and stood up at the front of the room. She squared her shoulders and faced the FBI agents in the room. "I think we'll get started without Agent Trask."

That was a lie. She'd asked Tom Trask to keep out of this meeting, her first meeting with the new Homegrown Recruiting Task Force. The next thirty minutes were going to decide if her leadership emphasis was going to be more about *task* or *force*. Liz smiled to herself. She'd have to remember that line.

As Trask had told her when she took the job, the internal politics of this new role were a bear. The assets of the previous al-Shabab Task Force had been folded into her new Homegrown Recruiting Task Force. As was FBI policy, the leader of a JTTF was promoted to Supervisory Special Agent. However, when your stint as leader ended, you went back to plain old Special Agent.

There was nothing wrong with it and everybody knew how and why it happened, but we're all human and demotions, even ones done for good reasons, still hurt.

Liz locked eyes with Special Agent Arnie Jannsen, formerly Supervisory Special Agent Jannsen, head of the al-Shabab Task Force. She could see the resentment in his eyes, and at a certain level, she could understand it. Jannsen had a decade of experience on Liz and his task force had done some good work. The fact that Liz was a woman didn't help the situation.

She didn't believe for a minute that Jannsen was a misogynist, but the FBI was still mostly a man's world, and that came with a man's worldview. Liz only had to look at this room to see it: eight people, all men except for her and one other technical specialist, a young African-American woman named Solange.

Jannsen held her gaze without flinching. It seemed that he was not planning on making her transition any easier.

Game on, Arnie.

"I asked you here this afternoon so we could talk about overall engagement strategy of the new task force before the full JTTF call tomorrow." In addition to the eight FBI personnel in the room, the full task force consisted of another thirty "partner personnel," or affiliated law enforcement agencies: mostly local police departments, sheriffs, Immigrations and Customs Enforcement, and the like.

"Up to this point, we've relied on traditional law enforcement tactics to stop international terrorist recruitment. We get a lead, maybe pop a FISA warrant, and do what cops do: build a case and make an arrest." She was pacing now, and out of the corner of her eye, Liz saw Jannsen shift in his seat. She held up her hands. "Don't get me wrong, it works. The arrest record from the al-Shabab task force has been excellent. Not a single arrest was overturned, and we all know how hard it was to build those cases."

All true. The task force had arrested almost two dozen young men, all of them Somali-Americans, trying to leave the country to fight for one international terrorist group or another. That was more than any other city in the entire United States.

Liz stopped pacing and faced them, leaning down on the table on planted fists. "Here's the cold, hard facts: it's not enough. There are not enough FBI agents in the world to surveil every potential young person who might be being radicalized right now. Just take the Somali population alone: over a hundred thousand, and that group skews young. We're talking about trying to find a few dozen possible bad guys—remember, they haven't actually committed a crime yet—among tens of thousands of candidates." She punched the table with her fist. "We need a better way."

The room was silent. Kamen and Adams, better known around the office as Cain and Abel, exchanged glances.

Please, someone ask the question.

Silence.

"Okay, Liz, I'll bite. What's the better way?" To her surprise, it was Jannsen who spoke first. If she listened really carefully, she thought she could hear a touch of bitterness in his tone. But he deserved better than that. Special Agent Jannsen had just sent a signal to everyone in the room that he was engaged. That didn't mean he agreed with Liz, but she'd rather have an open disagreement than a backstabber in her ranks any day.

"I'm really glad you asked, Arnie." She smiled at him in an attempt to show him just how much she appreciated his participation. "We need the Somali community to become self-policing. I don't mean informants, I mean families and faith groups who recognize the signs of a young man being radicalized and take action before he does something wrong. The rehab program that started earlier this year has had some success. We can get them into that program before these kids get criminal records."

Adams pulled a face. "That's a pretty tall order, Liz. How do we even start?"

Liz nodded. "It is a tall order, but think about the problem we're trying to tackle here. Two years ago, the recruiting threat was al-Shabab and the target was the Somali community. Then it was al-Qaeda. Now it's the Islamic State. Daesh has nothing to do with Somalia—nothing! Tomorrow it could be some other group, but the common thread in all these cases is *who* they're targeting: young Muslim-American men.

"Our law enforcement tactics will never be able to get ahead of these recruiters. We need to flip the problem. The immigrant communities need to take responsibility for their own policing and we need to give them the space to do that."

Adams raised his hand. "You still didn't answer my question, Liz. Where do we start?"

Liz picked up a sheaf of papers and passed them to the nearest agent. "We're going to make some friends. Everyone here— including me—is being assigned an imam. Let's try to build a deck-level relationship with these men that shows some trust in the community. Let's try to get them to talk to us not as FBI agents, but as people."

Kamen spoke this time. "Doesn't the local sheriff's office al- ready have outreach people on staff?"

Liz leveled a look at him. "They do, and I'm sure they're good people. But showing this community more love is not going to hurt us."

"So this is the kinder, gentler FBI?" The bitterness in Jannsen's voice was plain now. He folded his arms and leaned back in his chair. "Instead of arresting people, we have coffee with the imams?"

Liz bit back the smart-ass comment that rose to her lips. Any benefit of the doubt that Arnie Jannsen might have been offering seemed to be gone.

"I think it's a good idea, Liz," said Solange. She rarely spoke in meetings, and her voice stopped the chatter in the room. "My grandmother had a saying: you catch more flies with honey than with vinegar. Maybe the same thing applies here." She paused and blushed. "Just saying."

Adams raised his eyebrow and looked at Kamen. Kamen nodded.

Liz caught Jannsen's gaze and held it.

Game on, Arnie.

CHAPTER 8

When Reza entered the office of Iranian President Hassan Rouhani, the great man himself was seated in front of the television. The cleric's grandfatherly face was carved into a scowl as he stared at the Al Jazeera news anchor. He made no move to get up, so Reza waited.

". . . Iranian officials are reeling from the news of the murder of Muslim cleric Aban Rahmani in his home in Tehran last night. Officials close to the investigation say that Rahmani, who had been under house arrest since August of this year on unidentified charges, was shot to death in his home. Another man, presumed to be a bodyguard, was also found dead—"

Rouhani snatched up the remote and silenced the television. "How could this happen, Reza?" He threw the remote onto the couch. "Murdered, right under our noses. I tell you, the Quds Force

41

is behind this. They're cleaning up after one of their own." Rouhani stormed across the room to a window overlooking his garden.

Reza stayed silent, letting the mood pass. After more than thirty years as a faithful servant and sometimes confidante to one of the most powerful men in the world, he knew Rouhani's moods better than his own.

Still, it was all he could do not to curl his lip at the term "unidentified charges." He would gladly sacrifice his left testicle to tell the world how the holier-than-thou Imam Aban Rahmani had betrayed his country. The depths of Rahmani's treason, along with that of his two brothers, was beyond imagining.

Nuclear weapons. In the midst of negotiating with the so-called P5+1 Western powers over a nuclear agreement, President Rouhani had been shocked to find out that one of his own countrymen was harboring nuclear warheads from Iraq—and planning to use them against Israel during Rouhani's state visit to that country. Even more embarrassing, it was the Americans who had discovered the treachery. The only thing that saved Iran from entering another thirty years of international exile was Reza's relationship with CIA agent Donald Riley.

The three half-brothers—the holy man Aban, the Quds Force operative Hashem, and the Hezbollah agent Rafiq—had managed to get access to Saddam Hussein's cache of nuclear weapons. Together, the three had spun a plot that, had it worked, would have resulted in Rouhani's fall from power and decades of Iranian hard-line rule.

Lucky for all concerned, the only thing Aban loved more than power was his own skin. He gave up his half-brothers with barely a second thought. Hashem, the Quds Force operative, had died in the raid on a secret underground bunker in the mountains. The other half-brother, Rafiq Roshed, had escaped.

Reza studied the muted TV, which was showing more pictures of Aban Rahmani in his full clerical garb. Truth be told, Reza was glad to see Aban Rahmani gone. His only regret was that he'd not been there to ensure it was performed as painfully as possible.

Rouhani turned back from the window, an apologetic smile on his face. He embraced Reza. "I'm sorry, old friend. The blatherings of an old man, that's what you have to listen to these days." With a lock of gray hair peeking out from under his turban and a smile on his face, the president of Iran looked more like a grandfather than the leader of the most powerful Shia nation on the planet.

"I understand, Mr. President," Reza replied. "The elimination of Rahmani is unfortunate in the timing, but surely not without benefit, sir?"

Rouhani tugged on his gray beard, the way he always did when in thought. "Perhaps you're right. We were never going to put him on trial, but it's the way it was handled by Quds that infuriates me. An assassination of a cleric on Iranian soil—it's barbaric."

The Quds Force was the division of the Iranian Army of the Guardians of the Islamic Revolution (IRGC) responsible for clandestine operations. The half-brother Hashem had been one of their own and used his office to funnel money and materials to his secret nuclear operation. Like rats from a sinking ship, the Quds hierarchy—the precious few who knew of Hashem's treachery—had been doing their level best to ensure that all links to the rogue agent were cauterized. Aban Rahmani was one such loose end. It all made perfect sense, but it seemed just a bit too neat for Reza.

"There is another possibility, sir," Reza said.

"You have information." Rouhani studied his face. "Tell me."

"Not information, sir. Suspicions only. There's a possibility it could have been a revenge killing by the half-brother with Hezbollah, Rafiq Roshed."

"Impossible! I'm sure this is a Quds operation." Rouhani returned to the window.

Reza let the idea sink in before he spoke again. "I agree that Quds is responsible," he continued, "but they may have, shall we say, contracted the work out?"

The Iranian president put his hands behind his back and bowed his head in thought. "Roshed would be willing to risk coming to Iran just to kill his brother?"

"Half-brother, sir, and yes, I believe Roshed would take that risk. If he had help—from inside Quds, for example—to assassinate Rahmani and get out of the country safely, I think he would jump at the chance. Rahmani gave both of his brothers up without a second thought."

Hashem Aboud had been an extremely cautious and secretive man, the kind of man who understood the value of a fail-safe backup plan. After weaponizing the primitive Iraqi nuclear devices, he'd sent one warhead to a sleeper cell in South America under the care of his brother the Hezbollah agent. Reza only learned of the existence of the backup plan from Aban after the Americans had destroyed Hashem's nuclear operation on Iranian soil—a fact that still rankled the Iranian president.

Reza had taken it upon himself to track down Rafiq Roshed and the last nuclear warhead. But it was a fool's errand; Roshed was always one step ahead of him, and in the end, Reza was forced to go back to the Americans for help. Using his friendship with CIA analyst Donald Riley, they'd averted a nuclear disaster on American soil that would have been blamed on Iran—and on President Rouhani.

And Roshed had escaped—again. The thought that the

Hezbollah agent might have been right here in Tehran, only a few days ago, was almost more than he could bear.

"So you agree Quds was behind Rahmani's death?" Rouhani was saying.

Reza directed his focus back to the conversation. "Pure speculation on my part, sir, but Quds had the means and the motivation—"

"I agree, Reza," Rouhani interrupted. "You said it best: Quds is responsible for this assassination. They either knew about it and let it happen, which is treason, or they should have known about it and failed to stop it, which is incompetence."

Rouhani's reasoning was a bit simplistic, but not incorrect. Reza studied his mentor, a man who had saved his life more than thirty years ago on a battlefield in Basra. Rouhani smiled at him, a baring of teeth that did not leave one with a friendly impression. Reza knew that smile and it did not mean his boss was happy.

"I want you in charge, Reza," he said. "You're the only one I can trust. I leave next week for the international trade mission and I need someone minding the home front for me."

Reza had been planning the security details of the trade mission for months. They were set to visit France, Germany, the United States, the United Nations, and half a dozen Asian countries, all with the goal of increasing trade since the lifting of the nuclear sanctions.

"I don't understand, Mr. President."

Rouhani turned back to his desk and picked up a file folder. "It's all in here. I'm reactivating your commission as a Brigadier General in the Iranian Army, effective immediately. You are assigned as the head of the Quds Force Special Operations branch."

"But, sir, the trade mission leaves in—"

Rouhani held up his hand. "There's one more thing, Reza. And it's not in the folder."

"Yes, sir?" Reza clamped his lips shut. Rouhani had clearly made up his mind and nothing Reza said was going to change it.

"The elimination of Aban Rahmani may be a sign that it's time to put the entire *issue* behind us."

Reza tried not to smile. Finally, he would have the opportunity to complete some unfinished business. "You mean Roshed, sir."

Rouhani nodded. "In your new position, you will use all assets to find and eliminate Rafiq Roshed. I want this matter extinguished, once and for all."

"That search may require international cooperation, sir."

"Your friends in the CIA?" Rouhani frowned and made another trip to the window, waving his hand for Reza to join him. The trees and bushes in the garden were stripped bare of leaves and the grass had turned brown. "You're sure you can trust them?"

"*Trust* is a funny word, Mr. President. I'm sure I can use them."

"Very well, Reza. You have my trust in this matter. Use it wisely."

CHAPTER 9

Liz knocked gently on the door labeled Jamie Patterson, PhD. Jamie was one of those names that could be male or female, and she regretted that she hadn't taken the time to at least figure out if she was meeting a man or woman. Trask had made the appointment and then sent her at the last minute.

"Just listen to what the professor has to say and see if it offers any clues about how we can find some of these kids before they turn to the dark side," he said. He handed her a web article titled "Why ISIS Is Like a Gang."

Dr. Patterson, who was also the head of the Criminology Department at Metro State, turned out to be a short, balding white man in his mid-fifties. He smiled up at her from his cluttered desk. "What can I do for the FBI, Agent Soroush?" Dr. Patterson's speech had a trace of a British accent and Liz spied a diploma from Oxford University on the wall behind him.

She pulled the article out of her purse. "Your article makes a strong linkage between gang behavior and terrorist groups. I'm hoping you can help me build a profile to help us find kids that might be susceptible to messages from terrorist organizations like al-Shabab or ISIS."

The professor waved her to a chair in front of his desk. Liz needed to move a sloppy stack of graded papers from the chair to the floor before she could sit down.

Calling this space an office was being generous. More like a cave. The floor-to-ceiling bookshelves were crammed with a crazy assortment of magazines, textbooks, and mass market paperbacks. The shade on the narrow window was drawn such that the only light came from the green-shaded desk lamp between her and the professor. His eyes were hidden behind the light reflecting off his spectacles.

The older man steepled his hands. "How old are you, Agent Soroush?"

Liz shifted in her seat. "Thirty-five. Why?" *Didn't anyone ever tell you it was impolite to ask a lady her age?*

"Do you remember being a teenager?"

Liz shrugged. "It was a while ago, but yeah, I guess I do."

"Who did you look up to? Who was your role model?"

"That's easy—my father. We always had a good relationship."

"And did your Iranian heritage ever make you feel like an outsider with your peers?"

"How did you know I was Iranian?"

Dr. Patterson smiled beneath the pools of light on his glasses. "Accents are a hobby of mine. There's a very slight flatness in the way you pronounce the 'th' sound that suggests a Farsi influence. I'm guessing you're first-generation American but grew up in a home where Farsi was spoken."

Liz sat up in her chair. He'd nailed it, all from a one-minute conversation. "That's exactly correct."

The smile grew broader. "It's an indulgence of mine. I also find it helps to establish credibility with law enforcement types. Sometimes they see a late-middle-aged white man and doubt my credibility on more worldly matters, like gangs. Perhaps we could get back to the question at hand: did your heritage ever make you feel like an outsider with your peers?"

Liz thought for a moment before answering. "There were times, but I went to a private school. The kids around me cared more about getting into a good college than getting in trouble."

The professor nodded. "Can you imagine what your life might have been like if your father was absent and you didn't have that private school education?"

"I might have turned out differently."

Patterson chuckled. "I daresay you might have. And what if your skin was dark, not like these Minnesota Scandinavians, and you practiced a faith other than Christianity in a predominantly Christian country?"

"Things could have been a lot different."

"Undoubtedly, Agent Soroush. The Somali population here in Minnesota and all over the US are a people caught between two cultures. When the average Minnesotan sees a Somali man, they see a black man—an African-American, to use the politically correct vernacular. But they couldn't be further from the truth. The Somalis don't consider themselves "black" in the American sense—they actually see the traditional African-American label as a slur. They're a proud people who have been displaced from their homeland. That's not the issue that you have to worry about, though."

Liz frowned. "It's not?"

"The Somali diaspora happened as a result of a civil war. That generation arrived in this country en masse in the early 1990s, all within a span of a few years. The people you're concerned with are eighteen to twenty-four years old. In other words, they were all born here, in the US. That presents another problem."

"Which is?" Liz avoided looking at her watch. The professor's method of forcing her to draw every piece of information out was wearing on her patience.

"They're teenagers, Ms. Soroush. And like teenagers the world over, they see everything in black and white, right and wrong. Grownup bodies, but lacking in adult judgment. These young Somali men have a foot in both cultures. On one hand, they live in traditional Muslim homes, surrounded by the trappings of a homeland they've never seen. On the other, they live in a twenty-first-century world of Twitter and Facebook and malls and movies with half-naked women to tempt them. And that's where the gangs come in."

Liz felt in her purse for her notebook and pen while she waited for him to continue, but he just sat there grinning. Clearly the professor was enjoying the attention. "Could you elaborate on that, professor?" she said, doing her level best to keep the exasperation out of her tone.

"Many of these young men live in poverty. Poor job prospects, no authority figure in their lives. Enter the gang culture—and it is a culture. At the time in their lives when these men feel the most adrift, gangs offer a sense of camaraderie, adventure, purpose. These teenagers feel like they're a part of something bigger than themselves. For a gang, it's a piece of turf, a city block that is 'theirs,' and they need to protect it.

"ISIS, al-Shabab, or any other terrorist group is no different. They prey on the disaffected, the ones looking for something to aspire to as their real lives come apart at the seams. Social media has made the job so much easier for these groups. Remember, these are normal American teenagers, just as attached to their phones and their apps as any white kid. I assume you've seen the YouTube video 'Ambush at Bardale'?"

Liz shook her head. The professor turned to his computer and hammered away at the keys for a few minutes. Then he rolled his chair back and angled the screen so Liz could view it.

The semiprofessional video showed a band of armed insurgents on patrol dressed in camouflage, their heads covered in balaclavas. A narrator in English filled them in on the purpose of the raid while eerie Arabic music played softly in the background. Liz was reminded of some of the US military recruiting videos she'd seen. All this lacked was a slogan.

"Slick," was all she said.

"Very effective," the professor acknowledged. "Of course, the leader of that raid was killed almost two years ago, but his martyrdom only makes the video that much more valuable as a recruiting tool. It's all there: a sense of purpose, an element of danger and adventure, a higher calling. The exact same elements that gangs use to recruit members."

Liz cleared her throat. "So if I understand you, professor, there's not really a way to find these young men before they become radicalized."

He laughed. "No, not unless you're planning to lock up every teenager with brown skin and a mobile phone. We've been working on gang violence in this country for decades, and while it's gotten better, the problem is far from solved. Our society produces a crop of vulnerable young men every generation. The best we can do is try to minimize the size of that pool and intervene as soon as we see signs."

Liz slid her notebook back in her purse and stood. She held

out her hand to Dr. Patterson. "Thank you, sir. This has been eye-opening for me." She paused at the door.

"One last question, professor. You keep mentioning young men. Is there any evidence to suggest women could be recruited by these terrorist groups?"

Dr. Patterson shook his head and gave her a fatherly smile. "No, my dear, this is one area where your gender plays in your favor. Islam, especially the more radical sects, sees the role of women as subservient. They would be suitable as wives or nurses, but as fighters? Never."

CHAPTER 10

Chantal Deveraux untangled her sweaty legs from her lover and dropped from the four-poster bed to the floor. Victor snagged her wrist as soon as her feet touched the cold flagstones.

"Stay," he whispered.

"I'm hungry, my love. My body is still on US time."

"I'm hungry, too—but not for food." His smile was wolfish in the gloom.

"I need a drink." She pulled away gently.

The flagstones were deliciously cold under her feet and the whirling fan overhead dried the sweat on her back. She crept to the window and cracked the heavy wooden blinds. Late afternoon sun streamed in; the muffled sound of the surf sounded clearer.

She could pick out two of Victor's security team: one on the edge of the jungle, another closer to the beach. She knew there were more. Victor had once told her that his security team was like cockroaches—if you saw one, you knew there were ten you didn't see.

"That's a view I could get used to," Victor called from the bed, sitting up now. She shook her ass at him and laughed when he threw a pillow.

"Come back to bed, Chantal." His steel-gray eyes locked with hers and she felt that familiar weakness in her knees.

"I told you, I'm hungry," she said in a small voice.

"I know—and I'm going to fix that." Victor slid from bed and she let her eyes travel the length of his naked body. The thought of food slipped away again.

Chantal stepped across the room and into his arms. She ground herself against his thigh and felt him respond. She licked at the knife scar on his chest. "I've decided I'm not hungry anymore."

Victor picked her up and threw her onto the bed. "And I've decided you need your strength—for what I'm about to do to you." She watched him pad out of the room, her eyes lingering on his muscled back.

Chantal dropped back against the pillows and blew out a long breath at the fan turning slowly overhead. Victor Darwish was unlike any man she'd ever known.

She'd met him only six weeks ago, when she'd been on tour in Tunisia. It was a small club, smaller than was warranted for the great Imaan. They'd done an acoustic set, just her voice, a guitar, and a small percussion ensemble.

Victor occupied a private table to stage right and his eyes never left her all evening. He sent her a cocktail at intermission with an invitation to join him.

He rose when she approached his table. His dark suit fitted his lanky frame perfectly, the white silk shirt open at the neck.

When he pulled out a chair for her, his shirt slid open, revealing the puckered skin of the knife scar on his pectoral muscle. Chantal perched on the edge of her seat, every nerve tingling with anticipation.

She was twenty-eight years old and she'd never been with a man. The moment she sat at Victor's table, she knew that was about to change.

Chantal had grown up in Toronto, the daughter of a Somali mother and a Canadian diplomat father. Vague childhood memories of Somalia and Mogadishu were crowded out by the cold weather and bustle of Toronto. Her mother always told her how happy she was in Mogadishu, but Chantal recalled almost nothing from that time. It was only a few days after her seventh birthday when her parents divorced. She remembered it so clearly because her life changed so completely. Her mother, who retained sole custody of her daughter, underwent a religious reawakening and took Chantal with her on the spiritual journey. Overnight, her Canadian friends became "infidels," they were praying at the local mosque five times a day, and she was wearing a headscarf everywhere she went.

Chantal became Imaan at seventeen, after a YouTube video of her singing a Somali folk song went viral. Newspapers called her the next Celine Dion. Fluent in English, French, and Somali, the music of Imaan resonated with pet causes all over the world and across the political spectrum. Her life became a merry-go-round of recording, touring, and doing it all over again. Half the time she didn't even know what country she was in, let alone which cause was paying her.

The night she met Victor, she hadn't had a real vacation in over five years. Chantal rarely drank and the cocktail went straight to her head, adding to the euphoria and the surreality of the moment.

"I'd like to see you after the show," Victor said in a low voice, covering her hand with his own.

Chantal felt the space behind her belly button quiver. She nodded. Her voice had somehow stopped working.

All through the second set, the only person in the room was the intoxicating man sitting to her right. Every song was sung to him, every word seemed to be about him. His gaze felt like a living thing traveling up her thigh, across her breast, touching the hollow of her throat.

Victor, a Syrian businessman displaced by the war in his country, lived on a yacht, a sixty-foot behemoth with every imaginable luxury aboard. But Chantal saw none of those luxuries on that first glorious night—only the man who had brought her there.

When Chantal Deveraux woke up the next day at half past noon, she was a woman—and completely in love with Victor Darwish.

Even now, the memory of that first night made Chantal's breath catch in her throat. She slid her hand down the softness of her belly . . .

"Am I interrupting something?"

The sound of Victor's deep voice made her start. She sat up, blushing. "No, I'm just—is that for me?" She pointed to the tray.

Victor lowered the breakfast tray over her thighs and shook out a napkin. Chantal dug into a plate of scrambled eggs with spicy salsa, her hunger getting the best of her manners. "You're not eating?" she mumbled between mouthfuls.

"I ate in the kitchen." Victor slid into bed next to her. "I just want to watch you satisfy yourself." He dipped his face to her breast, gently tweaking her bare nipple with his teeth. She shivered.

Chantal took a sip of the sugar-rimmed cocktail that

accompanied her meal. Sweet and heavy with alcohol. "What is this?"

Victor smiled at her. "It's called a caipirinha. It's a South American drink made with sugarcane rum. Do you like it?"

Chantal shook her head. "Too sweet, too much alcohol. I'm a good Muslim, remember?"

"I'm not." Victor plucked the glass from her tray and took a long pull. His eyes went distant for a second.

"Tell me about Minneapolis," he said.

"It couldn't have gone better, my love. The FBI actually raided one of my concerts. A Somali was killed—accidentally. A tragedy, but it roused such a feeling in the community. I met a young woman named Ayana. She's perfect. Smart, driven, committed to me."

"A woman?" Victor took another sip of his drink. He licked his lips. "You plan to use her to recruit men?"

Chantal shook her head. "No, she is recruiting other women— girls, really, high school seniors mostly."

Victor studied her for a long moment. Chantal's heart beat faster. Just like in London and in Berlin, she'd been sent to Minneapolis to recruit men for Victor's plan. But the idea to develop an all-woman sleeper cell had been hers. In Minneapolis, the pieces seemed to come together organically, like it was meant to happen this way.

But now, as she told Victor about her plan, it seemed like less of a great idea.

He rubbed the cold glass against her bare breast. "Hey!" She pulled away.

He caught her arm and his icy gaze pinned her against the pillow. "I'm sending you to Helsinki next. I want you to recruit men this time, understand?"

She nodded, her mouth suddenly dry.

His gaze softened and he lay back on the bed. "So you really think a woman can lead what we have planned?"

Chantal placed her tray on the floor. In one move, she straddled Victor and plucked the drink from his hand. She took a long swallow of the cocktail, grimacing at the sharpness of the sweet alcohol. She arched her back, moving her hips against him.

"Absolutely."

CHAPTER 11

National Counterproliferation Center (NCPC), McLean, Virginia
19 December 2016 — 1330 local

Don Riley clicked over to the last slide in his briefing, a summary of the global nuclear threats he'd covered in the past ninety minutes: North Korea, Pakistan, Russia, separatists in Chechnya, the list went on. The older guys in the WMD Security Directorate, the NCPC "shop" where Don worked, still called them the Axis of Evil.

Thank God Iran was off the list—at least for the next decade or so. The world was complicated enough without adding another nuclear power in the Middle East.

He resisted the urge to pluck at his dress shirt where the sweat had made it stick to his back. Don did his best to meet retired Vice Admiral Daugherty's wintry blue gaze. He hadn't been exercised in a briefing like that in quite a while. In Don's opinion, this guy was totally ready to be the next Director of National Intelligence.

"What question haven't I asked you today, Mr. Riley, that I should have?" Daugherty rubbed his fingers along his jawline.

Unexpected. Guys like this never asked about what they *didn't* know. The obvious answer flashed into Don's mind, but he pushed it away. "Um, nothing, sir. I think we covered it."

Daugherty sniffed and shut his leather portfolio. He nodded at the two other analysts at the table—including Don's boss—and his own aide. "Give us the room, gentlemen."

Clem, Don's boss, backed toward the door, mouthing *what the fuck?* at Don. Don replied with a quick shrug of his shoulders.

"Sit down, Riley." Daugherty's tone sounded a touch warmer. Don pulled out a chair opposite the retired admiral and balanced the base of his spine on the last few inches of seat. He met the older man's gaze.

The admiral sat back in his chair. "It was a good briefing, Don. Do you prefer Don or Donald?"

Alarm bells tingled. *First-name basis with the prospective DNI? What did he want?*

"Don is fine, sir."

"I was curious about why you didn't mention Project Caveman."

And there we have it. The secret operation of Iranian hard-liners with three nuclear-tipped missiles had been discovered last year in a cave in the middle of the Gerash Mountains in Iran. Outside of the Joint Special Operations Command that had assaulted and destroyed the underground bunker, there were maybe a couple dozen people in the entire US government who knew about Caveman.

And everyone currently in power wanted it kept that way. It had happened during a state visit of Iranian President Hassan Rouhani to Tel Aviv. If the Israelis ever found out how close they'd been to nuclear annihilation, the political ramifications would be cataclysmic on so many levels.

"Sir, I can neither confirm—"

"I'm not asking you to talk about it, Don. I just want you to know that I'm aware of the operation—and its sister operation, Touchback."

Don kept his face perfectly still. *Don't say anything. Don't even blink.*

The name "touchback" was Brendan's contribution, a sly football reference that was still lost on Don. Even breathing that there had been a nuclear weapon on American soil in the hands of terrorists was grounds for rendition. That's what the paper said that Don had signed, and he had no desire to test the veracity of that particular nondisclosure agreement.

Daugherty gave him a thin smile. "I like your poker face, Don. Look, part of me wants to string you up for collaborating with an Iranian intelligence officer on a matter of American national security." He pinched his chin between his thumb and forefinger. "On the other hand, I admire the balls it took to do the right thing when it counted."

Don kept his tone neutral. "Thank you, sir."

"Don't thank me yet, Riley. I like your initiative. I think it's something that we've lost in our senior ranks in the intel community. If I'm confirmed by the Senate in January—or whenever the hell they get around to it—I want to send you over to the National Counterterrorism Center as a deputy director. You interested?"

Don gripped the arms of his chair. Deputy Director? He'd outrank his current boss by a paygrade or two, and he'd heard the tools over at Counterterrorism were much better than what he was used to in NCPC.

"Of course I'm interested, sir. What shop do you want me to lead?"

"I was thinking Strategic Threat Assessment."

"I'm not familiar with that division, sir."

Daugherty laughed. "That's because I made it up, Riley. Just for you."

"Sir?"

"You'll be in charge of keeping an eye on how these terrorist groups are growing their networks. Who are they making alliances with? How are they getting their money? How are they growing their organization?"

Don managed to keep a straight face. "I see."

Daugherty's eyes bored into him. "You seem disappointed, Don. Did you have something else in mind?" His voice had a slight mocking tone to it.

"I want to track down Rafiq Roshed." The words were out of Don's mouth before he'd even engaged his brain. No wonder—for the last few months, the mastermind behind the foiled nuclear attack in Minneapolis was never far from his mind.

"I thought you might say that, Don, which is why Strategic Threat Assessment is only a cover for your primary duties as a director of High-Value Target Prosecution, reporting directly to me. You go in-depth on the worst of the worst and come up with ways to take them out. Your first customer is Rafiq Roshed. How does that sound?"

"That sounds like something I could really get behind, sir." He swallowed. "There's something else, sir." Don's tongue scraped across the dry roof of his mouth.

"Yes, Riley?" Daugherty's gaze had hardened again. Don noticed they were back to "Riley" again.

"To find Roshed, we need the Iranians. I want your permission to confer with Reza Sanjabi of Iranian intelligence. He can be trusted, sir, and we need their help to—"

Daugherty held up his hand. Don snapped his mouth shut. The admiral pursed his lips as he surveyed Don again. "I'll consider it," he said finally.

"I can't do my job if you don't give me the tools, Admiral." Don thought he saw the ghost of a smile flit across Daugherty's face.

"You win, Riley. You get access to the Iranians for this one job, then we go back to radio silence. But remember: just because you colored outside the lines once and it saved the world doesn't mean you can do that twice. Be careful, Mr. Riley."

"I will, sir."

"You know what I'm going to say next, right, Don?"

"Yes, sir." Don paused. "We never had this conversation."

CHAPTER 12

Roosevelt High School, Minneapolis, Minnesota
02 January 2017 — 1145 local

Aya sat down at their normal table and folded her hands on the Formica surface. The other girls were eating the school lunch off the scarred plastic trays. Although Aya qualified for free school lunch, she was not eating today. She steeled herself for the questions.

"You're not eating, Aya?" Caaliyah asked.

"I'm fasting," she replied.

The other girls stopped eating and exchanged glances. "You're trying to lose weight?" They often made fun of the popular girls—mostly white—who were always talking about losing weight even though they had no butt and sticks for legs and arms.

"No, it's . . . it's my way of showing my faith." She looked around at her friends. "What did you all do over the holidays?" she said, trying to change the subject.

The diversion worked; the complaining started almost

immediately. America was a Christian land, no doubt about it. From Thanksgiving through the end of the year it was nonstop sales and Christian messages. Television, stores, newspapers— everywhere they were bombarded with Christianity. This year seemed worse than others. In the run-up to the 2016 presidential elections, the underlying tone often carried an us-versus-them message—and the implied "us" in that equation were the Christians.

Aya had been able to vote for the first time last fall. At the time, voting filled her with a sense of pride, but since then she'd been through the FBI raid on the Cedar. Now, especially after she talked with Imaan, that feeling of pride was replaced by a sense of anger.

"My brother went to the Mall of America last week," said Leylo. "He told me the police stopped him and made him turn out his pockets—right in front of everyone."

Aya nodded along with the others. She'd seen that happen to her own brother, Zacharia.

Hodan pushed her tray back. "I was at Southdale Mall last weekend. Three white boys from Edina made fun of my *hijab*." Her eyes filled with tears. "I was there to apply for a job. I was so embarrassed I just went home." Aya covered Hodan's hand with her own. Her friend was the most fragile of their group. It didn't take much to start Hodan crying.

Madino leaned in and lowered her voice. "My cousin—the one fighting for al-Shabab—was killed last week. My mother said he was killed at a wedding by a drone strike."

Aya wasn't sure if she believed Madino's drone-strike-at-a-wedding story—the girl had a way of stretching the truth—but based on the angry looks from the rest of the group, they seemed to be buying it. She tried to find that peaceful feeling she'd been cultivating over the holidays. She had spent hours reading the Qu'ran and praying—so much so that her mother asked her if something was wrong. After a few days of fasting and prayer, she managed to find the "calm center" that Imam Nabil at her mosque was always talking about.

By shutting out the world with prayer, she found a sort of peace.

But the world wasn't going to go away. After only a few hours back in school, she was lost in the slights of everyday life as a Muslim in America. Her clothes, her food, her language, her faith—none of it was welcome here.

"We're just as good as them," she said out loud. The other girls stopped talking.

"What?" said Caaliyah.

"We have just as much right to this country as any of them. We were born here—all of us are natural born citizens. They need to recognize us for who we are. They need to listen to us."

"Aya, we're just girls," chided Yasmin. "What can we do to make them take us seriously?"

"We're not just girls! We're strong Muslim women. Did you forget what Imaan said to us? We have the power in this world, the power of influence. The power to change our world."

The other girls stopped talking, their gazes on Aya. She felt herself sitting up straighter on her chair, as if her backbone was stiffening.

Imaan was right. Aya was the leader here and she needed to start acting like it. The singer said she was planning a protest, a demonstration to make the world recognize them as strong Muslim women. She asked Aya to be part of the cause. Aya had balked at the idea, but Imaan was right. She could see that now. Her group needed to take action, and she was the one to lead them.

"Has Imaan contacted you?" asked Caaliyah. Her eyes were wide and full of excitement.

Aya nodded.

"Well?" said Madino. "Tell us what she said."

One by one, Aya looked at each friend. Imaan had told her how to gauge whether each girl was with her or not.

Their eyes will tell you everything you need to know, Ayana.

Aya shivered as Imaan's rich voice echoed in her head. The singer had warned her to be absolutely sure about the trustworthiness of each friend before she took the next step. Aya's gaze settled on Hodan.

Maybe not tell them the whole plan. Yet.

"First," she said, "we're going to get jobs."

CHAPTER 13

Don Riley followed Terence Dawkins, his new deputy, through a maze of cubicles to his new office at NCTC. The guy was probably in his mid-fifties but sported a bushy gray mustache and walked with a stoop, making him seem a decade older. Old enough to be my father, Don thought. Well, older brother, at least.

When Daugherty had finally called with the details of his new assignment, Don could not have been happier. Officially, he was Deputy Director of the newly-formed Strategic Threat Assessment group, reporting directly to the DNI. Unofficially, Don headed a special department inside NCTC that hunted down elite-level terrorists who operated independently from organized groups. "The worst of the worst," in Daugherty's parlance.

"I trust that assignment will suit your needs, Mr. Riley?" the retired admiral had asked dryly.

"Absolutely, sir. When can I start?"

"You already have, Mr. Riley. Get your ass over there first thing in the morning."

"This is your office, sir." Terence stood to one side to allow Don to enter.

Don held himself back from whistling. The room seemed like an entire apartment after his cramped little cubicle back at NCPC. He strode to the window—a window!—and gazed out over the duck pond. In the reflection, he could see Terence watching him. Don assumed his poker face.

"This will do very nicely, Terence. Thank you for setting this up so quickly."

"The admiral ordered this arrangement weeks ago, sir. We've been expecting you."

"Oh." Don spied a door on the far side of the room. His own bathroom? "What's in there?"

Terence's smile was almost obscured under the mass of his mustache. "That's your comms suite, Mr. Riley." He opened the door to reveal a small desk and a video screen backed by a computer setup.

"At the DNI's direction, you have direct video-teleconference access to British SIS, Mossad, Australian SIS, French DGSE, German BND, Russian FSB, and the Iranian Ministry of Intelligence. Those last two circuits were the hardest ones, sir. Until a few months ago, no one anywhere in the US intelligence community had any access to their Iranian counterparts."

"Really?" Don kept his voice neutral.

"The DNI wanted you to know that when you are in contact with Russian FSB, you need to maintain two-person integrity at all times."

"I understand, Terence." He noticed the older man's frown. "Is there a problem?"

"Well, sir, I'm sure the DNI meant to extend the two-person rule to Iran as well as Russia."

"I think the DNI says what he means and means what he says, Terence. Maybe you can show me how this rig works?"

After ten minutes of instruction, Don had the procedure down. "I think I've got it, Terence. If you wouldn't mind shutting the door on your way out, I'm going to make a few calls."

"No problem, sir."

"Terence?"

The older man turned.

"Please call me Don."

Don used the directory to call up Liz's name at the FBI in Minneapolis. He composed his face into a frown as he hit the send button.

Liz's face filled the screen. "This is Special Agent Elizabeth—"

"Very important person from Washington DC calling to harass the minions in the field." He broke into a laugh.

"Don? The incoming call said it was secure from NCTC." Her face cleared. "You got a promotion!"

Don nodded. "I hunt down bad guys now. Really bad guys, especially the lone wolf kind." Even on this circuit he didn't dare mention Roshed's name.

Liz understood exactly what he meant. "I see," was all she said.

"How's Brendan?"

A pained look crossed her face. "Damned if I know. Haven't heard from him in a few weeks. He can't call when he's at sea and I have no idea when he pulls into port again." The edge in her voice made Don study her more closely. The area under her eyes was dark and she slumped in her chair.

"How're you doing, Liz? You look tired."

She scooted in closer to the camera and lowered her voice. "I'm in the middle of Boystown up here. I'm heading up a new JTTF on terrorist recruiting in the Twin Cities and it's a bear. We changed our operating philosophy and it's taking time to catch on. I'm running into a brick wall with the Somali community and the internal office politics here are . . . well, let's call them strained." She glanced over her shoulder. "And I miss Brendan. I don't know what's the matter with me. I lived without him for years and now it's like I'm dependent on him or something—emotionally, I mean."

Don thought about the gunshot wound she'd received only a few months ago during the nuclear terrorism incident at the new Minnesota Vikings stadium. "Have you been seeing anyone about these feelings? You know, professionally."

"You, too?" Liz sat back and crossed her arms. "Yes, Mother, I have completed the required psychological screening before returning to full duty. Anything else you'd like to know?"

"Liz, I didn't mean—"

"I know." She held up a palm and closed her eyes. "I'm not getting a lot of sleep these days and every time I check the local intel I feel like I'm sitting on a powder keg, but there's just not enough info for me to act." She sighed. "So we wait."

"I know that feeling. You know who I'm looking for, right?" A look of mutual understanding passed between them at the thought of Rafiq Roshed. "I'm going to get him, Liz. I just wanted to call you and make sure you knew that."

Don's next call felt historic.

He consulted the time zone planner that was part of the video-teleconference setup. Just after 1900 in Iran. He might just catch Reza at his desk, working late.

71

The secure video connection took about ten seconds to connect before Reza Sanjabi's round face filled the screen. Don and the people of the United States owed a lot to this baby-faced Iranian intelligence agent. In an act of bravery, he'd shared Iranian state secrets with Don that uncovered the plot to detonate a nuclear weapon in downtown Minneapolis. If things had gone differently, Reza Sanjabi would be sitting in an Iranian jail and there would be a radioactive crater where the Vikings stadium now stood.

"Donald, is that really you? When I was notified that I could receive calls from the US, I should have known you were behind it." His eyes narrowed. "This is not a social call, is it?"

Don shook his head. In terse terms, he outlined his new job and his plan to pursue Rafiq Roshed. Reza nodded thoughtfully as he listened.

"So that's my proposal," Don concluded. "We work together, you and I, to find Roshed and take him down. We'll involve other agencies as necessary, but this is personal for me—and for you, I'm sure."

Reza reached into the open safe behind his desk and pulled out a thick file folder. He smiled thinly at the camera.

"Let's get started."

CHAPTER 14

In the end, he almost had to call off the attack because he couldn't get a ticket to the game.

Faruq Hassan stood on the corner of Kellogg and Seventh Street in downtown St. Paul, letting the people flow around him. Despite the frigid winter weather, the Friday night crowd was loud and large. He shivered as he drew his long overcoat tighter against the icy winter wind. The steel barrel of the AR-15 pressed against his hip, stiffening his resolve.

On other side of the street, across the open plaza, the bright neon colors of the Xcel Energy Center billboard danced and swirled: Minnesota Wild versus the St. Louis Blues. A banner ran along the bottom saying the arena was sold out.

Faruq smiled to himself. He'd never been to an ice hockey game. Tonight would be a night of firsts in more ways than one.

A bearded man on the opposite street corner, his winter jacket stretched tight across a broad belly, held two tickets in the air. "Two for tonight!" he called out.

Faruq ran across the crosswalk just as the light was changing. The driver of the last car he passed flashed his high beams and laid on the horn. Faruq ignored him. "I'll take one," he said, stopping in front of the man with the tickets.

The man lowered the tickets and looked Faruq up and down. He could feel the man processing him: black skin, ratty overcoat, no hat, no gloves. The man shook his head. "Gotta sell 'em as a pair." He turned away and held up the tickets again. "Two for tonight's game," he shouted.

"Wait!" Faruq grabbed the man's shoulder and spun him around. A dark look crossed the man's heavy features as he shook off Faruq's hand.

"Back off, kid," he said in a loud voice. "I told you. They come as a pair."

Faruq saw a policeman on the other side of Kellogg. The cop was watching the exchange, watching him. "I'll take them."

The man's face broke into a yellowed smile. "Now that's more like it. Two hundred for the pair."

Faruq looked at the tickets. $53 each. The man was charging him almost double! He looked back at the policeman on the other side of the street. The light was about to change. "Alright." He dug into his pocket and pulled out the wad of money he had stashed for his getaway. Five hundred dollars. He peeled off ten twenty-dollar bills and handed them to the man.

The man eyed the wad of money. "What, are you like a drug dealer or something?" Despite his words, he didn't hesitate as he stashed the cash in his jacket pocket.

Faruq smiled at him as he turned toward the entrance underneath the neon billboard.

"I'm a Soldier of God."

Xcel Energy Center, St. Paul, Minnesota
27 January 2017 — 2030 local

Liz pulled her BMW into the lot next to the Xcel Energy Center
and hurried across Seventh Street. The entire corner plaza outside
the sports arena was awash with St. Paul police department squad
cars and ambulances. Despite the frigid temperatures, people were
milling about outside the police tape that ringed the area, watching as teams of paramedics treated injured people on the plaza.
Liz counted four bodies covered with sheets on the icy bricks of
the sidewalk.

She pulled her coat tighter around her and wished she'd remembered to bring a hat. Her breath steamed in front of her then
was whipped away by the wintry breeze. With the windchill, it
had to be well below zero tonight.

The SPPD command post was just inside the door of the Xcel
Energy Center. Liz stepped into the welcome warmth and approached the man in charge. She flashed her badge.

"Liz Soroush, FBI antiterrorism task force. Can you give me
a rundown, Captain?"

The precinct captain's eyes shifted over Liz's shoulder. She
turned and stifled a groan as she recognized the local chief of
police. Pushing sixty, sporting a mane of silver-gray hair with a
mustache and a belly to match, the man looked like a poster boy
for old-school politics. His face, always ruddy in complexion, was
deep red. Clearly tensions were running high for the chief—not
that she blamed him.

"We've got this one, young lady. No need for the FBI to get involved." He spoke loudly enough that people around them stopped what they were doing and turned toward the sound of his voice. To make matters worse, two of her agents, Kamen and Adams, had just stepped in the door. They exchanged glances.

Liz's face grew warm. "Chief, I believe you just told the press not ten minutes ago that this was a terrorist attack. Apart from the fact that you're jumping to conclusions on camera, that automatically makes this a federal case. I'm sure you were speaking out of concern for the citizens who lost their lives tonight." She forced a smile and moved close enough to smell his cloying aftershave.

"If you want me to get the mayor's office involved, I'll do it," she said in a lower tone, "but we both know that's not going to go well for you, Chief. My name is Special Agent Soroush, by the way. If you call me 'young lady' again, I will not be responsible for my actions."

The chief had a politician's smile painted on his face, but his complexion turned a deeper shade of crimson. "Captain, please brief our FBI colleagues on the situation."

The captain led her into the deserted interior of the Xcel Energy Center, her agents trailing them. "He's going to retire in June, ma'am. Not soon enough for me."

"Unfortunately, Captain, in my line of work assholes are an occupational hazard." She ignored the captain's stifled laughter. "So what have we got?"

The officer stopped in the center of the hallway. Concession stands lined the walls between entrances to the ice arena. Everything seemed in a state of suspension. Spilled popcorn, a half-eaten hotdog on the ground next to a trash can, an open beer tap dripping.

"African-American male—no ID yet, we're still running prints—entered through the main entrance. That's the one you just came through. He purchased a scalped ticket outside. We have the scalper for questioning, but all he says is he sold a pair of tickets to a black kid who seemed jumpy. Paid cash. When the guy asked if he was a drug dealer, he said he was a 'Soldier of God.'"

"Pair of tickets?" Liz asked. "There was a second person involved?"

The captain shook his head. "The guy was playing him. Said he would only sell a pair. Charged him double, too."

They kept walking and Liz began to see bullet holes peppering the walls and ceiling.

"He started shooting outside," the captain said. "The best working theory at this point is that he bought the tickets before he realized he'd have to pass through metal detectors to get inside the building. We think he panicked and tried to shoot his way in. He took out four civilians on the plaza, then two more inside as he went through the metal detectors. He had an AR-15 with three magazines of thirty rounds each, plus a 9mm Glock handgun." The captain pointed to a line of bullet holes in the ceiling.

"Kid was a lousy shot. Acted like this was the first time he'd ever fired a weapon. Couldn't control the recoil and took forever to reload. Never even used his third magazine." The captain gestured at a covered body thirty feet in front of them. "He never got inside the arena. One of my guys dropped him right there."

"Is your officer okay?"

The captain barked out a laugh. "Better than the six civilians who bought it. My guy caught one in the chest—he had his vest on—and lost a piece of his ear before he put the kid down."

Liz knelt next to the body and pulled the covering off the face. Her first impression was how young he seemed. To her eye, he looked maybe seventeen. She pulled the sheet back further. Three bullet holes, center mass.

"Nice grouping," Agent Kamen murmured behind her. Liz stood and pulled the sheet all the way off the body.

Dark jeans, black shirt, black overcoat. Under the jacket he'd fashioned a sling for the assault rifle using a belt and had sewn extra interior pockets in the coat for the banana clips. Everything screamed homemade.

Liz turned to her team. "Alright, let's figure this guy out. Adams, get the security footage and see what we can get from people's mobile phones. Anything on his prints yet?"

The captain checked his phone and shook his head.

"Once we have an ID, let's find out where he lives and search his place. See if we have a suicide note or video or something— what's this?" She knelt next to the body and held up his arm, pushing the sleeve of his overcoat down past his elbow. Through the latex glove, she could feel that the man's flesh was already cooling.

On the inside of his forearm was a tattoo. A stylized flame.

The captain leaned over her shoulder. "Gang sign, maybe? Never seen it before."

Liz gestured at Kamen. "Get a picture of this and see if we can find a match with a gang or some other group."

"What do you think, Liz? Lone wolf HVE?" her agent asked.

Liz lowered the corpse's arm and covered the body again. Homegrown violent extremists were the nightmare scenario for the FBI. An American citizen, disaffected and anxious to find a sense of worth in whatever twisted way he could get it, just like the San Bernardino shooters in 2015. No border fence or visa screening was going to find these people—they were already here, feeding off the dark side of the Internet. Most of them were as unprepared in their attacks as they were at life, and most were picked up long before they were a danger to the public. But a few—like this guy—met a bloody end and took innocent civilians with them.

The nightmare was another Timothy McVeigh. A lone wolf with smarts.

"Let's hope that's all it is."

CHAPTER 15

Liz stared into the mirror and blinked the Visine drops out of her bloodshot eyes. She still looked like she hadn't slept—which was true. She made a few halfhearted swipes at the dark circles under her eyes with a concealer pad and gave up.

A soft knock came through the restroom door. "Boss?" Kamen said. "We're almost ready to start the briefing with DC."

"I'll be right there," Liz called. *Showtime with the elephants in Washington—what a joy.* She slipped on her rumpled suit jacket and pasted a confident smile on her face.

The videoconference room was set up such that she and Trask shared the head of the table. The other FBI agents in her task force filled in the seats along the side. Liz drew in a sharp breath when the screen for DC went live. The leaders of Department of Homeland Security, FBI, and Director of National Intelligence filled the screens and numerous staffers were undoubtedly listening in. Trask had warned that an attack only days after the new administration took office was bound to get political fast, but this surprised even her.

Trask took the lead. "Good morning, ladies and gentlemen. I'd like to introduce Supervisory Special Agent Elizabeth Soroush, head of the very recently formed JTTF on Homegrown Recruitment here in Minneapolis. She will be briefing you on the events of last night."

Liz realized she had left her bottle of water in the restroom. She cleared her throat. "Good morning. At approximately 1946 central time last night, a lone gunman entered the Xcel Energy Center in downtown St. Paul armed with an AR-15 assault rifle and a handgun. He began firing into the crowd outside the building, then used the ensuing chaos to get through the security checkpoint. He was engaged and killed by an on-duty St. Paul police officer in the hallway outside the arena proper. Casualties were six civilians killed and fourteen injured, two in critical condition. The officer also received a minor injury."

She touched the keyboard and the screen showed the face of a young Somali man. "This is our shooter, Faruq Hassan. US citizen of Somali descent. Twenty years old, worked part-time for a local recycling company until he was laid off six months ago. Lives with his mother, no father that we can find. No employment history since and no criminal record. We had his fingerprints on file from an application for a job at the airport. We searched his apartment last night and found two things of interest. First was this video found on an SD card." Liz touched another button to start the video.

A shaky picture of Faruq taken from a mobile phone appeared. The young man looked sweaty and uncomfortable. His eyes were focused to the right of the camera and tracked along as he read his statement.

"By the time you see this testimony, I will have done my duty as a Soldier of God. I will have performed His will on this Earth and gone to a better place. American politicians talk about the land of opportunity, but what you mean is white opportunity. You mean that the rich get more wealth. And what about Muslims in your land of opportunity? You mock us because we dress different. You demonize our faith. You treat us like animals and expect us to stay in our herd. No more!

"I am a Soldier of God. I am His sword; He is my shield."

Liz let the video end and waited a few seconds before she continued. "Despite the rhetoric, there are some inconsistencies in his actions. He was well-armed but seemed unfamiliar with the weapon he carried. Mr. Hassan only managed to fire two of his three magazines for the assault rifle and never even drew his handgun. Indications are that he had not visited the site prior to the attack, as he appeared to be surprised by the metal detectors at the entrance. In his apartment, we found a high-end laptop that was completely wiped using a sophisticated shredder program. Both of these facts are inconsistent with an unemployed garbageman. Additionally, all of his social media accounts were closed about two hours before the attack. We're getting a warrant to recover all of his social media records."

"What about his religious habits?" asked one of the DHS analysts. "Did we see any increased devotion in recent months?"

Liz nodded. "We're canvassing the mosques in Minneapolis now. As soon as we find out where he worshipped, we'll interview the person in charge."

The line went quiet when Director of National Intelligence Daugherty spoke. He had the kind of voice that, even though he spoke softly, carried an air of confidence that forced Liz to hear him.

"Special Agent Soroush, let me recap what I've heard this morning. You describe all the classic signs of a candidate for radicalization—minority, male, unemployed, lacking an authority figure. You also tell us there are indications of outside support, such as a laptop and sophisticated software, which would suggest a local contact. To round it all out, this guy clearly just had a death wish. What am I missing?"

Liz cleared her throat. "You're right, sir, it doesn't add up. The 'Soldier of God' terminology does not align with any known terrorist group or gang element, but we did find one other item on his person that may have significance."

She showed the picture of the tattoo. "We found this mark on the inside of his right forearm."

"So what is it?" the DNI asked. "A gang symbol?"

"We have no idea."

CHAPTER 16

Liz pulled her BMW into the parking spot marked Visitor and switched off the ignition. From the outside, the Shaafici Mosque looked more like a warehouse than a place of worship, but she supposed every church had to start somewhere.

She closed her eyes and rested her head back against the leather headrest. After thirty hours without sleep, every muscle in her body told her she was running on empty, but this was her last stop before she went home for a few hours of shut-eye.

She'd deliberately planned to come between prayer times, and the foyer was deserted. Liz pulled the dark blue and silver headscarf over her hair and slipped off her shoes. She padded through the empty mosque, following the signs to the imam's office.

The inside of the worship area in the mosque was decorated with wall hangings and the lights had been softened, but it still had a slight industrial feel. Even the door to the imam's office looked like an ordinary cheap office door. She knocked.

There was a murmur from inside that she took to mean come in. Imam Nabil's office looked exactly the way she expected the office of a holy man to look. Heavy bookcases of dark wood were filled with thick tomes and a rich woven carpet felt good under her tired feet. Nabil rose from behind his desk, where he had been reading a newspaper under the soft light of a desk lamp.

"Ah, Special Agent Soroush, welcome."

Liz accepted his double handshake and inclined her head, unsure how to address him. Imam Nabil was in his late fifties with a frosting of gray on his close-cropped hair. He wore a business suit over a white shirt with a clerical collar and a white shawl covered his shoulders.

"Would you like some tea?"

Liz detected a scent in the air that she could not quite place. "Is that cardamom?" she asked.

Nabil laughed, a hearty chuckle from the belly. "Very good, Agent Soroush, very good indeed." He handed her a cup of steaming amber-colored liquid. "My own special recipe—and I love cardamom."

He settled behind his desk and waved her to a chair opposite him. "Before we get to the purpose of your visit, please tell me about yourself. I've never met an actual FBI agent before—and a woman at that. Your ancestry, is it Persian?"

Normally, Liz would have bristled at a man suggesting that a female FBI agent of Middle Eastern descent was somehow unusual, but Nabil seemed genuinely interested and open. She found herself returning his grin in spite of herself. She sipped her tea, letting the spices add some life to her tired muscles.

"Yes, my parents were both born in Iran—they left in

seventy-nine, when the Shah fell. I was born here, but my family keeps a strong cultural connection to our Persian heritage." She broke off, hiding her embarrassment with another sip of tea. "I'm sorry, I'm not used to talking about myself."

Nabil dropped a lump of sugar into his drink and offered the bowl to Liz, who declined. "Fascinating. How did you become an FBI agent?"

"I was in the Marine Corps." Nabil's eyes widened. "I graduated from the US Naval Academy and became a Marine. Later, I joined the FBI as a Farsi translator during the war in Iraq."

"Your parents must be very proud." Nabil beamed at her.

Liz buried her face in the cup of tea. He was half right. Her father was proud of her; her mother, not so much. When she looked up, Nabil's expression had darkened. "I have said the wrong thing." He put a hand over his heart. "I am truly sorry. Let us discuss why you wanted to see me."

Was she that easy to read or was this guy that good? Liz handed him a photograph of Faruq Hassan. "Do you know this man?"

Nabil studied the picture, then handed it back. "No. Has he done something wrong?"

"He was involved in the shooting at the Xcel Energy Center last night."

Nabil scowled. "A dark topic, Agent Soroush. How can I help you?"

"Please, call me Elizabeth."

Why had she said that? This was an official visit; no need to get on a first-name basis with this man. And why Elizabeth? No one called her Elizabeth.

"And you must call me Nabby—that is my nickname among my friends."

Liz frowned. "I'm used to religious leaders having more formal names, like calling a priest 'Father,' for example."

Nabby nodded. "A common misconception, Elizabeth. The leaders of our mosques are appointed by a bureaucracy, like other religions. I am the spiritual leader of this mosque, but I serve at the pleasure of the community. In that respect, Islam is a religion of the people." He offered a wry grin. "That approach has advantages and some drawbacks."

"And the issue of terrorist organizations recruiting your young people?" Liz asked. "Is that talked about in the mosques?"

A pained expression crossed Nabby's features. "Oh, yes, but in very different ways, depending on the imam. As you might imagine, an imam builds a following that mirrors his preaching. My community is very concerned about this issue. It goes against everything we stand for as Somalis and as Muslims. Destructive radical groups like Daesh and al-Shabab are the reason we left our homeland in the first place."

"But there are imams here in the Twin Cities who support those groups?"

Nabby shifted in his chair. "Yes, I suppose so, but that is what you call a 'red herring,' a distraction from the truth. There is no reason for a Somali boy to be attracted to Daesh—we share no cultural ties." He leaned forward, scowling, all traces of his good-natured smile wiped from his face.

"My generation fled our homeland in civil war, but our path to this country was not a straight line. I spent a year in a refugee camp in Kenya. It was hell—little food, filthy water, dirty—and then I came to America. Clean cities, friendly people, a warm place to sleep. I owe this country everything.

"The young people who are targeted by Daesh recruiters have never seen a refugee camp or gone hungry night after night. They fight a different battle, a battle of ideas. They were born here just like you, but this society does not really treat them like citizens. They are marginalized, on the outside looking in on the real America. They watch television and see big houses and fancy cars and they think: 'is this all there is?' That's when they find Daesh." He sat back, carving the air with his hands.

"We were all teenagers once, Elizabeth. Whether you were born in Mogadishu or Minneapolis, every young person experiences this rite of passage, a time of questioning, a time when the heart leads the head. This is when Daesh finds their recruits. When young people look for answers, Daesh makes it look easy. A caliphate—a state run by the pure ideals of Islam—is a fiction, but not to a young man on the edge of manhood looking to make his mark on the world."

Nabby paused and Liz realized she had moved to the very edge of her seat. He grinned at her. "I get wrapped up in my own words, Elizabeth. My apologies."

Liz realized she had not taken a single note in the meeting. She cleared her throat to buy some time. "Is there a way these young men can be identified early?"

Nabby stroked his beard. "We are dealing with the fires of youth, my FBI friend. Did you know what you were going to do when you were a teenager? I certainly didn't—and nowhere in my future plans did I expect to be an imam."

He chuckled, then his face turned serious again. "We have the expected responses, such as increased youth outreach, sports leagues, and so on, but the first and last line of defense is the family. A sudden change in behavior, a turn to devout practices for no obvious reason—these are possible signs of recruitment." He sighed. "Unfortunately, these are also signs of being a normal teenager."

CHAPTER 17

Minneapolis, Minnesota
29 January 2017 – 1030 local

Aya peered through the peephole in the door of their apartment. The gray-bearded face of Imam Nabil, made large by the curvature of the lens, filled her view. She closed her eyes. What could he want?

Aya forced a smile as she opened the door. "Imam Nabil, peace be upon you." The smile froze on her face as a short dark-haired figure stepped out from behind the Imam.

The FBI agent from the Cedar. The woman who had killed Hamza.

"What do you want?" Aya demanded. She struggled to keep her tone steady.

"Aya! That's no way to treat a law officer," the imam chided.

The woman placed her foot so that Aya could not close the door on them. "Is your brother Zacharia at home?" she said. The agent was short, but her shoulders were square and strong beneath her suit jacket. She stared at Aya with intensity.

"Why do you want to know?" Aya said. The door would not budge.

"Aya!" The imam tried to step between them.

"Please, Aya," the FBI agent said. "I just need to ask him a few questions. We're investigating the shooting at the Xcel Energy Center."

"He's not here." Aya increased pressure on the door, but the woman had her foot firmly wedged against the floor. Down the hall, Aya saw nosey Beydan, her mother's friend, peek out her door then shut it again when she saw the FBI agent. No doubt that witch would be on the phone to Aya's mother right now.

"Let them in, Ayana." Zacharia's voice sounded deep and manly behind her. Like he knew what he was doing.

The woman and the imam followed Zacharia into the tiny sitting room. Aya hung in the doorway to the kitchen, studying the FBI agent. She was barely taller than Aya, with Middle Eastern features, but her accent was pure American. The woman's eyes roamed around the room and Aya felt a flush of embarrassment at their worn couch and battered coffee table. By the cut of her clothes, this woman was used to finer things.

"Thank you for seeing me, Zacharia," she was saying. The agent and the imam sat side by side on the couch while her brother occupied the armchair opposite them. The agent held out her ID. To Aya's surprise, after Zacharia had seen them, she held her credentials out to Aya.

Elizabeth Soroush, the ID read. The accompanying badge was gleaming gold and looked heavy. Aya nodded and the agent snapped the leather folio shut.

"You said you were here about the shooting," Zacharia said. His eyes flitted between the imam, who was nodding and grinning like an idiot, and the intense woman.

"How well did you know Faruq Hassan?"

Zacharia shrugged. "I knew him from school. He graduated a year ahead of me at Roosevelt."

"You played on the same soccer team?"

Aya raised her eyebrows. How would they know that? She barely recalled that fact and this was her brother.

"Yeah, we did." Zacharia hunched forward and avoided the FBI agent's gaze. "What of it?"

"Were you involved in any other activities together?"

"No."

"Zacharia, my son," began the imam, "if you have any information that—"

"I don't know him!"

The agent studied Zacharia, letting the silence in the room build. Aya realized she was holding her breath.

"Are your parents at home?" Agent Soroush finally asked.

"My mother is at work," Zacharia said. "My father is sleeping. He has a bad back."

Aya stifled a laugh. Her father was stoned, that was the truth of it. Sure, he had a bad back, but his biggest problem was his addiction to painkillers.

"Could you wake him up? I'd like to talk to him."

Her brother crossed his arms. "That's not possible. I told you he's not feeling well. You came here to talk to me, right? Well, I'm talking to you, so what's the problem?"

The imam was shifting in his seat like he had to pee. He knows about my father, Aya thought, and he doesn't want her to find out either. "Elizabeth, perhaps we could come back another time?" the imam said.

Soroush pulled a small leather-bound notepad from her purse. "No, I think Zacharia's right. We can talk to him." She flipped the pad open. "What can you tell me about terrorist recruiting in the Minneapolis Somali population?"

"Why would you ask me that?" Zacharia sat up straight, his eyes blazing. "You think because I knew someone who joined al-Shabab, that I'm part of that movement?"

"Hamza was your cousin. At the Cedar, you tried to protect him." The agent's eyes narrowed as she stared hard at Zacharia.

"So that brands me one of them, does it?" Zacharia snapped back. "My parents fled a civil war with nothing but the clothes on their backs. They came here to build a new life. My sister and I were born here—we're as American as you, Agent Soroush. And yet you come into our home and imply that I am part of a group that kills people."

"I'm not implying anything, sir, I'm just asking questions." The agent's voice was calm, but she watched Zacharia's eyes. She's baiting him, Aya thought. She's trying to get him to say something that will let her arrest him.

"You call America a land of tolerance?" Zacharia pointed at Aya. "Do you know what they say to my sister about her *hijab*? She's just a girl!" Aya bristled at his term, but he was right. Her brother pointed at the imam. "How many times have you had to clean graffiti off the walls of the mosque? How many? If the same thing happened to a Protestant church, it would be on the front page of the newspaper." Zacharia spoke in an intense, fiery tone and Aya saw little flecks of spittle rain down on the coffee table separating him from the agent and the imam.

"You people do the terrorist's work for them!" he said. "You alienate, you oppress, you discriminate, and they go running to Daesh."

"We weren't talking about Daesh, Zacharia."

"You will be."

The agent exchanged glances with the imam, who had a stunned look on his face. "Would you care to explain?" she said.

Zacharia pulled his smartphone from his hip pocket and held it up. "This is the recruiting tool. You create the conditions, Daesh does the rest."

"Was Faruq active in a gang here in Minneapolis?"

Zacharia slipped his mobile back into his pocket. He took a deep breath. "Not that I know of."

"We have reason to believe he may have recently joined a gang. He had a tattoo, a gang symbol, we think." She passed a photo to Zacharia.

He shook his head and held it up so that Aya could see it. "I don't recognize it. Have you seen this, Aya?"

The photo showed a teardrop-shaped flame tattooed on the inside of someone's forearm. Aya felt sweat break out on the back of her neck. She shook her head, not trusting herself to say anything.

She had seen it before. On Imaan.

CHAPTER 18

Dark and cold, with a dampness that never quite left her body. That was how she thought of Finland. Chantal longed for the heat and humidity of the tropics and Victor's touch . . .

She was so lost in her thoughts that she walked right past the cafe and had to backtrack to the dingy door. Chantal peered in the window. The place was deserted except for a group occupying a table in the corner. The sun—what little they saw of it in the typically overcast months of January in Finland—had set hours ago. Any self-respecting Finn was home with his family next to a source of warmth.

But the group she was about to meet were not self-respecting Finns. Kahin looked up from his drink and saw her face in the window. He broke into a wide smile, white teeth set off against the mocha color of his skin. Chantal waved back and pushed through the doorway.

The interior of the cafe was oppressively hot, forcing her to unwind the scarf from around her neck. The group stood and applauded her. She had gotten them all tickets to her evening show. Chantal found the afterglow of a performance was the best time for recruiting. The shine of her star power was still intact and she always closed her concerts with a sweet Somali lullaby arrangement that brought even grown men to tears.

Kahin came forward, his hand outstretched. "Sister, it was a marvelous performance. Thank you for the tickets."

"Peace be upon you, brother Kahin." Chantal kissed him on both cheeks. Like her family, Kahin was a member of the Hawiye clan, one of the largest in the region in and around Mogadishu. She'd found that playing to the community aspects of the Somali clan culture worked well, especially in the closed Finnish society.

Like most of the Somali diaspora, the first wave of immigrants hit the shores of Helsinki in the early 1990s during the fallout from the Somali civil war. With the country in recession, the Finnish government crammed the new arrivals into hastily built rental buildings in the Meri-Rastila neighborhood of Helsinki. The area quickly became known as "Little Mogadishu."

She let Kahin handle the introductions while she surveyed the group the way Victor had taught her. Kahin was the idealist of the group and the self-appointed leader. Two of the men were brothers who looked at one another before either said anything—definitely followers. She studied the close-set eyes of the man Kahin introduced as Bashir. He was older than the rest, with a short, stocky frame and a way of jutting out his jaw when he spoke. Definite self-esteem issues, she thought. She would need to watch that one.

Kahin guided her to a seat next to the only other woman in the group, a young girl barely older than Ayana from Minneapolis. But where Ayana was plain with thick features and round cheeks, this girl was beautiful. Her doe eyes met Chantal's with a surprising steadiness.

"Peace be upon you, Imaan," she said in Somali. Her voice sounded alive with color and Chantal was sure the girl was a singer. "My name is Leymoon."

"And with you as well," Chantal replied. She touched the girl's *hijab* with her cheek as she kissed her. Chantal had an eerie feeling that she was looking at herself from a decade ago.

Kahin cleared his throat and Chantal took her seat. She folded her hands in her lap and lowered her eyes as if in prayer. The first few minutes of these meetings were the most critical. That was when most of her recruits made up their minds. Once they were committed, their own selective bias kicked in to allow only the inputs that validated their worldview.

"I have lived a blessed life," she began in a soft voice that she knew came across as humble. "Allah has seen fit to grant me the gift of song. I can touch millions of people with His gift—like all of you." Chantal raised her gaze and smiled—not too broadly, she was still going for humble at this point.

"I travel around the world bringing my message of hope and faith. But sometimes I am called to make a deeper connection with those who listen to my music." She scanned the group. The right signs were all there: parted lips, direct eye contact, dilated pupils. Even Bashir was engaged.

"I asked my brother Kahin to gather a group of . . . like-minded people—people he can trust—to talk about a deeper mission. Everywhere I travel, I see my Somali brothers and sisters suffering under the heel of Christianity. We did not choose this life. No, living as a Muslim under the yoke of Christianity was thrust upon us by circumstances beyond our control." She leaned forward and lowered her voice, noting with satisfaction how the group mirrored her actions.

"Our parents made a pact with these countries. 'Live here,' they said. 'We are free societies. We do not see color or religion— only the person.'" Chantal pretended to spit on the table. "That is a lie. And now, we come to your generation. You were born here. You are citizens of Finland. For you, there is no homeland but this one. And the time has come for you to demand your rights as free Muslim citizens."

Chantal stopped, breathing heavily, her cheeks flushed with color.

"What is it you ask of us?" Kahin asked, his voice hoarse with emotion.

Chantal took her time answering, gazing at each face around the table one at a time. Waiting until the person grew uncomfortable under her gaze and looked away. She finished with Kahin.

"What is it you have to give, my brothers and sisters? What are you *willing* to give? Time, money . . . your life?"

She stood and leaned over the table.

"Put steel in your hearts and answer that question for yourself. The time is coming when you will be asked to choose. The true believers will know their answer."

CHAPTER 19

Don Riley wanted to tug at his collar in the worst way, but he gripped the side of the lectern instead. He knew he should have worn the blue dress shirt with the size-seventeen-and-a-half collar. That last half-inch made all the difference since he'd been less frequent in his gym visits—

"Mr. Riley?"

Don stiffened, realizing he'd missed the last few seconds of conversation.

"Sir." He focused on the room again.

Vice Admiral Daugherty, the newly appointed DNI, bored into him with his wintry blue eyes. His three closest staffers—all of them career bureaucrats—exchanged knowing glances. Daugherty did not suffer fools. Don had been caught daydreaming, and he could see them practically licking their lips at the imminent bloodbath.

"I'd like to hear more about these partnerships you've formed with outside intelligence agencies in the search for Roshed," said the other man in the room.

Brian Bunkerage was the exact opposite of what you might expect from the new head of the National Counterterrorism Center. Soft, wavy brown hair, soft brown eyes, and a belly that strained at his shirt buttons made him look more like a pastor than a man in charge of keeping the country safe from terrorists. He'd been confirmed by the Senate just yesterday and Don had only met him moments prior to the meeting. In fact, the meeting was for his benefit, to bring him up to speed on the NCTC projects that Daugherty was watching especially closely.

Don realized his new boss had just thrown him a lifeline.

"Yes, sir," Don began. "The BND and the DGSE both claim to have sniffed out some leads on the whereabouts of Rafiq Roshed, but in the same breath they say they have no resources to put on it. Since the Germans and the French have their hands full with Syrian refugees anyway, I can't say I expected much help from them.

"The Brits and the Aussies are focused on South America and Southeast Asia, respectively. South America is a blank, but the Aussies have reason to believe he may have been in Myanmar recently. They're still following that lead for us. The Russians claim to have intel that Roshed is operating in Syria, against ISIS. It's a single-source lead, and while it's a possibility, I don't believe it. Roshed is a lone wolf with a lot of enemies. The fluidity of Syria would expose him to too many personal threats. In my opinion, it's doubtful that even his old Hezbollah friends would associate with him now.

"It's clear to me that the Iranians want him dead. So far, the support from Iran in this search has been invaluable and I believe that Reza Sanjabi has all the support he needs to track down Roshed. If the Iranians get to him before we do, Rafiq is a dead man."

Daugherty's lips twisted into a thin smile. "That would be fine by me—as long as they can prove he's really dead. This guy has a nasty way of staying alive when we least want him to." He shifted his gaze to the new head of the NCTC. "Do you want to tell Riley about his new assignment, Brian?"

Bunkerage nodded. "Thank you, Admiral. Mr. Riley, I assume you know about the failed raid on al-Shabab a few months ago?"

"Yes, sir. The raid didn't capture any al-Shabab leaders, but we did net indications of a new linkage between Daesh and al-Shabab."

"Exactly. The Islamic State threat continues to grow and our new President would like to send a message to any other extremist groups out there that association with Daesh is a sure ticket to a short life. We've been given a green light to carry out a direct action against al-Shabab leadership."

Don raised his eyebrows. As the Seal Team Six raid had proved, even with the best forces, military actions in Somalia were extremely difficult. With clan-based warlords ruling patches of territory, the lines between civilian and enemy were blurry on a good day. Add to the mix a severe lack of in-theater HUMINT and you had a recipe for a public relations disaster if the raid went sideways. Going after al-Shabab again so soon after the last raid was a gutsy move. He shuffled his feet and gripped the lectern a little more firmly.

"How can I help, sir?"

"We want you to pull double-duty, Mr. Riley," Daugherty said. "Lead the hunt for Roshed and quarterback the effort to nail down a location on the al-Shabab leadership. We want to take down

Ikrima. When you're satisfied you have them, we'll use JSOC to take them out."

"What's your timeline, sir?" Daugherty's plan to use Joint Special Operations Command forces to take them out showed he was not planning on this mission being anything but successful.

Daugherty's steely gaze didn't flinch. "Yesterday."

"What assets do I have, sir?"

"What do you need, Don?" *So we're back to Don now.*

Don's size-seventeen shirt collar suddenly felt a lot tighter. He was in the deep end of the pool now. Bunkerage was watching him closely, those soft brown eyes turned gleaming and hard. The little voice in Don's brain screamed: *This is how you become a scapegoat!* He slid a finger into his shirt collar and gave a sharp tug.

"You'll have my list by close of business, sir."

CHAPTER 20

Minneapolis, Minnesota
02 February 2017 — 1530 local

Imaan was even more beautiful than the last time Aya had seen her. Her rich dark hair spilled out from under her loose headscarf, shining like a living thing when she moved.

The singer had contacted her only last night, saying she was stopping in Minneapolis for a few hours on her way to California—just to see Aya. Just as Imaan instructed, she met the dark town car on the corner of East Franklin and 21st, across from the Blue Nile restaurant. When the car door opened, Imaan was there.

It was like a dream, the way the singer embraced her, kissing her on both cheeks with an extra kiss on the forehead, just below the tight line of Aya's *hijab*. She smelled of jasmine and some other rich scent that Aya couldn't identify. Imaan held onto her hand after the embrace, squeezing her fingers.

"It is so good to see you, my little flower," the singer said.

"Email is so impersonal. Necessary, but impersonal all the same." She looked out the car window at the houses flashing by in the winter twilight.

"Tell me, Ayana, have you seen your homeland through different eyes?"

Aya nodded. Imaan had indeed opened her eyes to seeing the everyday slights of life as a Muslim woman in America. Under her friend's liquid gaze, Aya told her of the men who stared at her traditional dress, the drivers who called her horrible names from the safety of their speeding cars. And then there was the Internet. The *Minneapolis Star-Tribune* had done a front-page story about a Syrian refugee family who bought a home in Minneapolis. Between the smiling man and woman in traditional *hijab* and robes stood a grinning four-year-old boy. The comments in the online article were the worst sort of Internet bile, shocking even Aya's dulled senses. Even recalling some of the slurs, Aya felt her face flush with anger.

Imaan's fingers tightened as the girl spoke and she nodded, her own eyes seeming to mist over. "You do see it, Ayana. I'm proud of you. The only way to fix the problem is to be able to see it first."

"So that's what we're doing? Fixing this discrimination?"

Another squeeze of her ringed fingers. "Patience, Ayana. Patience." The bangles on her wrists jangled as she raised Aya's hands to her lips and kissed her knuckles.

Imaan kissed my hands. Aya felt as if she'd passed into an alternate universe.

"Tell me about your circle of friends," Imaan said. "Can you trust them?"

Aya nodded. "They've gotten jobs at the mall—just like you said. Hodan and I are janitors." Aya wrinkled her nose and Imaan laughed. "Madino and Caaliyah are at the aquarium and Yasmin and Leylo work at the bookstore. We're saving the money, like you said, but for what?"

"Patience, Ayana!" Imaan laughed, then looked at her from the corner of her eye as if deciding whether or not to share a secret. Aya's heart beat faster as Imaan caught the edge of her red-painted lip with her perfectly white teeth. "Okay, maybe you are ready after all."

She twisted in her seat to face Aya. "You are part of a much larger organization—a worldwide network—to protest the treatment of Muslim citizens in Western countries. In a few months, we will stage demonstrations across the globe to show the West the power of Muslims, especially Muslim women."

"It's a secret?"

Imaan's fingers crushed hers and her face went still. "Please, Ayana, tell me I haven't made a mistake in trusting you with this information. If word were to leak out prematurely, the police would stop everything. The West wants Muslims to be silent, to live like the way you described to me just a few moments ago. You and all your sisters are native-born Americans. You don't deserve that kind of treatment, do you?"

Aya shook her head. "Will the demonstrations be violent?"

Imaan cocked her head. "Why do you ask?"

Aya turned Imaan's wrist faceup and pushed aside the jangling bangles to show the tattoo on Imaan's forearm. "This mark was on the boy who attacked the Xcel Energy Center. The FBI showed it to me."

Imaan snatched her hands away. "You spoke to the FBI?"

Aya's own hands felt suddenly cold and naked without Imaan's warmth. "No, Imaan, they came to our apartment to talk to my brother. I watched them from the kitchen. The woman FBI agent—you met her at the Cedar, Soroush was her name. She showed me the picture, but I told them I'd never seen it before."

"And they believed you? You're sure?"

Aya nodded. Imaan took her hands again, but her grip was different now. More intense. She felt the heat of the singer's gaze. "What happened at the Xcel Center was a mistake. A young man tried to make a real difference in this world—tried to make people see the truth as you and I see it. But he lacked patience. Instead of waiting for the right moment, he rushed into a situation and got himself killed. And for what?"

"So you knew him?"

"I knew . . . of him." She watched Aya from the corner of her eye again. "But let me ask you, Ayana. How did you feel when you heard about Faruq's actions?"

Aya felt her face grow hot. "I—I felt proud, in a way. I know the Qu'ran says that taking a life is wrong, but he made non-Muslims notice us—even if it was for the wrong reasons." She covered her face with her hands. "Then I felt ashamed."

Imaan put her arms around Aya, rubbing the space between her shoulder blades with long strokes of beautiful hands. She hummed softly in Aya's ear, the golden bangles making a soft accompaniment. When she spoke, it was in a whisper.

"Sometimes our first feelings are our truest feelings, Ayana."

CHAPTER 21

National Counterterrorism Center (NCTC), McLean, Virginia
17 February 2017 — 1355 local

Don paused in the hallway outside Admiral Daugherty's office to catch his breath. As usual, the stairs had winded him, but he was sticking with his New Year's resolution to get more exercise, and that meant stairs. Sometimes he thought that just spending time with Daugherty gave him a decent cardio workout—the man's presence was enough to spike anyone's heart rate. Don squared his shoulders and walked into the outer office.

"Is the admiral ready for me, Elaine?" he said with his best approximation of a confident smile.

Elaine, the only person in the building who would talk back to Daugherty, looked at Don over her reading glasses. "He's expecting you, Don. Go on in. Be warned: he's in a bitchy mood today."

Don felt his stomach muscles contract as he tried to maintain his composure. "Thanks." He knocked twice on the heavy wooden office door and opened it.

Jack Daugherty sat behind his desk, his eyes focused on a report in front of him. "Riley. About damned time. Take a seat," he said without raising his gaze. He waved at the large conference table that occupied the far side of his office.

The armchair at the end of the table was open, but that was the admiral's chair. Don steered toward the only other open seat. He glanced at the four other people around the table. Three of them wore suits and Don took them to be the typical Washington alphabet-soup crowd: CIA, DIA, NSA. The fourth wore the uniform of a Navy one-star admiral with a SEAL Trident gleaming beneath a wall of ribbons on his service dress uniform. They all had a copy of his just-released operations order for the al-Shabab intel plan in front of them.

Daugherty joined them at the table, slapping the oporder down in front of him. He made last-name introductions and agency affiliation in rapid fire. No one shook hands. Daugherty tapped the cover of the folder with a thick index finger. "These gentlemen have some questions for you, Riley, so how about you tell us what you have planned."

Don took a deep breath. Despite his brusque manner and "I'm in charge" attitude, Don knew this was a key buy-off meeting for Daugherty. Any one of the agency reps around the table had the power to kill this operation before it even started.

"Yes, sir. The overall objective is to capture or kill the senior leaders of al-Shabab, but we need to find them first. Since they've formally associated with Daesh, al-Shabab has upped their game. They move frequently, minimize mobile phone chatter, and keep interactions with the local population to a minimum. That means our usual means of locating them are much less effective—and if we can't find them, we can't kill them."

The glare of the CIA bureaucrat could have frosted the water bottle in front of Don, but the SEAL admiral had a thoughtful look on his face.

"We need agents on the ground," Don continued. "HUMINT. That's the only way we can be sure we're targeting the right people. I've scrubbed the database for suitable candidates for this mission—CIA, both case officers and covert ops, DIA, spec ops—everyone. I screened out anyone who came to the US from Somalia or anyone from the Somali diaspora unless they came from a completely clean source. Bottom line: we've got no one."

"And so you went looking outside?" the CIA man said. His icy glare had only gotten more intense the longer Don spoke. Daugherty kept his eyes on the open oporder.

"That's correct, sir." Don kept his voice neutral. "I took the liberty of reaching out to our intelligence counterparts to see if they had any suitable assets they might be willing to lend us."

"You took the 'liberty,' Mr. Riley? You're a CIA agent on loan to NCTC. How exactly did you manage to contact the intel operations of other countries without going through the CIA?" The NSA rep, an Asian woman, leaned in as if she wanted to hear the answer as well.

"I have a way to contact other agencies for another project. I asked my contacts if they had any assets that might work for this type of operation." Don tried not to sound defensive.

The CIA man flipped the oporder closed and folded his hands on the cover. "Really? Perhaps you could—"

"Marcus," Daugherty interrupted, "Mr. Riley has additional duties leading a special task force. That project is classified beyond the scope of this meeting." CIA and NSA exchanged glances. The DIA rep studied his fingernails and the SEAL just watched the show.

The CIA man tried a different tack. "Jack, please, if you're asking us to sign off on an intel mission of this scope, we should be clear about the working arrangement."

Daugherty closed his copy of the oporder and lined it up with the edge of the table before he spoke. "I think we're being very clear about the mission, Marcus. Let's face facts: our assets in that part of the world suck. If you want to have a dialogue about why they suck, schedule another meeting because it's going to take a while. Mr. Riley had a job to do—a job I gave him—and he used the tools at his disposal to find us a suitable agent. He is doing exactly what I asked him to do."

Daugherty drummed his fingers on the table as he stared down the CIA rep. "Does using an outside asset make the CIA look bad?" He shrugged. "Take it up with Congress if you need more money, but we've got a job to do now."

Marcus, the CIA man, reddened as Daugherty spoke, but it seemed to Don like the other three agencies were backing the DNI. "Who did you find, Mr. Riley?" Marcus's tone dripped with barely controlled anger.

"The Israelis have an agent that's perfect for this mission. Ethiopian Jew, looks and speaks like a Somali native. She's willing to undertake the mission and Mossad is willing to lend her to us. All I need is final approval from this group to make it happen."

Daugherty took over. "Let's assume you get your Israeli asset, Mr. Riley. Talk to me about the rest of the plan."

Don opened the oporder. "Page eight lists the assets I've got scheduled. Satellite coverage has been requested and I've got Global Hawk drones on tap as well. The map shows the planned insertion and extraction point for the agent."

"What about getting the asset ashore?" the SEAL admiral asked. "Will you need spec ops to get her on the beach?"

"No, sir," Don replied. "We have a Navy asset for that. Lowest possible signature for this kind of op."

"So I see." The SEAL studied the folder. "Tell me, Mr. Riley. What exactly is a Feisty Minnow?"

"It's a sailboat, sir."

CHAPTER 22

Brendan held the Zodiac inflatable boat tight against the stern of the *Arrogant*. Above him, he heard Rachel whisper goodbyes to the rest of the crew before she slipped into the boat next to him. She stood for a moment to receive her swim fins, mask, and a small dry-pack bundle that contained her disguise.

"Ready, boss," she whispered, her teeth white in the darkness. Brendan pushed away from the fifty-four-foot sailboat, letting the larger craft draw away before he started the small outboard on the Zodiac.

The engine noise made talking impossible, not that he had anything he wanted to say. Or should say. What he wanted to do was call up Baxter and tell him this plan was the most harebrained thing he'd ever been a part of. But that wasn't going to happen.

Rachel knelt in the bow of the small craft, a pair of night-vision binoculars to her eyes. Brendan let his eyes roam over the curve of her wetsuit-clad body. He focused on the GPS in his lap and made a tiny course correction. No matter how attractive, no good could come of his staring at a Mossad agent's ass.

The only warning Brendan had about Rachel Jager coming into his life was a cryptic message from Baxter two weeks ago telling him to expect a passenger when they docked in the Maldives. No name, no description, just a passenger. Brendan had expected another analyst. Baxter sometimes sent specialists to meet the boat in the field with an urgent hardware update or specific signals request, but having visitors to a Feisty Minnow asset was a pretty rare event.

As part of the highly classified Feisty Minnow program, the mission of the *Arrogant* was intelligence gathering. Electronic, acoustic, signals—if it radiated from the shoreline of any nation, Brendan and his crew would be there to capture it. As captain of the *Arrogant*, his cover was that of a rich software executive with a penchant for adventure, especially sailing.

When Rachel made her way down the pier in the late afternoon sunshine, Brendan took her for a local at first. He was alone onboard, standing in the mechanical compartment hatch, covered in grease from a recent wrestling match with the engine. Rachel was on the shorter side, maybe five foot four, with long black hair pulled into a ponytail that hung down her back. She was dressed in a pair of ragged denim shorts that hugged her hips and left a tantalizing gap at the waist. A sheer crop top covered a barely there string bikini halter.

Brendan was surprised when she stopped next to the *Arrogant* and draped a slim, caramel-colored arm across the railing. Still, his job description was a rich dilettante playboy, so technically speaking, talking to this beautiful woman was his job. He climbed out of the engine compartment and stood over her. She met his gaze without hesitation, and lowered her sunglasses to reveal a pair of striking hazel eyes.

The illusion of grace and beauty evaporated as soon as she opened her mouth.

"This boat?" she said with a sneer in her voice. "This is the one they call *Arrogant*, yes?"

Brendan stepped back like he'd been slapped. "Yes, who are you?"

"They call me Jager." Her eyes roamed over the rest of the sailboat before coming to rest on Brendan. "You are the mechanic?"

"Um . . ."

"I need to speak to the captain," she demanded. "At once."

Brendan did his best to keep his tone in check. "Look, lady, let's start over. I'm Brendan and I'm the captain of this vessel. Can I help you?"

"You were told to expect a passenger, no? I am the passenger. My bags are at the end of the pier. You will fetch them, yes?"

Brendan leaned over the railing until his reflection filled the entire space of her sunglasses. "I will fetch them, no. Everyone on this boat pulls their own weight. Got it, Jager?"

They stared at one another for a few seconds, then the woman grinned widely, revealing even white teeth in a generous mouth. "I got it, Captain," she replied, all trace of her haughty accent gone. "Just checking to see who I was dealing with. I'll be back with my gear in five."

The mission for the *Arrogant* was pretty simple: transit to the coast of Somalia, get Mossad agent Rachel Jager ashore by whatever covert means possible, then head south to wait for her extraction message. To fill the time, they were to spy on the Russian and

Chinese warships that plied these waters as part of an international antipiracy operation. With that much international firepower around, they were unlikely to run into the Somali pirates that often patrolled this coastline.

In the two weeks it had taken them to transit from the Maldives to the Somali coast and receive operational clearance for the insertion, Brendan had grown fond—maybe more than fond—of Rachel. And very skeptical of her mission.

He checked the GPS readout again. Another fifteen minutes to the drop-off point where they would wait for the signal. Brendan shifted so he could stretch out his bad knee. A carpet of jeweled stars hung over the tiny, darkened boat. Most nights, a scene like this would relax him. Not tonight.

The GPS screen flashed, indicating they had arrived at the targeted coordinates. Brendan killed the engine; silence cloaked them. Without a word, Rachel slipped to the rear of the craft, nestling next to Brendan. The wetsuit was slick against his skin, but the firmness of her flesh beneath the neoprene covering felt alive. She placed one hand on Brendan's thigh to steady herself as she held the binocs to her eyes. Her hand was warm on his leg—his bad leg, courtesy of a North Korean sailor with a rusty knife.

They were roughly a half mile offshore. The plan called for Rachel to swim to shore, change into the native dress she had in her small pack, and make her way to Haramka, a tiny Somali town a few miles inland. From there, she would travel south to Jilib and the suspected al-Shabab hideout. After endless reconnaissance flights and satellite passes, that was the intel community's best guess for where the terrorist group's leadership was holed up now. But they needed to be sure. No one wanted a repeat of the last raid on al-Shabab.

And the person who was going to provide that on-the-ground assurance was sitting next to Brendan, floating on a dark ocean under a world-class star show.

"The coastline looks all clear," she whispered, pointing into the night and handing the binocs to Brendan. He peered through the eyepieces, scanning the distant shoreline in the ghostly green night-vision display. No headlights, no sign of activity on the empty beach.

Rachel had her flippers on and the neoprene hood pulled up over her head. Her eyes glistened in the starlight. She dipped her mask in the ocean.

"I'll be fine, Brendan." She caught his hand. "Really."

He squeezed her hand back. "Watch out for sharks—and not just the ones in the water."

Rachel leaned forward and brushed her lips against his. It was no more than a fleeting moment of salty warmth, but it made his stomach drop.

"Goodbye, Brendan McHugh."

She slipped the mask over her face, tossed the small pack into the water, and slithered over the side of the Zodiac. Brendan snatched up the binocs and scanned the ocean. She was already thirty feet away, swimming in a strong breaststroke to minimize any splashing, the waterproof bag trailing behind her on a tether.

"Goodbye, Rachel Jager—and good luck," he muttered. Brendan started the Zodiac engine and steered the craft back out to sea.

CHAPTER 23

Liz kept one eye on the door as she checked her messages, hoping for something—anything—from Brendan. It had been more than two weeks now since any word from him, and even then it had been uncharacteristically cryptic.

Please don't forget to send Uncle Joe a card on his birthday. Love you—B

"Uncle Joe" was their personal code for Brendan going on an operation. For her boyfriend, an Uncle Joe could be anything from sailing the Mediterranean to taking part in an assault on an underground nuclear bunker in the Gerash Mountains of Iran. She blew out a long breath. The last she knew he was in the Maldives. Given two weeks on a sailboat like the *Arrogant*, he could be anywhere in the Persian Gulf now or along the Horn of Africa.

"Good morning, Elizabeth."

Liz jumped as the imam's deep voice interrupted her reverie.

So much for keeping one eye on the door. Her face flushing, she stood and extended her hand. Imam Nabil took her hand in both of his and held it for a second.

"May the blessings of Allah be upon you this fine morning, Elizabeth." Liz caught her breath. His simple act of containing her hand somehow stilled the mad rush of emotions in her brain. She swallowed, aware that the other patrons in the shop were watching them.

"Thank you, imam."

He chuckled and released her hand. "I told you to call me Nabby, Elizabeth. You are not of my faith. We are just two friends, having coffee on a cold winter morning." He shucked his heavy winter coat to reveal a herringbone-patterned sport coat over a white shirt with a clerical collar. He left the red and white patterned *kufi* on his head.

Liz slid a large mug of specialty tea across the table. "I took the liberty of ordering for you, imam—Nabby."

The older man wrapped his hands around the mug. "Thank you, Elizabeth. I'm afraid my African blood will never get used to these Minnesota winters." He nodded at her phone. "Have you heard from your young man? The one in the sailboat?"

Liz shifted in her seat. She'd told the imam that Brendan worked for a high-end sailboat design company—a lie. In a misguided effort to make the lie seem more real, she'd even hinted that he was associated with the America's Cup, a detail that fascinated the imam. The cleric was easy to talk to and she found herself confiding in him how much she missed her boyfriend. She worried that these personal details made her seem weak, but she always felt better after a talk with Nabby. In a way, he was the closest thing to a friend that she had in her life right now.

"He's—um—out of radio contact right now. Temporarily. It happens in his line of work. Nothing to be alarmed about." She was babbling under the imam's calm stare. *Stop talking, you idiot!* She took a long sip of her coffee, then blurted out: "He's getting a transfer back to the US in a few months."

"That is good news, Elizabeth." He raised his mug toward her. "You will be together again. Your life will go on as one."

Liz grimaced. "Not exactly, Nabby. He'll be stationed in Virginia—near the company headquarters. We'll still have a long-distance relationship." *Shut up! Why are you telling a total stranger about your personal relationship?*

The imam blew a ripple across his tea. "What you both do now is temporary, Elizabeth. What you are, how you care for each other, is permanent. Time and distance are just distractions."

"That's beautiful, Nabby. Is it from the Qu'ran?"

He stroked his salt-and-pepper beard, giving her an impish smile. "My mother." He took another sip of tea, then his expression turned serious. "But we have much to discuss this morning, Elizabeth."

"Of course." In the midst of the conversation, Liz had completely forgotten that the imam had asked for this meeting. The holy man leaned forward and she mirrored his movements.

"I've been in contact with my brothers at the other mosques in the area," he said in a low voice. "We are very concerned."

Liz nodded, eyeing her mobile phone. She wanted to record this conversation, but was afraid the request would reduce his willingness to share. The imam took a deep breath and glanced around the room. Better to not interrupt the flow of his thoughts.

"We are split about whether or not to go to the authorities on this matter. We don't have any specific information, just rumblings of discontent."

"Can you be more specific?"

He shook his head. "I am not a user of social media. The young people with their Twitter and their Facebook—that's how al-Shabab first infiltrated our communities here. It seemed like a good thing at first. The original al-Shabab was an organization that fought for peace and stability in a Somalia torn apart by civil war and famine and disease. Yes, it was an Islamic organization, but it had as its goal the peaceful rule of Somalia." He shook his head. "Sadly, we were wrong. Al-Shabab turned out to be no better than the al-Qaeda terrorists they associated with."

"What's changed, Nabby?"

"The attack at the Xcel Energy Center. Most of us assumed the young man was sick. He was troubled, yes, but not mentally ill. He was radicalized in a way that infected his mind with hate for this country that has supported us for the last two decades. It has made me and all my holy brothers look again at those who hijack Islam for their own reasons."

"But you said this meeting was urgent, Nabby. What has changed?"

The imam gripped his mug of tea. "Al-Shabab had a cultural connection to the Somali community. We did not condone our young people going to fight for al-Shabab, but we understood it. After all, they had been raised from the time they were babies on stories of Mogadishu and the beauty of their homeland. It was only natural some of them might want to return home." He paused to sip his tea, his face set in a frown.

"But fight for Daesh? This surprised us, worried us. There is no cultural connection, no reason for Somali youths to want to fight for ISIS! But still, we see a few of our young men answer the call of Daesh."

Liz frowned. "Forgive me, Nabby, but there's nothing new here. We've known all this for at least a year, maybe more."

"But now there is something else, Elizabeth. Not al-Shabab, not Daesh." He plucked a pen from his pocket and drew a tear-drop-shaped flame on a napkin. He spun the napkin around so it faced Liz. She watched as the ink bled into the soft paper.

"This is new, Elizabeth. And we have no idea what it is."

CHAPTER 24

Private island resort, Sao Tome, Gulf of Guinea, Africa
10 March 2017 – 0600 local

Chantal Deveraux stretched her hands to the ceiling, letting the early morning sun and the ocean breeze play across her bare breasts. Underneath her, Victor grazed his fingers along her belly, reaching upward. She slapped his hand.

"I said no touching!" She ground her hips against him. Victor responded with a low moan.

"You're a tease, you know that?"

Chantal bit her lip but said nothing, determined to make this feeling last as long as she could. Determined to push aside the thought that she was leaving in three hours. She felt the man she loved shiver beneath her and she dug her knees into his sides. *Not yet, my love. Not yet.*

Afterwards, she let the sea breeze cool her heated skin as she drowsed in the crook of Victor's arm. After three days, she was spent in every way possible—emotionally, sexually, spiritually, physically. Her body ached in muscles she didn't even know she had, but every twinge brought a smile to her face.

It was a good thing her next concert in London wasn't for another week. She'd need that much time to recover.

Victor rolled to face her, keeping Chantal's body cradled in his arm. She kissed his bicep.

"Eat," he said. He touched her lips with a piece of pineapple, letting the juice dribble down her chin. He licked it away, then pressed the fruit to her lips again. "I need to nurse you back to health." This time she ate it.

Piece by piece, he fed her breakfast. First pineapple, then tiny bites of banana, then chunks of fresh bread slathered with butter, until Chantal finally sat up in bed. He passed her a cup of coffee. "I thought I lost you on that last go-around," he said, tweaking her nipple gently.

Chantal blushed, suddenly aware of her nakedness. "I just wanted to make it last . . . give you something to remember when we're apart. I know there are other women, Victor—"

He put a finger to her lips. "Only you, my love. Only you."

Oh, how she wanted to believe that. But a wealthy man with a magnificent yacht . . . who was she kidding? It was weeks, sometimes months between her visits with Victor, and always in a different place. With his Syrian homeland in shambles, he was a man without a country. As Victor said often, he was one of the lucky ones, a man of means who was able to leave the Middle East and live in peace on the world economy. He had opened her eyes about how their Muslim kinsmen were treated on the world stage.

But soon, she and Victor would change all that. Together, they were planning a protest on a global scale. Daesh, Bashar al-Assad, the Iranians, the Wahhabists—a pox on all their houses. The future for Muslims was in the West, and it was time for Muslims to stand up for their rights as citizens. Too long, the Western powers had defined the Muslims within their borders by the acts of a few extremists in the Middle East. No more.

"Chantal?"

"Yes, I'm sorry, my love." She blushed at having been caught daydreaming.

"I said we should talk about your work before it's time to go."

"Of course." She sat up straighter in bed and pulled the sheet over her belly. "London is in good shape, as is Berlin, but in Paris it's difficult to get anything organized. The police presence is just too overwhelming since the attacks in 2015."

Victor nodded, his eyes distant. "What about Minneapolis? Your band of feminists, how are they doing?"

"Ayana is a strong woman. She will do well."

"How much does she know?"

Chantal peered at him over the rim of the coffee cup. What was his interest in Minneapolis? New York or Chicago would be much more iconic targets, but Victor insisted on Minneapolis as the site of the US protest.

"I've told her only the basics so far. She's placed trusted friends in the kind of jobs we need, and they're raising money."

"What about weapons?"

"Patience, my love. She'll be ready. I guarantee it. She reminds me of myself at that age."

Victor grinned. "Then I truly have nothing to worry about." The smile vanished as quickly as it had appeared. "What about Finland?"

Chantal placed her coffee cup on the bedside table and turned to face Victor. She crossed her legs, feeling the delicious twinge of overworked muscles on her inner thighs. She entwined her fingers with Victor's. "I'm worried about the Helsinki cell."

Victor said nothing. She couldn't bear to meet his gaze. He was depending on her to help him send a message to the world and she was letting him down. "The leader there, Kahin, I'm not sure he's right for the job. Too passive. His people don't respect him. I'm sorry."

Victor extracted his fingers from hers and left the bed. He paced the room, ending up at the window behind her that over-looked the ocean. Chantal hung her head, tears almost ready to rain down on her naked thighs. *You should have told him right away. Now you've waited until the last minute and Victor will go away angry—maybe for good.*

Behind her, Victor's hand on her shoulder made her jump. Gently, he gathered her hair behind her neck and lowered something over her head. A line of cold metal touched her bare chest. Chantal blinked away the tears to see a diamond necklace glittering in a shaft of sunlight. She touched it, letting her fingers slide over the cool sharpness.

"It's beautiful, Victor," she breathed.

He snapped the clasp at the nape of her neck and spun her body around. His strength surprised and excited her at the same time. Victor gripped her jaw, forcing her to meet his fierce gaze. Chantal felt the space under her breastbone grow tight. He kissed her. Hard.

"There is no sorry, Chantal. We *must* have Helsinki." He hesitated. "I need you to do something for me."

"Anything," she whispered.

"You must deal with this Kahin fellow as soon as possible. But you need to make sure he stays quiet. He could spoil every-thing we're planning." Victor kept his grip on her jaw.

"I understand," she said. "I'll ask Bashir—he's the former

soldier—to help me persuade Kahin to keep quiet. I can do it, Victor. I won't let you down."

"You could never let me down, my darling. But that plan will leave the cell lacking a leader, right? From what you've told me about Bashir, he's unpredictable. He needs supervision."

Chantal tried to nod her head, but Victor still had her in a tight grip.

"You will lead the Helsinki cell, Chantal," he said. "You're the only one I trust."

But that's not the plan, she wanted to say. They were supposed to sail off together on his yacht, safe in the knowledge that they had elevated the cause of global Muslim citizenry. He was asking her to go into danger . . .

"But how will I get back to you?" Her voice sounded small in her own ears, petulant.

Victor relaxed his grip and slid his hand behind her head. He drew her forward and kissed her again, gently this time. The diamond necklace swung between their bodies. Victor rested his forehead against hers.

"Do you trust me?" He looked deep into her eyes.

Chantal slipped her legs around his waist and pulled him close.

CHAPTER 25

The hardest part of being a spy was the waiting. Rachel once had a mentor who told her that more intelligence operatives died from impatience than from bullets. Timing was everything, he told her. Know when to make your move.

It took Rachel two days to walk and hitchhike the fifty kilometers from Haramka to Jilib, then another week or so of hanging around to find the lead she needed. Jilib was a medium-sized city of about 50,000 residents, so it was easy to blend in with the crowd.

The locals slowly opened up about an al-Shabab compound east of the city. No one went there—at least not voluntarily—but they all said the men there paid for fresh food. In cash. If you had the brass to make the trip out to the compound, you would be rewarded.

Two days later, Rachel had purchased five goats and herded

them to a crossroads a few miles east of town. She needed an escort to the compound and this was the most likely place to meet one. She hid her mobile phone under a rock and sat in the dusty road in the predawn darkness. With the goats curled up on the ground around her, she looked like some kind of biblical shepherd with her flock.

It worked.

Abdi was a rail-thin kid of seventeen or eighteen whose eyes lit up when he saw Rachel's goats. She stayed seated as he approached and shielded her eyes from the morning sun as she peered up at the young man, waiting for him to speak.

"Are your goats for sale?" he asked in the local dialect.

Rachel shrugged. "Maybe."

Abdi looked down one of the roads, the one that ran along the coast. "You alone?"

"My husband's dead." Somalia was full of widows, and the lie offered lots of avenues for backstory if anyone asked her why she was traveling alone or how she'd managed to afford five goats. Abdi accepted her explanation without even bothering to ask how he'd died.

"I know where you can sell them." He gestured at the goats. "Good price."

"Not interested." Rachel slipped an arm around the slim neck of the closest goat. The animal struggled, so she held it tighter. "I don't know you and these goats are all I have."

Abdi squatted down, his brown eyes pleading with her. "Sister, I can get you the best price. Better than anywhere else. They pay me to bring them fresh food."

Rachel took her time meeting his gaze. "Who?"

Abdi looked around and then leaned in close. "Freedom fighters."

"Al-Shabab?" Rachel brought a hand to her heart. "Will I be safe?"

Abdi stood and thumped his chest. "With Abdi you will be safe. I guarantee it." He held out his hand to help her up.

They walked for another two hours in the midday sun, Rachel keeping a tight leash on the elder nanny goat to make sure the younger ones followed close behind. She knew they had the right location when a roving patrol stopped them a mile from the walled compound. Rachel sneaked glances at them while they talked to Abdi.

Three men, each armed with a Kalashnikov that looked to be in good working order and extra clips of ammunition. One of them even sported a pair of grenades on his belt. Only one radio for the three-man patrol, Rachel noted. At least there was no sign of dogs.

One of the men approached her, a leering grin on his beefy face. Rachel quickly put a goat between her and the man. Getting raped in a place like this was a real possibility. While confident she could handle herself, fighting back would almost certainly blow her cover. She'd done her best to make her appearance as unattractive as possible, even going so far as to sprinkle goat piss on her *hijab*, but maybe even that wasn't enough.

According to the intelligence in the pre-mission briefing, the leadership of al-Shabab acted more like crime bosses than religious zealots. Whereas Daesh might rationalize violence against women as an act of God's will, al-Shabab was about business and raping the local women was bad for business.

At least that was the theory. Pre-mission briefings weren't always right.

He was a big man with heavy yellow teeth, which were bared

in what he probably felt was an attractive smile. He kneed the goat out of his path. "Warsame," he said, tapping his broad chest.

Rachel looked away, trying to make herself small. Her mind settled into stillness as she calculated how to best disable this man without making her martial arts training too obvious. It was going to be a problem.

Warsame grasped her by the chin, wrenching her face toward him. He had fat cheeks and a lower lip that pushed out from his face.

Abdi appeared next her, waving his arms. "I told her she was safe here. Let her go, Warsame."

The soldier released Rachel and pushed Abdi in the chest. The young man sprawled in the dust. "Maybe later," he said to Rachel, turning back to his fellow soldiers.

They passed two more patrols before reaching the gates of the compound, where she waited while Abdi went to fetch the cook. The walls of the compound were solid, made of local brick and at least six feet thick. The gates were new: eight-foot-high steel between two freshly-poured concrete pillars. Lots of money—new money—was being used to fortify this place.

When the gates opened, Rachel got a good look at six buildings plus a covered common area that served as a mess hall. She counted twenty men, all armed, plus four "technicals"—pickup trucks with .50-caliber machine guns mounted in the beds and extra fuel tanks for extended range. A box of ammunition peeked out from under a large pile covered with tarp.

An old woman hobbled out of the gate. Sucking on her few remaining teeth, she ran her hands over Rachel's goats and nodded in approval. "How much?" Her voice was husky with age and one eye had a white film.

Rachel shrugged. "I need a fair price, auntie. These are all I have now that my husband is gone."

The old woman scratched her chin, offering a price only slightly below what Rachel had paid for them a few days ago. Rachel squatted in the dirt, drawing the white goat close to her. "Please, auntie, I need more," she pleaded. "These are all I have left in the world."

The old woman sucked her teeth and shot a glance back into the compound. Rachel followed her gaze to where the door of the main house stood open.

Rachel froze. In the entrance stood Ikrima.

For the most wanted man in all of al-Shabab, he looked remarkably at ease. He slapped the man he was speaking with on the arm and walked with a rolling gait toward the covered eating area. His ease with the men and their respectful response showed all the signs of a born leader. Once a top operative with al-Qaeda, Ikrima had escaped SEAL Team raids on two separate occasions. Now it was rumored he had switched alliances to Daesh. His presence combined with the fresh stockpile of arms and a newly fortified compound told Rachel she'd hit the reconnaissance jackpot.

"Auntie," she said, "just a bit more." She tried to keep the excitement out of her voice. Rachel had the information she needed, the last thing she wanted to do was blow her cover by seeming too eager to close the deal.

The old woman pulled a mobile phone out from under her robes and thumbed it on. As she sucked her teeth—a habit that was really getting on Rachel's nerves—she accessed a text-based livestock pricing service. Like many developing nations, Somalia had bypassed landline phone service in favor of nationwide mobile phone coverage.

The woman grunted and showed Rachel the screen with current livestock prices. Rachel nodded and replied: "In dollars."

With rampant inflation, Somali shillings were all but worthless, driving a strong black market in relatively inflation-proof US dollars. The old woman's lips worked as she considered the offer, then she nodded and the deal was struck.

The sun was just starting to set when Rachel departed the compound. She knew if she waited any longer, the old woman would feel obligated to ask her to stay the night. She spied the first patrol far off to her left as she rounded the first bend in the road. She hurried into the approaching dusk, anxious to get away from the compound.

Rachel cursed herself for not bringing the phone with her. While owning a mobile was not an issue, it hardly fit her destitute widow story and she hadn't wanted to risk having it confiscated by someone at the compound. Still, if she hurried, she could be back at the crossroads before full dark.

These were the thoughts that occupied her mind when Warsame stepped out from behind a thick stand of bushes. He gave a deep chuckle. "Goat girl. Maybe you can earn some more money tonight."

Rachel stopped, the dust swirling around her feet. She ignored Warsame, listening instead to the surrounding brush. Where were the others?

"Just you?" she replied. "Aren't you afraid I might be too much for you?"

Warsame scratched his beard. "I'm off duty. Thought I might just catch you on your way out."

"Please don't hurt me. You look like a good man." Rachel thought she should at least give him the opportunity to do the right thing, though she had scant expectation he'd take the high road.

Warsame made a step in her direction, his heavy boot setting up a cloud of dust. He reached for Rachel's arm.

She slipped back, evading his grip. "Please, let me go."

The only reply was a huffing laugh. This little game of chase was turning him on.

Rachel let him step closer, then she launched a kick into his crotch, feeling the arch of her foot bury deep into the softness of his groin.

Warsame froze in mid-grab, his eyes bugged out of their sockets. A noise like a strangled cat filled the air. Rachel used the heel of her hand across his larynx and the noise ceased. Warsame collapsed at her feet, alternately gagging and vomiting.

Rachel stepped back and closed her eyes, listening to the brush around her. She and Warsame were still alone. Her mind raced. If she killed him—which he deserved—Ikrima's men were sure to come after her, but if she made it look like a rape gone bad, she might stand a chance.

Working quickly, Rachel seized his ankles and dragged the man off the road into a depression behind a screen of bushes. Sweat covered her face by the time she managed to get him hidden from the road and kick at the dust to cover up the drag marks. She unbuckled his belt and pulled his trousers down to his ankles. Warsame's dull eyes focused on her, a light of fear in them now. His yellow teeth worked as he tried to say something.

"Warsame, this is going to hurt you more than it'll hurt me." Her hand flashed in the dusk and the man's nose blossomed with blood. She raked her fingernails across his cheeks and neck.

Then Rachel returned to the road and started to run.

CHAPTER 26

National Counterterrorism Center (NCTC), McLean, Virginia
12 March 2017 — 1100 local

Don unlocked his office safe and hefted the thick file onto his desk. It made a satisfying thump on the table. The exterior of the folder bore bright red classification labels and the tab said ROSHED in all caps. Everything he knew about the international terrorist Rafiq Roshed lived in this folder.

Despite the elaborate electronic filing system that existed at NCTC, Don still preferred paper for his most complex cases. Sometimes the change in medium helped him see things he might have otherwise missed. His brain just seemed to process information presented on a screen and a piece of paper differently. He perused his inked notes from his last call with Reza Sanjabi of Iranian intelligence, then he punched in the number for his Iranian contact.

It took three rings for Reza to answer. He was holding a napkin in one hand when his image went live on the screen.

"Donald," he said with a smile. "I'm afraid you've caught me eating a late dinner at my desk." He wiped his mouth and pushed aside a plate. "Pardon my manners, my friend."

Don studied the older man. He was aging fast in his new role. The once baby-smooth cheeks had sagged into jowls and dark circles filled the space under Reza's brown eyes. His friend had been circumspect about his new job in the Quds Force, but it was clear his new role was taking its toll on his health.

"I can call back—" Don began.

"No matter." Reza waved his hand at the screen. "Why don't you fill me in on any activity with Roshed's family while I finish eating."

"As far as we know," Don said, "Roshed's made no attempt to contact his children." He extracted a photo of two dark-haired children from the file and held it up to the camera. "The kids are still on the ranch living with the wife's extended family. We have them under surveillance, but I'm sure Roshed knows that."

Reza laid his fork down and pushed the plate away. Don realized his mistake too late. Reza had been in the raid that killed Nadine, Roshed's wife. As much as they both wanted Roshed stopped, orphaning two children took its toll on one's moral compass.

The uncomfortable silence hung in the air until Reza swiveled in his chair to snatch a file from an open safe behind him. "I have news of our mutual friend."

Don leaned forward. "I'm all ears, Reza."

The Iranian tapped at his keyboard and a map of Indonesia appeared on Don's second screen. The image zoomed into northern Sumatra, with the city of Pekanbaru in the center of the screen.

"Reza, you must be joking. Indonesia?"

The older man nodded. "I have a source who tracked him

from Syria to Malaysia to Indonesia. From there the trail went cold. He's positive about the ID and this source has been very reliable in the past."

"Okay, let's give your source the benefit of the doubt. Why was he there?"

"It's certainly the last place we would look for him." The Iranian barked out a laugh. "Maybe he really is on the run. If we assume he's out for revenge, are there any US assets in Indonesia worth hitting?"

Don pinched the bridge of his nose. "Nothing comes to mind, but I can check." He hated to sound dismissive of Reza's work, but Indonesia didn't fit with his profile of Roshed. "You said you had two leads?"

The map on the screen switched to a large-scale map of Africa.

"You recall that last month we were following up on a lead that he had been in Tunisia? My people picked up his trail in Tunis. We have confirmation he was in Tripoli, then in N'Djamena, capitol of Chad."

Don traced the trail on the screen with his finger. "So your theory is that he's pushing into Central Africa?"

"The source in Chad indicated he was headed east, towards Sudan, which we surmise could be a staging area to attack the US base at Djibouti."

Don sat back in his chair. Camp Lemonnier in Djibouti was the only permanent US military base in Africa. Situated on the Gulf of Aden, the tiny country of Djibouti was sandwiched between Ethiopia on the land side and Yemen across the narrow strait called Bab al-Mandab, the Arabic phrase for "Gate of Tears." This twenty-mile choke point was the shipping channel between the Mediterranean Sea, via the Suez Canal and Red Sea, and the Asian markets. If there was one target in all of Africa that would hurt US operations in the region, Lemonnier was it.

"That base is key to stabilizing Yemen and Somalia and is used to interdict extremist movements in the region." Don's thoughts immediately flew to the pending operation in Somalia. "This is the first solid lead we've had on Rafiq, my friend."

Reza bowed his head slightly in acknowledgment. "If we assume he's planning an attack, he'll be looking for recruits, weapons, explosives, and the like. The most likely places for him to show up again are either Khartoum or in Kampala, Uganda. We're checking both locations, but nothing so far."

Don leaned toward the camera. "Do you have any suggestions about where Rafiq would find willing partners in the region?"

He studied his friend's reaction. The US and Iran were "frenemies" at best, and Don's query went right at the heart of the differences between the two nations. Iran certainly wanted Rafiq Roshed eliminated, but the Middle East was a rat's nest of counter-allegiances. As the major Shia power in the region, Iran was fighting for Assad in Syria as well as opposing the Saudis in their campaigns in Yemen and Somalia.

Reza smiled grimly at the camera. "I'm not sure that Rafiq has any religious convictions worth mentioning, and the region is changing rapidly—thanks to Daesh. Our latest intelligence is that al-Shabab, once considered al-Qaeda loyalists, are now aligning themselves with Daesh. Money and power, that's the real religion of these people."

Don thought about the Mossad agent in Somalia. Without realizing it, Reza had offered another confirmation of their analysis of the situation in Somalia.

"I couldn't have said it better myself, Reza."

CHAPTER 27

Rachel didn't stop running until she reached the crossroads. The dusty place where she'd met Abdi this morning was bathed in faint silver moonlight from the quarter moon that had risen over the horizon. She retrieved her mobile phone from under the rock where she'd stashed it early that morning.

As she waited for the phone to boot up and find a signal, she considered her situation. With any luck they wouldn't find Warsame until the morning, but would they buy the staged rape scene? If they did come after her, they'd come in trucks, not on foot, and Abdi would lead them here to the crossroads first. From this point, the roads led north to Mogadishu, west to Kenya, east to Jilib, or south to the coast—where her extraction was waiting.

Rachel consulted the clock on the now-functional phone. 2130. Her extraction point was at least forty-odd kilometers down the coast. Could she get there on foot and make the swim out to the extraction point by 0200?

She needed to try. The information she'd gleaned from the trip to the compound was the kind of intel that could make a differ- ence, but only if she made it out of the country. Rachel punched a coded sequence into the instant messaging software and hit send. The message would arrive in Israel in seconds, route through Mossad HQ, then get bounced back to the CIA in Langley. The CIA would inform *Arrogant* to be on station for a pickup at 0200.

She was on the clock.

Rachel sprinted down the road, forcing her body to settle into a pace she could maintain for the next three hours. Once she was in the open countryside, she stripped off the *hijab* and the heavier outer robes, leaving only a long slip. She tied the heavier material around her waist and pressed on, alternating ten minutes of run- ning with two minutes of rest.

The moon moved overhead and her mind wandered. The last time she'd eaten was very early this morning and since then she'd walked miles in the heat of the sun. She was still sweating, which was good, but not anywhere near the amount of perspiration for this much exercise. Even moderate levels of dehydration dulled the senses; she needed to stay alert.

Still, a wandering mind made the miles go faster. She passed a *yehib* bush and the scent triggered a memory of her childhood home in Israel. She'd grown up in a tiny apartment on a tree- lined street where *yehib* bushes formed a hedge between the buildings.

Rachel had been studying for a doctorate in African languages and literature when Mossad approached her. A career in academia was her goal in life. She smiled as she recalled how the young woman said they were looking for "people of color" to join the

Israeli intelligence agency. Would she be interested in learning more about a career in Mossad? She'd accepted their invite to a weekend seminar on a lark, thinking it might be good fodder for a book someday. But Rachel came away from the encounter with something else entirely. The sense of purpose and personal drive in the people she met that weekend impressed her beyond measure. They were not the cartoonish zealot killers she expected them to be, but simple professionals who took their job of protecting their homeland very seriously.

And then there was Levi.

The cynical side of Rachel said that Mossad put them together hoping they would fall in love. The spiritual side of her thanked them.

With a headful of unruly brown curls and dark eyes that flashed when he laughed, it was hard for her to believe that he'd been a divinity student. Whatever he had been, Levi was a Mossad agent through and through. By the end of the weekend, Rachel Jager committed to the Mossad training program and to the love of her life.

The moon was setting now. She checked the time. 0035. For the last half hour she'd been running with the sound of the surf in her ears. Rachel needed to stay aware to make sure she didn't miss her landmark to guide her back to where she'd buried her swim gear.

The muffled slap of her sandals hitting the dusty road lulled her into another daydream.

Levi. The way his cheek dimpled when he smiled, the way she could see the flutter of his pulse in his neck when she leaned in for a kiss, the way he would nuzzle the spot between her shoulder blades . . .

The way they'd sent his remains home in a container the size of a shoebox. *It's a risk we take,* he used to say. *The price of freedom.* Rachel's vision blurred.

Her brain registered the bent tree that loomed against the starlit sky, and forced her to stop running. The landmark.

She pulled out the phone. 0105. She had to hurry.

Rachel scrambled through the low dunes that separated the shore from the road. She got down on her hands and knees, sweeping the dim light of the mobile phone in front of her until she found the three-rock arrangement that marked the spot where she'd buried the swim gear. Then she shoveled out great handfuls of sand. She had to hurry. She still had a mile to swim to the extraction point.

The black neoprene squeaked against her sweaty flesh and she felt the sand grate against her skin. She made certain the IR strobe beacon worked, then snapped it in place on her shoulder. Rachel stuffed her remaining clothes and the phone into the waterproof bag, then ran to the water's edge. The surf was gentle as she sat in the water to put on her fins and mask. She longed for a drink of water, but that would have to wait.

The sea was cool on her face as she fitted the snorkel into her mouth and dove into the waves. Head down, she drove her body forward with the flippers. *Keep your arms still, let the fins do the work,* some long ago swim instructor's voice rang in her head. The face of her dive watch glowed. 0154. She'd never make it in time for the rendezvous. That meant she'd have to go back to shore, assume her disguise, and try again tomorrow night.

Rachel wasn't sure she'd be able to make it back.

At 0212, Rachel treaded water. She snapped on the IR beacon and held onto the dry bag to buoy her up in the gentle swells. She was so thirsty and the salt had dried her lips until they cracked.

She tasted her own blood and wondered if a drop of blood from her lip could attract a shark.

0220.

Think about something else.

She could barely remember his face anymore. These days, she had to refer to a picture of Levi to see him in her mind again. Rachel concentrated. She could see him now, but his features were fuzzy, misty in memory.

But so real. She reached out and her hand touched a hard black surface. And Levi's face was there above her—blurry, but still there all the same.

"I've got you, Rachel," he said. He sounded so good, so real, that she started to cry. His hand gripped hers; she felt herself being lifted out of the water.

Something touched her lips and sweet water spilled into her mouth. Levi's face grew clearer and his hand cradled her head. She touched his cheek. He was real! He was alive! She knew they'd lied to her—if he had died she would have felt it.

"Levi." She slipped her hand around the nape of his neck and drew him down. "It's really you."

Levi removed her hand gently. The fuzziness melted away.

"No," a voice replied. "It's Brendan."

CHAPTER 28

Lieutenant Jon Washington squatted in the dim passageway next to his team, breathing slowly, trying not to sweat in the 3mm neoprene wetsuit he wore.

"Captain, depth is one-five-zero feet, sir," came the gravelly voice of the Chief of the Boat from the nearby darkened control room.

"Very well, Dive," replied the captain. His voice was sharper, edged with tension. *A submarine sailor doesn't like being this close to shore,* Washington thought with a wry smile.

"Sonar, Conn, clearing baffles to the left," the captain called out. "Helm, left ten degrees rudder. Nice and easy, Dive, let's just make sure we're alone before we offload our cargo."

One of the men next to Washington snickered. So they were cargo now.

The deck tilted slightly under his feet as the ship turned.

Through the open door, Washington could see the captain and the XO huddled over the sonar display.

"Conn, Sonar, I hold one sonar contact, designated Sierra four," came the sonar report over the intercom. "Bearing one-seven-six, estimated at two-five thousand yards and drawing away from us. Classified as a merchant." Washington wondered to himself how anyone could hear something over twelve miles away. He knew the captain was worried about a fishing boat floating silently above the sub with his nets out, just waiting to get snagged by this monster creeping along under the surface.

"Very well, Sonar. Diving Officer, take us to nine-zero feet. How's the trim look?"

"Steady at nine-zero feet, Captain," the COB called after a few minutes. "Trim is gnat's ass, Captain. I guarantee it." Someone in control chuckled and Washington smiled at the COB's brashness.

"We'll see, Master Chief, we'll see. Helm, all stop."

"All stop, aye, sir," chimed the sailor manning the helmsman station. It sounded like his voice hadn't even broken yet. Someone next to Washington chuckled and he shushed the man. They'd been through scenario planning and worst-case analysis; making cracks about the crew that was dropping them off was not part of the plan. *Stick to the plan, Washington.*

As the ship slowed, he felt the bow nudge up a bit. Looks like the COB's trim wasn't perfect after all. The low voice of the Diving Officer muttered commands to his team and the deck leveled out again.

"Gnat's ass, COB?"

"It was a big gnat, sir." A ripple of laughter followed, but was stilled by a hiss from the XO. "Ship is hovering, Captain."

"Very well, Dive. Weapons Officer, inform the SEAL Team they may enter the submersible."

Washington got to his feet. "That's our cue, boys. If you haven't gone potty by now, you're just going to have to hold it. No one pees in my ride."

The Weapons Officer, a muscled redheaded lieutenant commander, strode down the hallway and clambered up the ladder next to Washington. He heaved on the dogging mechanism and spun the wheel to open the hatch. There was a hiss of air as the officer equalized pressure between the ship and the water-tight docking capsule attached to the hull of the *Los Angeles*–class submarine. The Weapons Officer pushed the hatch up to reveal the underside of the *Proteus*, then dropped back down to the deck.

"Your chariot awaits, lieutenant." He gripped Washington's hand. "Good luck."

Washington gave him a tight smile. "Tell the captain I said thanks for the lift." He climbed the ladder, feeling the weight of his gear pulling him backwards, careful not to bang his air regulator or his sniper rifle against the rim of the hatch.

He entered the *Proteus* via the center compartment and stooped to walk forward to the pilot's seat. The twenty-six-foot submersible could take six SEALs with full gear, so their complement of four left lots of room. He settled onto the pilot's bench and plugged in his comms jack. "Chicago, *Proteus*, comms check."

"Read you five by five, *Proteus*. What's your loading status?"

"Copy that, Chicago." He twisted in his seat. "Last man is aboard. Closing the hatch now." His man gave him a thumbs-up and slid the bottom panel in the floor shut. "We are ready to get wet, Chicago."

"Roger that, *Proteus*. Flooding the docking station." The lights went out, leaving only the glow of the control panel in front of him. He felt a momentary surge of panic, but tamped it down.

The water level rose swiftly, filling the *Proteus* and the

external docking vessel at the same time. The *Proteus*, the latest in SEAL delivery vehicles, was designed as a "wet" delivery vehicle, meaning they would be wearing their SCUBA gear the entire trip.

"Confirm we are feet wet, Chicago." The water level rose to his chest, then over his face mask. He switched comm channels so he could talk to his team. "Alright, gents, confirm we have a go on our equipment." He received a thumbs-up from each man, then flipped the switch back. "Chicago, we are ready for launch."

"Standby for pressurization, *Proteus*. In three, two, one." The ship equalized the pressure of the external seawater with the interior of the docking capsule and Washington felt an invisible hand clamp around his body.

"Pressurization complete, Chicago," he gasped.

"Opening capsule door."

On the video screen, Washington watched a large bubble float away like a blob of quicksilver into the open ocean beyond the open door of the capsule.

The captain's voice came on the line. "You are free to depart when ready. Good luck, *Proteus*."

"Luck has nothing to do with it, sir. It's all in the training."

The transit was supposed to take two hours, depending on the accuracy of their drop-off point, currents, and any maneuvers needed to avoid contact with fishing boats. After leaving the *Chicago*, they angled upwards to verify their position using the foldable mast and set a course for land. The *Proteus* was remarkably easy to maneuver and their mast made barely a ripple on the calm sea.

No contacts and they were right where they were supposed to be. So far, so good. Washington steered the submersible back down to fifty feet and set the autopilot. And waited. Cold seeped into his wetsuit.

His hands fidgeted to do something, but he'd been warned to let the onboard computer do the work. After all, once it dropped them off, the *Proteus* was going to return to the *Chicago* without a driver. The water underneath them was shallower now, no more than one hundred feet and shoaling rapidly. The submersible changed to a contour-following driving profile that allowed it to ride fifteen feet off the sandy bottom.

Their mission was to get ashore on the coast of Somalia and set up two reconnaissance posts on a known terrorist compound approximately four miles inland. They were the eyes on the ground in advance of a possible full-out assault in the next three days. The Global Hawk UAV launched from Camp Lemonnier in Djibouti had provided them with detailed topographical maps and would be there to guide them to the target if necessary, but the Global Hawk carried no weapons. If they ran into trouble, they'd be on their own.

The *Proteus* slowed and the screen blinked to indicate they were at their destination. The submersible settled in forty feet of water, coming to rest on the sandy bottom with a soft thump.

The men behind him sprang into action, sliding open the fore and aft covers that separated them from the sea. Washington punched a command into the pilot's console to tell the *Proteus* to return to the *Chicago* and swam after them.

After days of inactivity on the submarine and two hours cramped into the *Proteus*, it felt good to stretch his muscles. He swam hard to catch up with his team. They kept a low profile as they came ashore in the surf, then removed their flippers and sprinted for the dunes a hundred yards away. One man dug a hole to bury their swim gear while Washington surveyed the surrounding countryside. Sandy and hot, with rolling terrain and plenty of scrub brush for cover. Within minutes, the whole team had stripped off their wetsuits and redressed in camouflage. Everyone checked their weapons again and the four set off at a fast trot in the direction of the compound.

The countryside around them was deserted and the few shacks they came across were half falling down and unused. It appeared that the al-Shabab leaders didn't care for neighbors.

It was nearly 0330 by the time they had the compound in sight. Washington and his spotter Petty Officer Beck took up residence on a low ridge overlooking the shallow valley that housed the walled compound. The second team made a long circuit around the base to a small rise a mile opposite his position.

After another thirty minutes, Washington got the expected radio confirmation that team two had taken position. He extracted a small phone from his cargo pocket and slipped an earpiece into his ear. He keyed the phone. "Homebase, this is Overlook. We are in position."

He knew the call was being relayed from the Global Hawk overhead to the Tactical Operations Center back at Lemonnier and from there passed to AFRICOM in Germany and back to Fort Bragg, headquarters for the Joint Special Operations Command.

"Overlook, this is Homebase. Acknowledge you are in position. Homebase, out."

Washington moved a rock out from under his belly and rested his chin on his fist. He stared up at the starlit sky, wondering which bit of black space hid the Global Hawk. Beck stretched out next to him. He was a good kid, still pretty green, but with a good head on his shoulders. "What now, sir? We just wait?"

"Welcome to the Navy, Petty Officer Beck. Hurry up and wait."

CHAPTER 29

FBI Field Office, Brooklyn Park, Minnesota
07 March 2017 — 1330 local

It didn't matter how many IT people you had on staff—when you were trying to set up a secure videoconference between the Department of Homeland Security, NCTC, Director of National Intelligence, and who knew how many other three-letter agencies, there were bound to be technical difficulties.

Minneapolis had earned the dubious distinction as the leading US supplier of young men to overseas terrorist groups like al-Shabab and the Islamic State. As leader of the homegrown radicalization task force, Liz was in the hot seat today. Since being appointed as Task Force leader in November, Liz and Trask had received more resources—and more pressure—than they knew what to do with.

And today—the first Tuesday of the month—was briefing day for the Washington DC providers of resources.

Liz was reviewing progress in the Xcel Energy shooter case.

In truth, they had precious little to go on. Faruq Hassan had covered his tracks well—too well, given his meager educational background.

"Our working assumption is that al-Shabab sent Hamza Abdul back to the US last November to set up the Xcel Center attack. We surmise that Hamza recruited Faruq, armed him and schooled him on how to cover his tracks. Unfortunately, Hamza Abdul was killed during his apprehension. After his death, Faruq decided to carry out the attack on his own." Liz mentally kicked herself. It also meant that if she had been able to capture Hamza Abdul alive, they might have prevented the Xcel attack. "That theory accounts for Faruq's lack of training with the weapons. He could have received help via the Internet in destroying his computer and deleting his social media accounts," she concluded.

"Which leaves us where, Agent Soroush?" Liz ignored the heavy tones of criticism in the voice of Admiral Daugherty, the DNI. She cleared her throat and flipped to the next screen—a row of half a dozen mug shots of young Somali men.

"Known associates, Admiral. These six men represent the common circle of friends between Hamza and Faruq. We're putting all of them under a microscope right now, but no solid leads so far."

"What about Somali community leaders? Are they cooperating?"

"It's a mixed bag, sir. We're viewed as part of the solution by some and part of the problem by others. The situation is complicated by the clan nature of Somali culture, especially the older generation. This tends to compartmentalize the information. We never seem to get the whole picture."

"If they want this problem solved, they're going to need our help," growled Daugherty.

"I agree, sir, but the trust is not there across the community. I've got an excellent resource in Imam Nabil, a Sufi—that's one of the more moderate sects—but have virtually no relationship with the more hard-line religious leaders. When these imams tell their people not to talk to the FBI, we're pretty much dead in the water."

"So what's our next move?"

"We keep talking to them, sir. Unless we have a firm connection, I think pulling them in for questioning is a mistake. It sets us back in terms of building trust. Using the imam as an intermediary, I was able to interview one of these suspects." She clicked on the picture of Zacharia Ismail and his image filled the screen.

"This man is a cousin to Hamza and was present at the Cedar the night Hamza was killed. He also went to high school with Faruq. A tenuous link, but still a connection. I conducted the interview at his home, brokered by the imam."

"And your conclusion?"

"I found no evidence that he was connected to the Xcel shooter. He showed no reaction to the tattoo, either."

"And you've got all of them under surveillance?"

"Yes, sir."

"Alright, our time's up for today, Special Agent Soroush. Unless you've got anything else to report, we'll convene again same time next month." Daugherty signed off without waiting for her to reply.

The air was filled with beeping sounds as the parties to the call logged off. Liz saw Trask's hand grip the arm of his chair at the DNI's slight. Not that Liz blamed the admiral. They were getting nowhere fast and had no reason to expect that to change any time soon. The plain truth to her was that law enforcement wasn't about to solve the problem of homegrown radicalization on their own. There was no way the FBI would ever understand the internal complexities of Somali culture enough to prevent another terrorist convert. The only way this would get solved was if the Somalis helped themselves.

Imam Nabil's words came back to her: "You're dealing with teenagers in the midst of an identity crisis. One foot in America, one foot in the Somali culture of their elders—and they don't belong to either. We have to help them find themselves."

"Special Agent Soroush?" Liz jerked her head up at the sound of her name. She consulted the directory of attendees still logged in. Donald Riley, NCTC. She smiled to herself.

"Yes, Mr. Riley?"

Don's pudgy face filled the screen. "Could I ask you to hang on for a moment? With Special Agent Trask, of course."

Liz nodded, her eye on the attendee list. When the last one logged off, she blocked anyone else from joining and turned to the screen. "What can we do for you, Don?"

Don cleared his throat. "I can't get into specifics, but there's some activity that's ramping up in my shop that might impact your workload. It's not a sure thing yet, but keep your ear to the ground. It might shake something loose on your end."

Trask and Liz exchanged glances. Don was pushing the bounds of operational security, but it helped to know there was an operation overseas that might spike activity in their community. It just might give them the clue they were looking for.

Liz had a sudden thought. Maybe Don was trying to tell her Brendan was part of the op.

"Thanks for the heads up, Don," Trask was saying. "We really—"

"Don," Liz interrupted. "Any mutual friends taking part in this activity?"

"Could be, Liz. I have to go."

CHAPTER 30

Don's first impression of the White House Situation Room was how small the space was. No bigger than a large dining room, really.

The half-dozen armchairs running down each side of the conference table were filled with a who's who of United States political, military, and intelligence communities. The Vice President sat stony-faced between the directors of CIA and Homeland Security. Against the wall, an outer ring of chairs held the Undersecretary of State for Political Affairs, as well as a layer of trusted staffers for the people at the main table. Down the opposite side of the table were the Secretary of Defense—widely considered to be the smartest guy in the room and not afraid to let anyone within earshot know it—and the Chairman of the Joint Chiefs, a stern Marine general.

Daugherty and the National Security Advisor, occupying the

two chairs closest to the head of the table, chatted in undertones. The people in the room seemed edgy but not frantic, the kind of tension you might feel at an important business meeting while waiting for the CEO to arrive. Don tried to stay invisible behind the podium at the front of the room. He was the youngest person in the room by at least a decade and a whole lot of pay grades.

He checked his secure video feeds again. The head of US Africa Command was an Army four-star general sitting in Stuttgart, Germany. US Special Operations Command, based in MacDill Air Force Base in Tampa, Florida, was represented by a Navy four-star admiral, and General Haskins, a three-star in charge of Joint Special Operations Command (JSOC), was calling in from Fort Bragg in North Carolina.

Daugherty got a ping on his mobile and gave Don the high sign. The president was on her way. Don took a sip of water and hoped he didn't need to pee halfway through the briefing.

The door snapped open; everyone jumped to their feet. The president stood behind her chair for a long moment, surveying the room. "Please, be seated, everyone." She adjusted her chair and looked up at Don. "Mr. Riley, I've been looking forward to meeting you. DNI Daugherty speaks very highly of you."

Don's mouth went dry in an instant. "Thank you, ma'am." He bent his lips into a smile.

Daugherty cleared his throat. "Madam President, we'll start with a short intelligence update from Mr. Riley, then we'll turn it over to General Haskins for the mission brief."

Don flipped the screen to show a satellite photo of the al-Shabab compound side by side with a headshot of Ikrima. The photo of the terrorist was a grainy image, probably shot from a mobile phone, showing a square-jawed black man, his face partially hidden behind a hood.

"Madam President, the mission target is this al-Shabab base located in southern Somalia. Using a variety of assets, we have positively verified the presence of Ikrima inside the compound. It is our belief that if we can capture or kill Ikrima, we will send a strong message to any other fringe organizations that might be considering joining Daesh. We feel this would be a strong deterrent to further Islamic State recruiting as it would demonstrate a weakness in Daesh, that they are unable to protect their own. Further, we missed Ikrima once. This is a chance to show that the US always gets our man."

"You have a positive ID on this Ikrima?"

"Yes, ma'am, a Mossad agent visited the compound three days ago and made a visual confirmation of the target. Since that time, we've monitored the site continuously using drones. No one has left the compound."

The president turned to Daugherty. "So we're going to get him this time, Jack?"

Daugherty offered a wisp of a smile. "I'll let General Haskins answer that one, ma'am." He indicated to Don to switch to the secure videoconference.

General TJ Haskins's face filled the screen, his face set in a customary scowl, icy blue eyes squinting over a pair of reading glasses. "Good evening, Madam President."

"General Haskins, good to see you again."

The general nodded to someone off camera and a PowerPoint slide popped up on the adjacent screen that read OPERATION VENERABLE PORPOISE in bold letters.

"That's quite a mouthful, General."

The Chairman of the Joint Chiefs spoke up. "We have a computer system that randomly generates names for top secret ops, so there's no chance of offering any clue as to the true nature of the mission. Speaking personally, ma'am, we got lucky this time. Some of the names that come up are pretty terrible."

The president nodded at the screen for Haskins to continue.

"We're not holding back on this one, ma'am. We have recon elements on the ground already. SEAL Team Six, using air assets from AFSOC—that's Air Force Special Ops Command—is standing by for the main assault." He flashed up a picture of the compound showing where the major ground forces of JSOC would be positioned. "Using the SEAL recon elements as spotters, we plan to surround the compound, then work forward, corralling everyone within the perimeter before we start the attack."

AFRICOM, the Army four-star, chimed in: "Madam President, the *Essex* Amphib Ready Group is off the coast. We have a Marine battalion landing team on standby—just in case. We can also use the *Essex* as a hospital platform, if needed."

The president pursed her lips. The rest of the room was silent except for the creak of an armchair as someone shifted in their seat. Don couldn't stop staring at the president. She'd been sworn in less than three months ago and now she was about to launch an attack against another country. If this thing went south—like the last time—it would set the tone of her foreign policy for the rest of her term.

"Ma'am," the Secretary of Defense said, "the recon elements are in place and JSOC assault forces are inbound. If we're going to do this, we need to do it now."

The president signaled the comms officer on the periphery of the room. "Get me the Secretary of State."

The connection was almost immediate. "Matthews here."

"Mike, it's the president. What's your status on notification to the Somalis?"

"I have the Somali ambassador scheduled for two hours from

now. I'm keeping it low-key, but they're suspicious, I'm sure. I don't often receive ambassadors in the evening."

The president shot a glance at Haskins on the video screen. "That's plenty of time, ma'am," the general said. "We're thirty minutes out. We just need a go from you to start the clock."

"I'll let you know, Mike." She nodded to the comms officer to kill the phone connection. The Secretary of Defense started to say something and she held up her hand. "Does anyone—and I mean anyone—have anything to say before I approve this mission?"

The room went so still that Don held his breath.

"Mr. Riley?"

Don started, expelling a noisy lungful of air. "Ma'am?"

"Can you please call up the drone video and play it on the screen?"

Don punched up the live feed from the Unmanned Aerial Vehicle (UAV) that was circling the al-Shabab compound. Global Hawks were Air Force recon assets that flew at high altitude with advanced sensor packages to track ground targets. Although Global Hawks did not carry any offensive weapons, they were able to relay targeting data to weapons-capable platforms for immediate strikes. This was also how the SEAL recon team was able to stay in contact with Camp Lemonnier in Djibouti.

The infrared video feed sharpened as the signal was assigned to dedicated priority bandwidth. The UAVs, launched from the US base in Djibouti and controlled from air-conditioned offices in Creech AFB in Nevada, had been continuously on station since the Mossad agent had confirmed the target in Somalia.

In the infrared image, the figures of men showed up brightly against a dark background. A bonfire in the center of the compound blazed with white light. Outside the walls of the compound, Don counted three groups of three men roaming through the terrain.

Those would be the enemy patrols the agent had described in her report. Further out, two stationary pairs of men were positioned on either side of the stockade.

Daugherty used a laser pointer to highlight the two pairs. "These are our recon elements. They'll guide the strike force on to the target so we can seal the area. As soon as the attack begins, the recon teams will take out the patrols and an AC-130 gunship will lay down a suppressing fire until the assault teams are on scene."

The president watched the screen for a full twenty seconds. The Secretary of Defense shifted in his chair, looking like he was about to say something, but he held his tongue.

"General Haskins?"

"Yes, ma'am."

"You have my permission to commence the assault . . . and, General?"

"Ma'am?"

"Let's get them this time."

CHAPTER 31

International waters, off the coast of Somalia
16 March 2017 – 0120 local

Lieutenant Commander Dave "Ringo" Ringler shifted in the jump seat of the MH-47 Chinook. Over the last three hours, the vibration of the massive twin rotors had numbed his ass to the point where he wasn't sure if he'd be able to stand once they got the go signal from Homebase. He laughed to himself. Who was he kidding? Like always, when they got the go signal, his body would be as amped up as the next guy.

He surveyed the dim cabin, where twenty-three other SEALs sat in various stages of wakefulness. They all dealt with the stress of upcoming action in their own way, but three hours in the back of a dark chopper was enough to put any man to sleep.

The deck of the helo banked again as they made another turn. He craned his neck to see out the window and thought he could make out the shape of another darkened MH-47 in the sky. There were five more out there—one more with another squadron of two dozen SEALs, two packed with Rangers, and two empties in case something went sideways.

They'd planned this mission like they were assaulting a heavily fortified castle. Two SEAL recon teams on the ground, two full squadrons of SEALs for the assault, four squads of Army Rangers on perimeter security, and an AC-130 Spectre gunship to provide high-accuracy fire support.

Too much for an al-Shabab compound of about fifty men with small arms? Probably, but the new doctrine of overwhelming force called for them to throw everything at the bad guys, including the kitchen sink if anyone thought it would help. Besides, the report from the last failed SEAL raid on Somali soil was required reading for every man jack in Ringo's outfit, and all of them had watched *Black Hawk Down*.

This was Somalia, and shit happened in Somalia. He set his chin. Not today, not on his watch.

Ringo keyed his mike. "Homebase, this is Eagle One. What's our status?"

"The elephants are still stomping around, Eagle One." Homebase was Camp Lemonnier in Djibouti, where they'd taken off three—make that four—hours ago. If they were forced to hold station off the coast much longer, the choppers would have to refuel again, an exercise that would set them back another hour. He glanced at the luminous dial on his diver's watch. 0137. Their attack window opened at 0100 and closed at 0300 local.

Elephants was slang for the bigwigs in DC. Ringo was sure that a raid decision like this one would go all the way to the top—to the president, most likely. He tried to imagine that meeting: the new president, in office less than three months, having to make a decision to launch an attack on another country—oh, and the last time we tried to get this guy we got our asses handed to us.

"Eagle One, this is Homebase. You are cleared for the mission, I repeat, you are cleared to go. Good luck, gentlemen."

"Roger that, Homebase." Ringo could feel the deck of the Chinook tilt forward as the huge machine accelerated forward. He activated the microphone for the internal comms circuit.

"Wake up, sleeping beauties, it's time to earn your paycheck. We are inbound; touchdown in thirty."

🔥

Al-Shabab Compound, Somalia
16 March 2017 — 0210 local

Muhammed eyed the shadowy bench carved into the wall. Tempting. He shook his head to clear his mind. If he sat down, he'd be asleep in nothing flat.

He climbed a rickety ladder to the top of the twelve-foot-high walls of the compound. From his perch, he could see for miles in all directions. Overhead, the star-filled sky looked like diamonds, so close that it seemed like he could reach out and scoop up a handful. That was the part he liked best about night watch: the stars. Back home in the US, with the city lights polluting the night sky, he'd be lucky to see any stars at night. On the rare occasions when the weatherperson said the Northern Lights had traveled down so they were visible from Minneapolis, he'd never seen them. Not even once.

The walls, six feet thick, made of brick and mud with a walkway on top that went all around the compound, made him feel strong, safe, invincible. Sure, fighting for al-Shabab wasn't all that it was cracked up to be, but it had its upside. Muhammed took a deep breath. Like the stars over the nighttime desert.

He blew out his breath . . . and his world exploded.

The earth vomited up great gouts of dirt and rock and fire. He was hurled off the wall into the courtyard, landing on his back, the wind knocked out of him. Then he watched as the wall he had just been standing on—six feet of impregnable brick and mud—disappeared.

Rock and dust rained down on him, a big chunk of shattered brick nailing him right in the forehead. Muhammed felt a warm stickiness cover his face and he struggled to stay conscious.

Just as suddenly as it began, the barrage from hell ceased. Another noise crept into his blast-deadened ears. A whirring sound, and the cloud of dust started to blow away.

Choppers.

We're under attack.

Around him Muhammed saw men—his al-Shabab brothers—racing for the break in the wall. They carried weapons—where was his weapon? Muhammed tried to get up, but none of his limbs responded. He called out, but his weak voice was barely audible in his own ears.

Shapes, like hulking demons spitting fire, swept through the gap in the wall, and his brothers dropped like blades of grass. One fell across Muhammed's body, but he couldn't feel the man's weight on his belly. That was bad. He tried to recall his battlefield first-aid training. Spinal cord injury? It all seemed to jumble together in his head, and he knew he was going into shock.

I'm dying.

Suddenly all he could see was his mother's face. At that moment, all he wanted in the world was to talk to her one last time, to tell her he loved her and that his decision to fight for al-Shabab had nothing to do with how she had raised him. They offered him a place, a way to show his worth in a world where all his friends talked about were tweets and apps and Facebook posts. He was different. He went to find a sense of purpose in their Somali homeland.

Be proud of me, Mother. I was a hero. I made a difference.

His mouth filled up with blood; panic clamped a cold hand around his heart. *I'm drowning.* Muhammed wanted to laugh. *I'm drowning in the desert.*

Using the last of his air, he spit out a mouthful of blood and called out to one of the soldier-demons.

"Help me. I'm an American."

CHAPTER 32

Ringo decided that of all the shitty places he'd ever experienced, being in the line of fire from an AC-130 gunship was his personal definition of hell on earth.

From 10,000 feet, the Hercules could rain down 105mm shells with pinpoint accuracy. The pilots liked to brag that they could shoot a golf ball off a tee from 10,000 feet. They neglected to mention that while they would hit the golf ball, they'd also destroy the entire green along with it.

The mission plan called for the SEAL recon snipers to take out the roving patrols outside the compound, then call in the AC-130 to soften up the compound and breach the walls.

Ringo's SEAL assault teams were the second wave, designated to take the compound. Their orders were to capture as many fighters as possible and preserve the physical intel—computers, maps, that kind of thing—for the HUMINT teams. But taking fighters alive was a tricky business. If they threw down their weapons and held up their hands, that was one thing. If they resisted at all, they were going down without a second thought.

Ringo didn't expect many prisoners from this crowd.

The MH-47 dropped the back ramp and she flared into a touch-and-go landing. The SEALs ahead of him stormed off the helo. He was the last man off. As assault leader, his job was to coordinate the attack. Behind him, the wind from the rotors of the bird increased as the Chinook took to the sky. From the time the ramp of the helo touched the ground until it was safely airborne again was less than twenty seconds.

"Eagle One is on the ground," he said into his mike.

The two SEAL assault teams had divided up the half-dozen buildings in the compound. By the time he made it to the wall, he could already hear shouts of "clear!" as his team split into groups of three and secured the facility room by room. Every so often, a staccato of shots would punctuate the darkness.

Ringo mentally ticked off the buildings in his head until he knew they had all been cleared. He called it in to Homebase and checked his watch. Twelve minutes had elapsed since they'd stepped off the chopper.

"All teams, secure the dead and bring your captives to the court-yard. Call in if you need a medic," he said into the radio. Standard operating procedure called for them to zip-tie the hands of all hostiles, no exceptions. The last thing anyone wanted was some terrorist playing dead. The SEAL teams frog-marched their prisoners into the courtyard and forced them onto their knees. Fifteen men and women in total. "Who has eyes on the prize?" he said into his mike.

"Team leader, Ikrima's dead. I nailed him in the top floor of the big house."

Ringo cursed. Although the possibility was small, they'd

wanted to capture Ikrima alive. He surveyed the motley crew of captives. They looked like lower-level associates, but that would be for the interrogators back at Camp Lemonnier to figure out. He keyed the radio.

"Big Bird, send in the intel teams. We've got a group of guests for you to transport back to Homebase."

The helo acknowledged his call and a few seconds later the rotors roared as the double-bladed monster settled to the ground. A team of six sailors descended, carrying black plastic Pelican cases. The HUMINTers would take biometric readings from all the dead and wounded for the terrorist database.

One of the intel officers knelt next to the big man sprawled across a pile of rubble and sporting two bullet holes on the left side of his chest. His blood made a large blotch across his beige nightshirt. The intel officer had a DNA swab in her hand, ready to insert into the dead man's mouth, when she sprang back and scrambled away.

"Sir, we've got a live one over here!"

Ringo spun around, drawing his Sig Sauer P226 at the same time. He advanced on the corpse, stepping to one side so he could get a better view.

A bloody face, covered with dirt and brick fragments, peered up at him. And spoke perfect American English.

"Help me. I'm an American."

USS *Essex* (LHD-2), off the coast of Somalia
16 March 2017 — 0343 local

Corpsman Daniel Rustom steadied the IV bag as the *Essex* medical crew carried the stretcher down the ramp of the helo.

The chances of the American kid making it were not good. He had no movement in his arms or legs—probably a spinal cord injury—and tons of internal bleeding. Daniel had done the best he could for the kid, but it was his own fault for leaving the US to fight for a terrorist group anyway. What did he expect would happen?

He'd regained consciousness during the chopper ride for about ten minutes. Sometimes the IV fluids did that, perked up the patient. He said his name was Muhammed, but the intel guys ran his prints and he came up as Tahlil Mufti. Nineteen years old. They even had a home address in Minneapolis, Minnesota.

"You're a long way from Minneapolis, Tahlil," Daniel had told him on the chopper ride.

The kid focused on his face. "Do I know you?"

Daniel shook his head. "You're on your way to the USS *Essex*. They'll patch you up in no time." That was probably a lie. Internal injuries were tough to diagnose, and Daniel was no doctor, but Tahlil's injuries looked as bad as any Daniel had ever seen.

"Do you want me to contact anyone for you?" Daniel asked.

Tahlil's eyes lost focus and Daniel thought he'd passed out again. He wiped a dribble of blood from the patient's mouth.

"My mother," Tahlil said. He was very hard to hear over the sound of the helo rotors and Daniel had to put his ear right next to the kid's mouth. He'd watched a few men die and all of them asked for their mothers at the end. "Tell her it's not her fault."

Tahlil remained unconscious for the rest of the ride to *Essex*.

Once he turned over the Minneapolis kid to the doctors on the amphib, Daniel was free. He took a quick shower and headed for the mess deck for a bite. The breakfast crowd was spotty this morning; most people were probably still on watch as they received choppers from the raid on the al-Shabab compound.

Daniel found an empty table and dug into his Wheaties.

"May I join you?" The voice was soft and belonged to a blonde woman about his age dressed in civilian clothes. "I'm Samantha," she said.

Daniel just stared.

She smiled at him. "Okay, I'm going to sit down. If you don't want me to, you just say so." Daniel nodded and she slid into the bench opposite him. "What's your name?"

"Daniel." His voice sounded like a strangled cat. He wondered if he had anything stuck in his teeth.

"It's nice to meet you, Daniel. What do you do around here?"

"Corpsman. You know, medical stuff, first aid . . ."

She laughed. "Yeah, Daniel, I know what corpsmen do." She winked at him. "Were you involved in the operation last night? The one in Somalia?"

"Yeah, but I can't really talk about it, you know."

"Of course! They already briefed us anyway. The attack and all that. Looks like it was successful—that's good. I guess you rode in with the casualties, huh?"

"Just one," Daniel said. Samantha had enormous blue eyes and a generous mouth. "He was nothing but a kid—nineteen years old. From Minneapolis, if you can believe it."

"Really?" Samantha's blue eyes grew a fraction wider. "Tell me more, Daniel."

CHAPTER 33

Don's face looked worn and pasty on the video screen. *Not that I look that much better,* Liz thought, finger-combing her own hair. She stole a look at her watch. 0620. Twenty minutes ago she'd been sound asleep until she was rousted out by the crisis of the day.

Coffee. She needed coffee.

"Start from the beginning, Don, and speak slowly. I'm not awake yet."

Don scrubbed his face with both hands and squinted at the screen. "Okay, here goes. About nine hours ago, we launched a raid on an al-Shabab compound in Somalia. It's believed to be a recent Daesh convert and we were sending a message from the new administration to the Islamic State. Between you and me, it was also a do-over on the raid that failed last fall."

"So the raid failed?"

Don winced. "On the contrary. It went off like clockwork. All of the top al-Shabab leaders were killed or captured, we freed a bunch of civilians and boosted a shitload of intel. Hard drives, maps, reports, money—you name it, we got it."

"So what's the problem?"

"Well, we found one of your kids there."

"My kids? I don't follow."

In reply, Don put an image on the screen of what looked to be a high school yearbook picture. "Meet Tahlil Mufti, Roosevelt High School, class of 2015. Member of the student council, captain of the soccer team, and international terrorist."

Liz hammered the name into the search engine box on her secure computer. "I don't have a record of him anywhere. Do you have him in custody?"

"Not unless you count a body bag as custody."

"Very funny, Don. Look, I realize I'm a little slow this morning, but can you please just tell me what's going on?"

"Lizzie, there's been a leak. Someone on the *Essex* heard about the ID on the body and called home and—"

"And now we're going to have a media shitstorm over why the FBI didn't know about this guy."

"You got it, sister."

The news coverage was even worse than she'd feared. Fox News ran with the breaking news headline: "From Soccer Star to ISIS Killer." The talk shows spooled up as the morning wore on and her phone rang nonstop with requests for media interviews. Trask had his door shut for most of the morning as he fielded calls from Washington.

At noon, it got worse. A local African-American imam called a press conference to denounce the FBI for smearing the good name of a local Somali boy who had made good in "the white man's society." He accused the FBI of fabricating the story to scare the Somali community into informing on their Muslim neighbors. He asked Tahlil's mother to speak. The older woman approached the microphone like she was stalking a snake. Her voice was soft, her English heavily accented.

"My boy is good boy," she said. "This is a lie. They lie about my boy." The imam put his arm around her, glaring at the cameras.

Trask appeared in Liz's peripheral vision. They stood side by side watching the TV. "I don't suppose we can produce a body and shut this idiot down?" he asked.

Liz shook her head. "Not unless you want to start a riot. Don said the body's pretty shot up. They'll do a burial at sea once they've collected DNA and such."

"We're going to need to do a press conference on this, Liz, and I want you to handle it. It's set for four o'clock this afternoon."

"What are we supposed to tell them?"

Trask shrugged. "Tell them the truth. The kid was radicalized right under their noses and no one in their community did anything to stop it. This is not about being Muslim or Christian or any other religion—it's about being a citizen." He pointed at the TV screen where the imam was pounding on the podium as he answered a question. "And this kind of crap doesn't help anyone."

"Thanks, boss. Can I quote you on that?"

"We'll do a prebrief at three in my office." He spun on his heel. "You might want to call your imam friend for some advice on how to message this."

Imam Nabil answered after the first ring. "Oh, Elizabeth, I have been expecting your call. My heart is heavy. Is it true? About Tahlil?"

"I'm afraid so, Nabby. He was killed in a raid on an al-Shabab

171

compound last night. The news of his death becoming public was
. . . unintentional."

Silence.

"How could this happen, Nabby? How could his mother not
know her son was fighting for Daesh?"

"Elizabeth, don't judge her too harshly. She's ashamed. She
makes up stories about her son with a big job in Vancouver or
some far-off place to tell her friends. She goes on and on about
how well he's doing until she begins to believe her own lie."

"And the imam? How do you explain him?"

Nabby barked out a short laugh. "Politics and religion are
twin sisters, Elizabeth. Not all imams are harmless old men like
me. Some imams believe we're in competition with each other,
that we need to market our 'brand' to grow our following. This
is what you Americans call a 'made-for-TV moment.' However
shameless the actions of Imam Zahir, I assure you he is speaking
to a very active segment of the Muslim community."

"So how do we counter his rhetoric?"

"You speak the truth, Elizabeth. The people that Imam Zahir
is speaking to are hearing what they want to hear. You must speak
to everyone else."

"Is there anything else you can tell me that might help us,
Nabby?"

She could hear the older man fidgeting on the other end of the
line.

"Nabby?"

"There is one thing, Elizabeth, but I'm sure it's no more than
a coincidence."

"In my business, there's no such thing as a coincidence,
Nabby. What is it?"

"As far as I know, there's only one person who has a direct

connection with Tahlil, Hamza, and Faruq. But I'm sure it's nothing."

"Who is it, Nabby?"

The old man sighed. "Zacharia Ismail."

CHAPTER 34

The news of Tahlil's death went through the Roosevelt High School Somali population like a shot. By the time Aya arrived at lunch, all of her friends were waiting at their normal table. No one was eating.

"Can you believe it?" Caaliyah asked, her dark eyes shining. "We knew him. A freedom fighter—from our school!"

"I heard Mr. Johansen called him a terrorist in class," Madino replied. She rubbed the scar on her chin when she spoke. "He said anyone who fought for al-Shabab was nothing."

Aya's thoughts were in a whirl. Terrorist? He was a freedom fighter. He gave his life to free Somalia from . . . what? It was all so confusing. Her parents sometimes talked about what their lives were like when they grew up in Mogadishu. They talked about beaches and fancy restaurants and it sounded like heaven—certainly better than cold Minneapolis. Her mother told her once that she didn't even wear a *hijab* growing up!

174

Then the Saudi clerics came and brought Wahhabism, their brand of Islam, to Somalia. She knew al-Shabab came after that, but . . . it was all so mixed up. Aya was American—whatever that meant. She'd never been to Somalia and never would. None of this affected her.

Hodan tapped her on the forearm. "Have you called Zacharia yet?" she asked.

Aya snapped herself out of her reverie, annoyed. Hodan was always asking about her brother. "No, why?" she snapped. "Wait—what do you mean?"

"You said the FBI came to question him after the shooting at the Xcel Center. He knew Tahlil. Won't they be back again?"

Aya fumbled for her mobile. Hodan was right. That FBI woman would be back. Had he heard the news? She needed to warn her brother.

Where are u? she texted.

Aya tapped the corner of her phone on the table as she waited. Zacharia normally answered her texts within a few minutes.

"What does Imaan say about all this?" asked Caaliyah. She snapped her fingers in Aya's face. "Aya? Are you listening?"

"I—I haven't talked to her recently." Aya checked her phone again.

"She said we would stand up for ourselves, right? We would claim our rights as citizens—make some noise, right? What are we going to do?"

"I don't know!" Aya stood up. Still no answer from Zacharia. Something was definitely wrong. "I'm going home. I need to find out if my brother is okay. And then I'll call Imaan."

She left immediately, not even stopping at her locker to pick up books for her math homework and definitely not signing out at the main office. Aya texted Imaan on her way home. It was a special number that Imaan had made her memorize, to be used only in emergencies.

I loved the last song on Rise Up, she texted. That was what she was supposed to send. *Rise Up* was Imaan's latest album and truth be told Aya was lukewarm on the last song. But that was the code—that's what Imaan called it. A code for a meeting.

1 hour. The response came fast. Faster than Aya had expected. She quickened her pace toward home.

The apartment was empty. Even her father was gone. She paced in the tiny kitchen, her fingers automatically smoothing the cloth on the table, straightening the wad of napkins into a neat bundle. What should she do? Call her parents? Call Imam Nabil? She settled for texting Zacharia again.

Z - where RU?!!

By the time the hour was up, Zacharia still had not responded to her texts. She went into her brother's bedroom and pulled his laptop from under his bed. It was a newer model, one that her brother had bought with his own money from a job in his senior year of high school. She waited as the device booted up and found a wireless signal. Normally, Zacharia's computer was off-limits to her, but she knew his password. Besides, she was doing this because she was worried about him.

Aya took a deep breath as she typed in the URL from memory exactly as Imaan had told her. The screen went blank, with only a blinking cursor in the upper right corner. Had she done it right? She checked the time on her mobile. She was maybe a minute early.

The computer jiggled on her lap as she tapped her foot, waiting for the seconds to tick by. Finally, the screen cleared as Imaan's face smiled up at her.

"How are you, my little flower?" Imaan said, her cool voice flowing through the computer speakers.

Aya's shoulders sagged. "I needed to speak with you, Imaan. The news about Tahlil broke this morning here in Minnesota, and I fear the FBI has taken my brother, and—and—" Her cheeks were wet and she was babbling. Aya dug her fingers into her thigh until it hurt. *Get a grip!*

"It's alright, Ayana. It's alright, but we only have a few minutes. You must be strong and clear in your reports to me. You can do that for me, right?"

Aya sat up straight and wiped her cheeks with the back of her hand. "Yes, Imaan." She could almost feel the reassuring grip of the older woman's fingers entwined in hers.

"Good. Now, from the beginning, tell me what has happened."

Aya took a deep breath and then slowly relayed the events of the morning to the older woman. She found if she watched Imaan's painted nails as they gently stroked the curve of her jaw, it relaxed her.

"Good," Imaan said when she'd finished. "You have done well, Ayana. Very well."

Aya felt a rush of pleasure at Imaan's words. The older woman pursed her lips as if she was thinking. Aya imagined those lips kissing her cheek.

"And your sisters? They are ready to take action?"

"Yes, Imaan, they said so—all of them."

"And they will follow you?"

Aya nodded. "Yes, I think so."

"And you are committed to this cause? To me?"

"Yes. Absolutely." Aya locked eyes with Imaan's image on the screen. "I would do anything for you."

Imaan held her gaze for a long moment, but Aya refused to look away. Finally, the singer smiled at her, a broad smile, a smile of love. "I believe you would, my little flower."

The smile faded and her eyes narrowed. "We don't have much time, Ayana, so listen carefully. This next step must be done with discretion and skill. In order to make the American government take you seriously, you need to appear serious." Her painted fingernails rested on her chin.

"Do any of your sisters have connections with gangs in Minneapolis?"

CHAPTER 35

The *Arrogant* pulled into the slip just as the sun was coming over the horizon. In contrast to the fishing fleet they'd passed on the way in, the marina was still and silent. The crew spoke in hushed tones as they tied up the boat and transferred trash to the pier. Brendan tossed his half-full sea bag onto the dock and jumped down after it, letting his good leg take the brunt of his weight.

It was hard to believe that meager sack of dirty clothes was all he had to show for the last few months.

"Heads up, Brendan."

Rachel tossed her much-heavier bag at his head. Brendan staggered under the weight. She dropped lightly to the dock and hoisted the bag out of his arms with a wink. "I'll take that. What a gentleman."

Rachel wore her dark hair loose around her shoulders. A few

weeks in the sun had brought out honey-colored highlights that emphasized her hazel eyes. Brendan watched her as she made her way down the pier with her gear.

What a completely baffling woman. One minute she seemed to be coming on to him, the next she was a withdrawn, brooding mess. After a few weeks at sea, even the most hardened introverts tended to share their life stories, but Rachel's identity was wrapped in a hard shell and buried under layers and layers of emotional concrete.

Still, in their weeks together, he'd grown as close to her as any of the crew. He wondered about the night he'd plucked her from the Indian Ocean, half-dead. She'd called him Levi.

Pretty much every clear night, Brendan went to the open deck on the bow and lay on his back to enjoy the stars. Although he never asked her to join him, Rachel invited herself. It was just such a night, with a full moon perfectly mirrored in the glassy sea, when Brendan asked Rachel about Levi.

"Don't ever say that name," she said, turning away.

"Is he your husband?"

"Leave it."

"Hey, when I pulled you out of the drink, you were the one who brought up the name."

She sat up. Brendan saw her shoulders quiver in the moonlight.

"I said leave it."

Brendan sat up next to her. He put his arm across her shoulders. "Sorry."

"You remind me of him," she said after a long time. "His name was Levi."

"He's . . . gone?"

She blinked as she nodded.

"Was he—"

Rachel shrugged off his arm and stood up in one movement. "I don't want to talk about this anymore. I loved Levi and he's gone—that's all you need to know. You remind me of him, and all this"—she swung her arm toward the flat sea—"lets me pretend that it might be alright if I . . . if I let someone in again."

She knelt down and placed her hands on Brendan's shoulders. Her eyes sparkled in the darkness, and for a moment Brendan thought she was going to kiss him.

"You have someone, right? Liz?"

He nodded.

"Don't ever leave her, Brendan. Take it from me: it sucks to be the one left behind."

She was still friendly to him after that, but it was like there was a wall between them now.

"Well, skipper, I guess this is goodbye."

Brendan tore his eyes away from the figure of Rachel hailing a cab on the road next to the marina. She was out of his life and good riddance. He focused on his lead tech.

As always, she made him smile. Dot Pendergrass's frizzy gray-blonde hair was forever escaping the bun at the back of her head and flying around her face. Her eyes were glassy and her lip trembled.

"I'm going to miss you, Dot."

"It won't be the same without you, skipper."

Brendan felt his face growing hot. Dot had been with the *Arrogant* since the very first mission. She'd taught him what a "major SIG" was, for God's sake. He might have been the captain, but she was the one who held the intel team together and made the kind of intelligence finds that had put the Feisty Minnow program on the map.

Brendan hugged her, blinking back tears. "I owe you so much, Dot. Thanks for everything."

The older woman tightened her arms around him. "Stay safe, skipper."

The official turnover was done at a local hotel. Brendan kept one eye on the new captain of the *Arrogant* as he introduced the man to his new crew.

Jim "Crime Dog" MacGuff had spent enough time as a naval aviator to acquire a call sign—and he liked to use it. Like Brendan, he was a Naval Academy grad and a member of the USNA sailing team, but their time at the Academy had not overlapped. Squat, with a barrel chest and bulging biceps, Crime Dog looked like his nickname.

"Call me Crime Dog or just Dog," he said when the introductions were completed. He waved toward the couches and armchairs on the far side of the suite where there was a continental breakfast laid out. "I'm loving this rich-guy cover story," he said as he plucked a piece of fruit from the tray and chomped down on it.

Brendan reminded himself that MacGuff had been screened personally by Baxter, but he watched the reactions of his crew all the same. He wished now that he had insisted Dot come for the debrief.

Crime Dog clapped his hands and rubbed them together. "Well, McHugh, I know you've got a plane to catch, so let's get started. Whatcha got for me?"

Brendan gave a rundown on the few maintenance issues and other logistical matters, then a short debrief on the intel package that Dot was prepping to upload. MacGuff sipped his coffee and nodded.

One of the analysts spoke up. "Skipper, what about the—"

"Let me stop you right there, compadre," said MacGuff. "This is not *Gilligan's Island* and I don't do 'skipper'—just so you know." He waved his hand. "Continue."

Brendan gritted his teeth as the analyst colored and finished his thought, a minor detail about the intel package. "I think that's all I have, Jim."

Three flights and thirty hours later, Brendan walked out of the automatic sliding doors at Baltimore/Washington International Airport. Despite the four Advil he'd taken on the final leg of the journey from Amsterdam, his bad knee throbbed with every step. He rubbed the grit out of his eyes as he peered at the slow-moving line of cars outside of baggage claim.

"Brendan!"

A silver Ford Taurus had pulled up next to the curb and Baxter jumped out of the driver's seat. His white teeth flashed against his dark skin as he made his way around the front of the car and embraced Brendan. "You look like something the cat dragged in." He pushed Brendan back. "You smell like it, too." He tossed Brendan's bag into the backseat. "Get in."

Baxter was silent as he eased the car into traffic. "How's the knee?" he said when he had maneuvered the vehicle into the far lane and picked up some speed.

Brendan shrugged. "Hurts like hell, especially after two days sitting on airplanes." He rubbed his face with both hands. "Where do they have me staying and how long before I can go home to Liz?"

Baxter slipped on a pair of sunglasses. "The intel package that Dot uploaded was good enough that your debrief is postponed until tomorrow. And you're staying with me."

"Aw, Rick, I don't want to put you out—"

Baxter slid the sunglasses down his nose so Brendan could

see his eyes. "I insist. We have much to discuss, grasshopper." He pushed the glasses back into place. "By the way, the promotion lists were posted today. You made commander."

With his injury and moving to the Office of Naval Intelligence, Brendan had pretty much given up hope of being promoted to commander on his first look, let alone below zone. He gaped at Baxter. "Are you screwing with me, Rick?"

His boss's face took on a serious look. "Brendan, what you've done for the Navy and your country is beyond measure. Feisty Minnow, the Middle East thing"—they shared a look about the operation that had taken out a rogue Iranian nuclear weapons site, the one they didn't dare talk about even now—"and now the Somali reconnaissance op. Man, you deserve this."

"Does Liz know yet?"

Baxter shrugged. "I didn't tell her. You can use my phone if you want to call her. But I'd wait if I were you."

"What does that mean?"

"Good news comes in waves, my young friend. If you wait a few hours, you'll have more than just a promotion to talk about."

"What could possibly be better than a promotion?"

"All in good time, Brendan."

Baxter's definition of "good time" included Brendan taking a shower while he put some steaks on the grill and opened up a pair of microbrews.

Brendan accepted the beer and sat in the lounge chair. "Alright, Rick, enough foreplay. Will you please tell me what's going on?"

"There's been some changes in the works for a while—stuff that I couldn't talk about—but as of yesterday, it's official."

Brendan refused to be baited by his boss. He sat back in his chair and took a long pull of his beer.

"The CIA's taking over Feisty Minnow," Baxter burst out.

"Ships, operational control, the whole works." Baxter's eyes shone and the pace of his talking picked up. "The op you did with the Mossad agent to help us nail al-Shabab was the icing on the cake for the powers on high. We're going to the show, buddy! Ten times the budget and less bureaucratic bullshit, what do you say?"

Brendan leveled his gaze at the grill. "I say you're burning the shit out of our dinner, boss."

As Baxter leaped up to attend to the steaks, Brendan considered the label on his beer bottle. Baxter had put his entire career on the line to launch Feisty Minnow, and Brendan was more than glad to have his friend's work validated. But maybe it was time for him to look for another career—one that kept him closer to Liz. His encounter with Rachel left him feeling unmoored. Was he really that shallow of a person? Put him with a pretty girl in a high-pressure situation and . . .

Baxter stood over him, holding a plate of steaming steaks. He pointed the meat fork at Brendan.

"What?" Brendan asked.

"I know that look, McHugh. Don't do or say anything stupid until I tell you the best part of this plan." He dropped the platter on the table and pointed to a chair. "Sit. Eat. Don't speak unless spoken to."

Brendan was glad for the cover. He tucked into his steak and savored the glass of Malbec that Baxter poured for him. When he finally pushed his plate back, Baxter topped off his wineglass and waited for Brendan to settle in his chair.

"Alright, we comfy now?" Brendan nodded and Baxter continued. "Look, I know the last deployment was longer than expected, but it couldn't be helped. How're you and Liz doing?"

Brendan shrugged, avoiding his friend's eyes. "Hard to tell. She got that promotion to Supervisory Special Agent for the task force on homegrown recruiting and it's been a tough transition for her. To be honest, the last few times we've been able to talk it's been more fighting than talking. I'm worried, Rick."

Brendan took a sip of wine. At least he'd said it out loud finally.

"I hear you, Brendan. Men and women have been screwing up long-distance relationships since the Odyssey. But I may have a solution for you."

"Well?"

"Our new bosses want us to set up a front business for Feisty Minnow, and they've settled on a travel agency—I know, talk about cliché, right? Our cover is selling high-end travel to rich people on our global fleet of luxury sailboats. We're to set up shop in a specially built office complex right in your hometown of Minneapolis, Minnesota. And you, *Commander* McHugh, get to go home to Liz every night."

"This is for real?" Brendan could feel the grin spreading across his face.

"As real as it gets, Brendan." Baxter raised his glass. "To Feisty Minnow."

Brendan toasted with his friend, then set his wineglass down with a thud. "Excuse me, Rick, I think it's time I made that phone call."

CHAPTER 36

Chantal arranged her skirt across her knee for the tenth time in the past ten minutes. Her apartment in Helsinki didn't have much furniture, so choosing how to set up the meeting with Kahin really had only two options: sit next to Kahin on the couch or opposite him in the armchair.

The armchair, she decided. It will make it seem less intimate, more like a meeting.

Her thoughts were interrupted by a knock at the door. Even Kahin's knock sounded timid.

When she opened the door, Kahin smiled at her shyly, without showing his teeth. "Good evening, Imaan. I am so sorry about the late hour, but . . ." He folded his hands and let the sentence fade into nothingness.

Chantal tamped down a flush of anger. Firstly, she had told

him to call her Chantal, not Imaan, and secondly, she had asked him to the meeting, so why apologize for the late hour?

She smiled and kissed him on both cheeks. "Nonsense, Kahin. I invited you. Please come in."

She served him tea as they made small talk. He sat on the couch, his knees drawn together, and spoke only when spoken to. His eyes followed her as she settled into the armchair. Chantal studied him over the rim of her cup.

Yes, she had not chosen well with Kahin. When she compared him with Ayana in Minneapolis, the difference was staggering. With Ayana, her plain looks and *hijab* hid a very organized and talented young woman. In the space of only a few months, she'd managed to recruit another five girls and prepare them for the next step. In contrast, although Kahin was a beautiful lad with flawless skin and doe eyes, he'd done next to nothing.

Victor was right. She needed to make a change.

"So," she said, setting her teacup on the table between them. "What do you have to report, Kahin?"

"Ah, well, it's been very difficult, Imaan—"

"Call me Chantal, please."

Kahin's smile was a nervous uncovering of his teeth. "Sorry— you said that before. Chantal, then." He took a sip of tea. "The economy is not very good, so getting a job in one of the stores you asked about is very difficult, Imaa—Chantal."

She nodded. "I understand, Kahin. Jobs are hard to come by. What about weapons?"

Kahin frowned. "Well, I'm glad you brought that up. I was wondering why we need weapons. This is a demonstration, right? Won't guns scare people?"

"We've been through this, Kahin. We're not going to hurt

anyone, but we must be taken seriously. How many weapons have you procured?"

"Well, so, that's the thing." He picked up the teacup and tried to drink more before realizing it was empty. He looked imploringly at Chantal for more tea. She ignored him.

"How many?"

The teacup made a rattling sound when he placed it on the table. "None," he said in a small voice.

"Have you even tried, Kahin?"

"No." He would not even meet her gaze.

"Kahin," she said with more force than she intended. "This is not working."

"Imaan—"

"Call me Chantal," she snapped, springing to her feet and leveling a finger at the man. He shrank back.

"But Chantal—"

"I depended on you. You've put this entire operation at risk and I cannot have that."

Three solid knocks sounded on the door. Chantal crossed the room in three strides and threw open the door.

Bashir's stocky body was almost as wide as the doorframe. His bald head gleamed in the dim light of the hallway. In contrast to Kahin's straight white teeth, Bashir's smile was yellowed and showed gaps. His beard jutted out before him as he stalked into the room.

Kahin got to his feet. "What is he doing here?" His voice had risen half an octave.

Bashir looked at him and grunted.

"I will be taking over leadership of the Helsinki operation," Chantal said. "Bashir will be my second-in-command."

Kahin looked like he might cry. "But what about me?"

"You will no longer be needed, Kahin."

"But, Imaa—Chantal, we're from the same clan. Practically family. How can you—"

"This goes far beyond clans, Kahin. We're making a difference for all Muslim citizens, regardless of their clan." It sounded righteous and high-minded when she said it like that.

"Why is he here?" Kahin pointed at Bashir.

"Bashir is here to make sure you understand that you will never speak about our cause—to anyone. Ever." She settled her gaze on Kahin's doe eyes. This was *the* moment. Kahin could choose to go peacefully or he could choose to fight.

Kahin chose badly.

"You can't treat me like this. I'll tell people about what's going on. I'll—"

For a stump of a man, Bashir moved like lightning. In the space of a split second, he'd crossed the room and slammed a beefy fist into Kahin's midsection. Kahin's thin frame doubled over, and he was reduced to a gasping, gagging mess on all fours.

Bashir cocked an eyebrow at Chantal.

Would that be enough? Even as she phrased the question in her head, she knew the answer was no. Victor had taught her that first feelings were invariably the truest feelings. Kahin would recover and he would expose their operation. That was her first feeling, her true feeling.

She nodded at Bashir.

Bashir's fist shot out again, catching Kahin on the jaw. His head snapped around and he collapsed to the floor, unconscious.

"I'll take care of it," Bashir said. He picked up Kahin's body with ease and slung the man's slim frame over his heavy shoulder. He let himself out of Chantal's apartment without another word.

The shaking started in her right hand a few seconds later. Her breath caught in her throat as the trembling spread to her entire body. She collapsed into the chair as her mind processed the enormity of what she had just done.

Enough! She clenched both fists until the shaking stopped. She had done what Victor had asked of her. No, she had done what needed to be done. Victor or no, Chantal Deveraux made her own decisions.

The shaking faded to a quiver and an emptiness inside her belly. She put the kettle on for another cup of tea. While she waited for the water to boil, Chantal found her mobile phone and thumbed her way to Victor's latest mobile number.

It is done, she texted. Then she powered down her phone without waiting for a reply.

CHAPTER 37

Reza ended the secure videoconference and stared at the blank screen. His right hand searched for the bottle of aspirin in his upper right-hand drawer. He automatically snapped off the lid and popped two pills in his mouth, chasing them with a gulp of cold tea.

His job as the head of Quds Force intelligence was wearing him down in every way possible: emotionally, physically, mentally. He couldn't remember the last time he'd eaten a proper meal with another human being. These days, his closest friend seemed to be the bottle of aspirin in his desk drawer.

His eye caught the black-and-white photograph on the corner of his desk, a much younger Reza in his Army uniform being awarded a medal by an equally younger Hassan Rouhani. Even now, after all these years, Reza felt a tingle of gratitude toward his mentor. He'd saved Reza's life that day, a debt that could never be fully repaid.

Reza's gaze fell to the photograph that topped the pile of papers in the file folder on his desk. The square jawline, stylish haircut, and icy gray eyes of Rafiq Roshed were worthy of a fashion runway model. At some point over the last few months, Reza had inked a bullet hole in the center of Rafiq's forehead. *That's what I'll do to you when I find you—and I will find you. Before the Americans.* The last of the three brothers who had nearly taken down his beloved Rouhani would pay with his life and it would be by Reza's hand, if he had anything to say about it.

He rubbed his face. *Enough daydreaming.*

Reza spread out his notes from the just-completed conference call with Donald Riley. It still amazed him that he had the authority to speak directly to the Americans on the issue of Roshed. Donald could be trusted; Reza knew that from their work together to stop Roshed from detonating a nuclear warhead on US soil. He smiled wryly to himself. *Another life debt owed.* Without Don's intervention, Reza would probably be moldering in an unmarked grave instead of leading the most powerful intelligence agency in the Middle East.

He stabbed at his notes with a pen. In his opinion, the Americans were "grasping at straws," as their saying went. The intel tracked Roshed to Kampala, Uganda, on the theory that he would use that as a base to launch an attack on Camp Lemonnier in Djibouti. While the US forces in the Horn of Africa made sense as a target, the idea that Roshed would align himself with Daesh in order to strike the Americans made no sense. Daesh had killed Roshed's mother; he was more likely to attack Daesh than align with them. Even terrorists had standards.

It wasn't until the very end of the call that Reza heard Donald's side comment on a possible sighting of Roshed in Ivory Coast. He closed his eyes to recall the exact wording.

Donald had said: "The last thing to report is that the French claim to have sighted Roshed in Ivory Coast. No photographs, but they say the man matched Roshed's description, except with blond hair. He stayed at the Sofitel in Abidjan a few months ago. The location on the western side of Africa makes no sense and the French say their source is marginal, but I offer it up for the sake of completeness. We agreed to share all leads, but this one—I think you'll agree—is pretty weak."

At the time, Reza had smiled for the camera and said something witty, but mention of Ivory Coast had tickled a memory. A whisper of something he had seen a few weeks ago.

Reza pulled a thin file out of a stack and reread the report from their man in Accra, Ghana. A blond man matching Rafiq's description was sighted in Ghana a few months ago. No photographic backup, no indication of any suspicious activity, but this source was very reliable—one of their best.

His headache returned in force. He should bury this file, walk away. There were so many more pressing duties for him these days. Despite signing a nuclear peace deal with the West and restoring a flow of funds to the starved Iranian economy, Iran's position as a major power in the Middle East had grown more tenuous.

Every day Assad in Syria grew weaker. An infusion of support from the Russians had gotten him off life support, but there was no way he'd be able to successfully rule Syria again. But at least the Russians checked the influence of the Americans in the region. In Yemen, his Quds teams supported the Houthi rebels against the Saudis, while at the same time, both Iran and Saudi Arabia made war on their common enemy, Daesh.

Move and countermove; that was his job now. It felt more like treading water. Reza considered another hit of aspirin.

And in the midst of all this chaos, he put his valuable time into the pursuit of Rafiq Roshed. His entire world teetered on the edge of collapse and he put his most valuable resource—his own attention—on the hunt for one man. *I wonder if this is what the Americans felt like when they hunted down bin Laden?* At least they got their man. Roshed was still at large.

Reza got to his feet and stood in front of the wall map of the world. Abidjan, Côte D'Ivoire. He stabbed it with his finger. And right next to it, barely a finger's width away, was Accra, Ghana. He strode to the window.

Night had long since fallen over Tehran. Yellow streetlamps, hazy in the smog, cast a warm glow over the city. Lines of tail-lights winked at him from the line of heavy traffic.

"Rayen?" he called out.

His secretary poked her head into his office. "Yes, sir."

"Send a cable to our station in Ghana. Have our lead officer fly back here for a meeting. Immediately."

Rayen nodded. "Anything else, sir?"

Reza settled behind his desk and reopened the file from Ghana.

"No—wait. Go home, Rayen. Your family deserves you more than I do at this hour."

CHAPTER 38

Brendan pinched the bridge of his nose to stem the impending headache. He cracked open one eye to stare at the pile of eighty-three personnel files still on his desk. The closest stack had only six folders left in it. He made a deal with himself to at least get through those before he left for the weekend.

Moving the Feisty Minnow program from US Navy control to a CIA covert operation had been anything but smooth. Baxter spent most of his time in Washington trying to sort out the bureaucratic details leaving Brendan in charge of running the Minneapolis operation. Odyssey Vacations was what was known in bureaucratic parlance as an intelligence commercial activity, or ICA. The principle was simple: an actual private company with real products and real employees also served as a front for intelligence operations. The practical application of Title 10, US Code 431 was far more complex. Brendan was actually supposed to run—and staff—a real business, while at the same time executing the Feisty Minnow intelligence-gathering activities. To make matters worse, the CIA actually expected their ICAs to make a profit, which was then rolled back into the covert operating budget.

The largest operation Brendan had run prior to this was a SEAL platoon of eighteen highly trained, highly screened warriors. Now he was in charge of a group of three dozen travel specialists, plus the crews for seven sailboats in the Feisty Minnow fleet. Another seven boats were planned for the next fiscal year, and they all needed to be staffed with crews.

Odyssey Vacations was meant to appeal to the über-wealthy, the kind of client who sought "signature experiences" where money was not an issue. In his two months on the job, Brendan had seen multiple chartered power yacht cruises around the Mediterranean, a penguin encounter in Antarctica that cost almost as much as his annual salary, and, of course, sailing adventures on the Odyssey fleet of sailboats, which were mixed in with the Feisty Minnow fleet on intelligence-gathering platforms.

Brendan dispensed with the last of the short stack of personnel files and logged out of his secure terminal. He glanced at his watch. 1810. If he left right now, he could get home in time to take a quick shower before the barbecue at his parents' house tonight. The annual Memorial Day cookout was the McHugh family summer season kickoff party. Everybody in his parents' circle of friends and family was invited. Liz had been dreading it for weeks, expecting to have to answer the inevitable "when are you two getting married?" question at least a hundred times. Snatching up his car keys, he headed for the door.

The long subterranean hallway was mostly deserted at this time on a Friday evening before a holiday weekend. A young man in khakis and horn-rimmed glasses poked his head out of a doorway. "There you are, Brendan. I was just about to call you. You're wanted on the watch floor."

Brendan gritted his teeth. "Thanks, Jenkins." He spun on his heel and headed back the way he'd come to the double doors at the end of the hallway.

The watch floor was dominated by a wall of floor-to-ceiling high-definition monitors showing a map of the world whose oceans were littered with colored dots. The CIA tapped into the US Navy's geolocation system for all allied and friendly shipping, as well as electronic signals emanating from less-friendly merchant ships. Layered onto that merchant shipping data were the positions of all warships of any nation gleaned from satellite coverage. The blue, yellow, and red dots signified friendlies, neutral, or high-interest ships. The handful of green dots showed the locations of the Feisty Minnow fleet.

Brendan made his way across the dim room to the side of the shift supervisor. "Whatcha got, Supe?" he asked the woman seated behind the desk.

She swiped at a strand of hair that had strayed from her ponytail. "Hi, Brendan. We've got a problem on the *Scimitar*." She signaled to one of the watch team and the area off the shore of Venezuela expanded into a close-up view. A lone green dot sat just outside the twelve-mile border for international waters. "They ran into some weather and their main SIGINT antenna was hit by lightning. It's totally fried."

"What's our closest port with secret facilities?" The mast was the heart of the intelligence-collection platform. Without it, the *Scimitar* was just another sailboat.

"That would be Puerto Rico. Even if we meet them in PR, they'll be off station for at least two weeks."

Brendan rubbed his jaw. In recent months, the political

situation had deteriorated in Venezuela. Enter the Russians, with Vladimir Putin only too happy to help his South American comrades. There were members of Congress calling the Russian intervention in Venezuela a breach of the century-old Monroe Doctrine.

"What've we got to backfill them with?" Brendan asked.

"From our inventory? Nothing," the watch supervisor said. "But you can call the Navy, if you want." She hovered a cursor over a dot in the waters off St. Croix, Virgin Islands. The tag read: USS Virginia, SSN-774. "The *Virginia* is a less-capable intel platform but she'll do in a pinch. I already checked and she's just doing routine war games at AUTEC," she said, referring to the US Navy underwater test range off the island of St. Croix. "I'm sure the Navy will let you borrow her if you ask nicely."

Brendan stifled a groan. There was no way he'd make it home by seven now. Liz would be pissed if she had to go to his parents' house by herself. He had a sudden thought. Baxter was still in DC; maybe he could make a few calls and get the *Virginia* assigned to the Venezuelan coverage.

"I'll see what I can do," Brendan said. He jogged back to his office and dialed Baxter's number.

"What can I do for you, Brendan?" Baxter's tone was clipped, far from his normal warm greeting. Brendan bulled ahead anyway.

"Hi, Rick, we've got an issue with our ship down south. Storm damage. There's another asset in the area, and I was hoping you could make some calls on our behalf."

"Have you released a sitrep yet?" A sitrep was a situation report, meant to inform the chain of command of a problem.

"Uh, no." Brendan snapped on his desk lamp.

"Have you formally asked for the asset to be tasked to your project?" Baxter's voice dripped acid.

"No . . . sir."

"No. You just called me to see if I could 'make a few calls' instead of doing your damned job, Brendan."

"What a minute, Rick. That's not fair—"

"Don't talk to me about not fair, Brendan," Baxter interrupted. "It's time you learned the hard truth: our operations run on paperwork—and you're not doing your fair share. I bet you haven't even finished reviewing the personnel files I left for you last week."

Brendan eyed the remaining stack of folders on his desk. "I'm mostly done," he said.

"Look, Brendan." Baxter's tone softened a touch. "You need to understand, you're being groomed. You were deep-selected for commander, but now you have to earn it. You need to show the admirals that you can handle the high-end stuff so that you'll be ready for captain in a couple of years."

"Wait a minute, Rick. I haven't even pinned on commander yet. And you're talking about captain?"

Baxter sighed. "Look, Bren, as soon as you make commander, they're already considering you for O-6," he said, using Navy shorthand for the rank of captain. "If you don't show you can make that cut in a few years, you're labeled as a terminal O-5. Look, you have the talent and drive to make flag rank if you want it, but from here on out, it's as much about politics and who you know as it is about talent. You need to be the face of the Feisty Minnow operation if you want to advance. Got it?"

Brendan powered on his computer and started the login procedure to his multiple secure systems. He eyed the stack of personnel files. He dreaded the call he was about to make to Liz.

"Yes, sir. I've got it."

CHAPTER 39

The cool nighttime breeze slipped past Aya's cheek, continuing on into the back of the minivan. No one spoke and Madino had turned the radio off the minute they left the highway.

Madino's face was lit by the dashboard lights, the greenish tinge catching the smooth paleness of the scar on her chin. The girl's heavy face was set in a determined cast and she gripped the steering wheel with both hands.

"How much longer?" Aya asked.

"Soon," Madino grunted without bothering to take her eyes off the road.

Caaliyah, Madino's sister, squeezed Aya's shoulder from the seat behind her. "Not much further, Aya."

Aya shrugged off her hand. She didn't need comforting, she was in charge. Facing Madino, she said in a louder voice, "How much longer?"

The bigger girl sniffed and pulled the minivan to the curb in the darkness between streetlamps. She glanced up into the rearview mirror at her sister. "Go," she said.

"Wait a minute," Aya broke in. "Where is she going? Why don't you—"

Madino put the car in park and twisted in her seat. Her look stilled Aya's voice. "Do you have any idea where we're going, Aya? Even if you knew what house, would you even know where to look for the guns?"

Aya tried to meet her icy glare and failed.

"I thought so," Madino continued. "I know what I'm doing, so why don't you just keep quiet and let me handle it."

Aya was glad that the other girls—all crowded in the backseat—couldn't see the flush of red that crept up her cheeks. This was not how it was supposed to be. Imaan said she needed to establish herself as the leader of the group and that meant giving the orders.

Caaliyah snorted. "You two keep arguing while I check to make sure the house is empty." She slid open the side door, which triggered the overhead light. Madino cursed as she fumbled on the dashboard for the switch to kill the light.

The minutes ticked by in the dark. Hodan, Leylo, and Yasmin made no sound and Aya and Madino stared straight ahead out the windshield, each pretending the other wasn't there. A mosquito buzzed through the open window, making a lazy circuit of the interior of the minivan before exiting again.

Aya's phone buzzed and lit up.

All clr.

She tried to keep the gloating out of her smile as she showed the text to Madino. The other girl wrinkled her nose as she started the car and drove into the street. A half block later, she turned into a narrow alley between the tiny backyards of bungalow-style houses. Single-car detached garages crowded against the alley and the sour smell of rotting trash wafted in the window.

Madino parked the car in the shadow of a dilapidated garage and shut off the engine. "You stay here," she said to Aya. "The rest of you come with me."

"I'm coming with you," Aya said, louder than she'd intended. She opened her door and stepped into the alley. Her foot sank into something soft and squishy, but she ignored it. She joined Caaliyah, who was waiting by the gate.

"Look, Aya," Madino began.

"I'm coming inside," Aya said, and for a second, Aya thought the bigger girl might hit her. Caaliyah intervened.

"Leylo, you stay with the van," she said. "If anyone comes, text us." Caaliyah lowered her voice. "And you two stop it."

They crossed the yard as a group, Hodan and Yasmin crowding close to Aya. The steps leading up to the open back door felt rotten under Aya's feet and the small kitchen had a scent of unwashed dishes. Caaliyah took an immediate right and led them down a narrow set of stairs into the basement. Madino closed the door behind them and switched on the light.

The basement of the tiny house was partially finished. Someone had painted the concrete walls a dingy white, but it was mostly masked by graffiti now, the centerpiece of which was a stylized inscription that read St. Paul Pistol Boys, framed with blazing guns on either side and bandoliers of ammunition.

"Welcome to the P-Boys hangout," Caaliyah said with a nervous laugh. "It's okay. The windows are blacked out."

Two couches and a pair of recliners surrounded a battered coffee table, which was covered with cigarette burns and an overflowing ashtray. The air held the sweet stench of marijuana.

Yasmin must have noticed because she said, "Caaliyah, where's their stash? Let's have a party—"

Madino grabbed Yasmin's arm and shook the smaller girl. "Do you know what they'll do to us if they find us here?" She pushed Yasmin into one of the recliners. "We get the guns and we get out. This is not a party. These guys will hurt us if they catch us." She pointed to the scar on her chin. "How do you think I got this?"

Aya saw her opening. "Madino's right. Let's get the guns and get out. Where are they?"

Caaliyah was pulling the cushions off one of the couches, a hide-a-bed model. Instead of a mattress, a custom-built wooden box filled the space under the cushions. She flipped up the lid.

There were more guns in the box than Aya had ever seen in her life. Madino and Caaliyah piled handguns on the coffee table. "The rifles are AR-15s—all bought legally. We don't want those. We need something we can hide under our robes." She held a gun in each hand. "These are 9mms, a Beretta and a Glock."

"What's the difference?" Hodan asked in a timid voice.

Madino handed the Beretta to Aya and the Glock to Hodan. "Mostly size and weight. They both shoot the same kind of ammo. The Glock is smaller and a bit lighter. The Beretta has a thumb safety." She flipped a lever above the butt of the handgun, revealing a bright red dot. "When that dot is covered, you can't fire the weapon. The Glock doesn't have that."

"So the Beretta is safer?" Hodan asked.

Madino sighed. "No—you know what? We have two of each. Aya and Caaliyah take the Berettas and Yasmin and Hodan get the Glocks. I'll find another 9mm for Leylo."

"What are you going to use?" Aya asked.

Madino reached into the box and pulled out a wide-bore

weapon about as long as Aya's forearm. She pumped the barrel, making a loud ratcheting sound.

"My weapon of choice is the sawed-off shotgun."

CHAPTER 40

Liz poured herself a glass of orange juice and nudged the refrigerator door shut with her knee. Wisps of steam rose from the plate of scrambled eggs Brendan had made for her.

"Thanks, honey!" she called toward the sound of the shower in their bathroom.

Honey. No, that didn't fit, either. Since Brendan had come home to live with her, she'd been trying out different pet names, but nothing seemed to fit. Every couple had pet names, right?

I need a girlfriend I can talk to. The fact that she was a workaholic and worked mostly with men had never bothered her before, but now . . .

Brendan's homecoming was everything she'd hoped for—and everything she'd feared. Liz twisted her engagement ring around her finger. They were a physical couple and sex was their go-to activity, but at this point in their relationship they needed more—*she*

206

needed more. They were supposed to be building a life together, for God's sake, and she didn't even have a pet name for her fiancé. She'd already been divorced once, and Liz was determined that was not happening again. Not with Brendan.

She scooped up a mouthful of eggs as she donned her shoulder holster and her suit jacket. Carrying her breakfast plate, Liz made her way toward the balcony, flipping on the TV as she passed through the living room.

"We interrupt this programing to bring you breaking news," said the authoritative voice of the WCCO morning news anchor. The newscaster frowned at the camera in her best serious news face.

"We're receiving news of a shooting in the vicinity of the Karmel Mall, off Lake Street." Liz's forkful of eggs stopped halfway to her mouth as the screen filled with images of squad cars bearing the logos of Hennepin County Sheriff and Minneapolis PD. "Initial reports are that the gun battle was between two Somali gangs. Several fatalities are reported. We'll update you as we learn more. Now back to our morning programming."

Liz's phone rang when she was in the elevator. "I assume you've seen the news?" Trask's voice sounded tired.

"I'm on my way," she said. "Can you have Cain and Abel meet me at the scene?"

The news updates on the way to the scene got progressively worse, with one anchor comparing the shooting to the Somali civil war in Mogadishu decades ago. *Great, nothing like throwing gasoline on the fire.*

Gang intervention was normally a local police issue, but Liz knew a bit from her investigation into the connection between gangs and homegrown recruiting. The greater Minneapolis–St. Paul metro area had four main Somali gangs roughly organized along clan and turf lines.

She had to park a block away and show her badge twice before she got close to the action. On the outskirts of the crime scene, she came upon two paramedics loading a Somali youth into the back of an ambulance. The young man was trying to remain stoic in the face of a nasty-looking gunshot wound in his shoulder. Liz's hand involuntarily went to the scar on her own shoulder. The doctors had dug two pieces of buckshot out of her arm less than a year ago. On the day of the attempted bombing at the Vikings stadium, if she'd been standing a few inches to the left, the shotgun booby-trap would have taken off her head.

A Somali man in his late thirties wearing an ID from the sheriff's office was questioning the youth on the gurney. Behind the ambulance, Liz could see five shrouded bodies lying in the street. Bright yellow evidence cones littered the area. A tall, bald man wearing the uniform of a Hennepin County sheriff approached her.

"Special Agent Soroush. I would say good morning, but that's not how I see it right now." The sheriff's face was tight and his voice had a rough, trembly quality to it.

"I agree, Sheriff. I'm not here to take over jurisdiction, by the way, just here to see if I can connect this to what I'm working on."

The sheriff barked out a mirthless laugh. "God, I wish you would." He waved his hand at the bodies. "Five dead, six injured—two of them probably won't make it. Kids killing kids. But here's the kicker: they were fighting about guns. See the irony? They were shooting guns at each other because someone stole someone else's guns." He clamped his hat back on his bald head and pointed to the Somali man who had been interviewing the youth in the ambulance. "If you need details, see Amin Mahad. He's had a chance to speak to all the injured."

With a nod of thanks to the sheriff, Liz approached Amin

just as the ambulance was pulling away. His close-cropped curls had a touch of gray at the temples and his eyes were a soft, golden brown. His shoulders sagged a bit as he stared after the ambulance.

"Mr. Mahad, my name is—"

"I know who you are, Agent Soroush." He forced a weak smile as he shook her hand. "We talk to a lot of the same people and our mutual friend Nabby speaks highly of you. What can I do for the FBI this morning?"

"Can you tell me what happened?"

Amin faced the street where the bodies lay covered with white sheets. "Two gangs. The Somali Outlaws are the locals here at the Karmel. The other guys are from a gang called the St. Paul Pistol Boys."

"The sheriff says they were fighting about guns?"

Amin's face twisted into a grimace. "Yeah. The St. Paul gang says the Outlaws raided their hangout and stole their weapons. The kid I just put in the ambulance is an Outlaw and he says they didn't do it. I've known him for a long time and I believe him."

"So another gang stole the guns?"

Amin shrugged. "Not that I can tell. Other gangs in the area normally give the Somalis a wide berth. This is very unusual."

Liz dug out her phone and scrolled through the pictures. She stabbed the screen when she'd found the one she wanted and held it out to Amin. "Ever see a gang member with this tattoo?" The phone showed the photo of Faruq's forearm with the image of the stylized flame.

"No," he said after studying the picture. "Nabby asked me the same question and I gave him the same answer: I'd know about it if a new gang was being formed." He handed her phone back. "The tattoo looks new. Any chance I can talk to the person wearing it? I might be able to pick up on something your team missed."

Liz grimaced. "Not unless you can communicate with the dead, Amin."

CHAPTER 41

FBI Field Office, Brooklyn Park, Minnesota
27 June 2017 — 1400 local

Liz tried to stretch the kink out of her neck in a way that wouldn't look too ridiculous to the people behind the sixteen videoconference screens in front of her. Too late, she realized her desk yoga had caused her to space out on the last few seconds of conversation.

"Mr. Riley, can you say that again? I'm not sure if I get your meaning."

"Absolutely, Agent Soroush. We have indications of a sleeper cell based in the Minneapolis area. It's not clear if it's linked to Daesh or to al-Shabab, but it appears to center in Minneapolis."

This was not the news she needed right now. Until this call, it looked like the US was finally making some gains against terrorist groups trying to recruit Muslim youth. The FBI had just stopped four potential ISIS recruits from traveling to Turkey and instead of jail time had placed them in a community halfway house for rehabilitation.

"Can you clarify how they are recruiting? Is it still social media?"

Don shook his head. "No, this is different. The NSA has been focused on the Dark Web for some time now. It's a real challenge for us with all the new encryption techniques, but we have been able to isolate the general location of IP addresses. No content yet, just general vicinity."

"And you know these are recruiting sessions how?"

"We don't know for sure," Don said. "It's just suspicious activity for now."

Liz pinched the bridge of her nose. "Okay, let's say you're right and this is recruiting activity directed at the Minneapolis Somali population. Where is it coming from?"

An NSA analyst who looked like she might have cut her high school classes to be on the call answered. "We are certain that one of the connections originates in Finland. There's another in London, and one in Africa."

"Africa? That's all you have? That's a big continent, miss . . ."

"Williams. Jennifer Williams. That's actually one of the things that makes these communications so suspect—it's too good. The level of sophistication for all of them is very high, but Africa is off-the-charts good. We were lucky to narrow it down to a continent."

"So what's our next step?" Liz asked.

"Focus on the Minneapolis end of the connection," Don spoke up. "For that we need a FISA warrant and some serious computer time. This will be like looking for a needle in a field of haystacks."

Liz made a note. "Alright, keep me posted, and unless anyone has anything else that we need to cover, we're adjourned for today. Mr. Riley, can you stay on the line?"

She waited until all the other screens went dark, then let out a breath and slumped in her chair. "Alright, *Mister* Riley, give it to me straight. How serious is this Dark Web connection?"

Don shrugged. "It's too soon to tell, really. It looks suspicious, but mostly because it's unlike anything we've seen before. The fact that all the nodes go to Minneapolis and you're the capitol of Daesh recruiting makes me worry a little."

"What about those names I gave you?" Liz had given Don a list of known associates of Hamza and Faruq, the shooter at the Xcel Energy Center, that had been provided to her by Imam Nabil.

"Zilch. We ran them through every algorithm and database and had collection tools running full time for the past few weeks and we got a whole lot of nothing. Nothing criminal, anyway. Two of them have a serious porn addiction, but that's not illegal."

"But they fit the profile! Lack of authority figure, unemployed, sudden religious fervor. The models tell us these are the at-risk people."

"That's the problem, Liz. We want to look for what makes sense, what fits the profile. This new network is playing by different rules and it smells bad."

"Don, you're not helping. I need fewer leads, not more. Basically, you're telling me that everything I know about finding potential terrorists is out the window."

Don offered a lopsided grin. "I know, and I hope this turns out to be nothing, but we have to check it out. Besides, it's not all bad, right? I mean, the love of your life is back and he's staying there permanently."

Liz closed her eyes. "Living with me right now is a challenge on a good day. It's . . . it's just not what it was."

"Hey, look at me, Liz." She raised her eyes to the screen. Don's face was stern. "That's bullshit and you know it. You two are a team, a natural team. You just need time to adjust. Let Brendan add some balance to your life, not make it harder. Give your relationship the focus it deserves. It will make you a better leader, and a better agent."

Liz stared at the screen. "Wow, since when did you become Dr. Phil? That was pretty in my face."

Don blushed. "Sorry. I watched you two fight the obvious attraction for so long that I can't take it anymore. You two belong together, always have." He wagged his finger at the screen. "There's more tough love where that came from, if you need it."

Liz held up her hands. "No thanks, Romeo, but I would really like some actionable intelligence from Washington for a change."

"Wouldn't we all, Liz? Wouldn't we all." Don Riley was still laughing when he signed off the call.

CHAPTER 42

Chantal found a corner in the coffee shop across from her hotel and plugged in her laptop. Victor had cautioned her to always use public Wi-Fi, not her hotel, where she'd be easier to identify. She pulled the headscarf closer around her face and hunched over the machine. The downside of a public place was that she might also be recognized.

She considered ordering another coffee before her call with Victor, but at the last moment switched to a hot chocolate with extra whipped cream. This was a celebration of sorts; she deserved to splurge a little on the extra calories.

Chantal sipped her drink, trying not to stare at the clock in the lower right of her screen. She bubbled with excitement inside at the news she had for Victor. There was no need for her to stay in Helsinki for the attack. With Kahin gone, Bashir had pushed the Helsinki cell to get back on schedule. They'd collected a cache of handguns and even produced four improvised explosives made from kitchen appliances. After reviewing the Helsinki plan with Bashir this morning, Chantal was convinced they were fully capable of pulling off the demonstration without her guidance. With any luck, she could be on a plane to meet Victor by tomorrow morning.

She took another sip of hot chocolate and licked the thick whipped cream from her lip. It had been nearly two months since her last rendezvous with Victor and her need for him now was like an ache deep in her belly. Chantal closed her eyes, imagining their next meeting, the way his hungry eyes would roam over her body, the way his touch made her quiver inside . . .

"Pardon? May I take your cup?" The busboy's heavily accented English jarred her back to reality. Chantal realized she was trembling.

"Yes, yes," she said, mentally cursing herself for allowing her mind to wander like that. Then her eyes fell to the clock on the laptop screen and she almost squealed. It was time.

Working in deliberate slowness, Chantal logged into an anonymous email account, collected the web link in the spam folder, and pasted it into her browser. She wasn't exactly sure what happened behind the scenes, but Victor had told her this action took her to someplace on the web where their activities could not be tracked. The chat screen opened to a blinking cursor as she waited for Victor to initiate contact.

It came a few seconds later, an innocuous line about a soccer game. Chantal typed in the required response to establish her identity, then they were free to talk.

I miss you, my love, Victor typed.

Not as much as I long for you, she replied. *But I have good*

news. The group here has made wonderful progress. I am no longer needed to lead the project! When can I meet you?

The cursor pulsed for a long time, so long that Chantal wondered if the connection had been broken.

I would like nothing more, my love, but you need to stay. Helsinki needs to be perfect. Only you can do that for me.

Chantal's face grew hot. This is not how it was supposed to be! He was supposed to tell her to fly to him right away.

I understand, she typed. *What are your orders?*

It took a long minute before the detailed instructions scrolled down the screen. She read them carefully, committing the details to memory. There would be no hard copy, only what she carried in her brain. Not for the last time, she wondered how Victor had so much information about the security procedures at all of the demonstration locations in London, Helsinki, Berlin, and Minneapolis. Private security locations, police response times, lockdown procedures—Victor had it all. She acknowledged the message after committing the details to memory.

The screen cleared again and Victor typed: *Remember, we need as much news coverage as possible in all locations. Social media needs to be saturated with all four demonstrations. The West will finally see that Muslim minorities will be heard! This is a great day for all of us.*

Chantal's fingers moved sluggishly over the keyboard, unable to reconcile the idea that her lover had the chance to shield her from harm and he did not take it. They'd planned for the demonstrations to be peaceful, but there was a chance she could be arrested or even hurt. Her secret worry resurfaced. Victor was using her; he didn't love her after all. She was nothing but a pawn to him—

And now, the most important part, Victor typed.

??

Your extraction, my darling. I need you to come to me safe and sound as soon as the mission is over.

Chantal's heart did a stutter-step. He did care after all.

Once the demonstration begins, go to the northeast corner of the parking garage in the Kamppi shopping center. This man will meet you.

A picture flashed up on the screen. A white man with blond hair and a bland face. A Finn? Of course a Finn, she was in Finland.

Follow his instructions. He will get you to safety . . . we will be together soon.

Until then, my love, she typed.

Chantal signed off, her mind a whirlwind of emotions. Her head told her that Victor was only being reasonable. They had planned these events together for months, and despite her recent progress, Helsinki was the weakest location. It was only right that she make sure their demonstration come off as intended.

But her heart . . . her heart said something else. She shook off the feeling. Only a few days now and then she'd be free. With Victor. Chantal pulled a mobile phone from her purse and thumbed through the contacts until she found the number of the burner phone she'd left with Ayana. She found herself smiling at the thought of her Minneapolis protégé. Unlike their concerns about Helsinki, there was nothing Victor could say about the all-female cell in Minneapolis.

Ayana. That girl was the future of Muslim women. Smart, passionate, Western-educated—she would make the world stand up and take notice.

I need to speak with you, Chantal typed into a text. Her finger hovered over the send key.

At the same time, Ayana was so young; she had so much

promise, so much to live for. The possibility of jail time as a result of these demonstrations was almost a certainty.

Chantal pressed the send button.

We all must make sacrifices, she thought.

CHAPTER 43

Minneapolis, Minnesota
02 July 2017 — 0600 local

In the darkness of her bedroom, Aya stared at the brightly lit mobile phone screen.

I need to speak with you.

The text was unsigned but it made Aya's heart pound all the same. Since her last meeting with Imaan in February, she had kept the mobile phone charged, carrying it with her wherever she went, all for this moment when Imaan called her to action.

Aya listened for sounds of her family. It was Sunday and her mother was long gone to the coffee shop. She heard nothing from Zacharia's room, either. The long, strangled draw of her father's breathing made its way through two closed doors. She'd walk down to the river, Aya decided, and take Imaan's call there.

One hour, she texted back.

Aya lifted the shade in her bedroom a few inches and dressed by the dim light, braiding her long hair loosely before slipping on her *hijab*. Her robes would be hot in the humid Minnesota summer air, but she was used to it.

Outside, it was the kind of day when every tree, every building, every bird seemed etched against the deep blue of the cloudless sky. A day of possibilities, promises of things to come. She was so excited about talking to Imaan that she even skipped a little as she walked.

Since the Fourth of July fell on a Tuesday this year, Aya knew many people were taking the whole week off. Minnesotans did love their summer holidays. Runners passed her as she neared the banks of the Mississippi. A few threw questioning looks at her headscarf and robes, but her mood today was such that even those ignorant looks couldn't disturb her mood.

She took a seat on an empty bench overlooking the expanse of slow-moving water. Aya smiled to herself. Ever since she'd met Imaan, her life had changed for the better. Her self-confidence, her ability to lead her sisters—all of it flowed from her relationship with the singer. Sometimes she would lie in her bed at night and imagine she was singing on stage with Imaan. The crowd would sway and chant the lyrics to her songs and Imaan would embrace her like a daughter, or maybe a sister, or maybe even more.

The phone buzzed in her hand. Aya jumped.

"Hello?"

"It is so good to hear your voice again, Ayana." The singer's voice dripped like honey in Aya's ear. She put her hand to her mouth to stifle a whimper. Imaan expected her to be strong and confident. Girlish antics would not do.

"Imaan, I have so much to tell you—"

"And I you, my little flower, but our time grows short already. Are you ready?"

Aya's heart skipped a beat. "We are ready, Imaan. We've done everything you asked. The seeds you planted have grown into flowers." Imaan had insisted they use coded language. "Flowers" meant that they had procured guns.

Stealing guns from the St. Paul Pistol Boys had been remarkably easy. Stupid men. They were completely blind to the idea that a group of girls could have stolen from them. Madino and Caaliyah had dated gang members the year before and oh how their boyfriends loved to brag about their guns.

After their high school graduation ceremony, Aya arranged a weekend retreat for the Muslim-American Women's Studies Club at a Boy Scout camp up near Hinckley, Minnesota. Imam Nabil was more than happy to let her borrow the van from the mosque. There in the stillness of the north woods, each girl had a chance to fire a weapon. Madino had learned quite a bit about guns during her time with the gang and she proved to be a very able instructor.

Aya could still recall the first time she'd fired her 9mm Beretta. The sound made her ears ring, the metal grip kicked in her hands, and she closed her eyes at the last minute so she missed the target, but the weapon gave her a feeling of power unlike anything she'd ever known. Even now, she carried it with her in her purse.

"I'm so happy," the singer replied, jerking Aya back to reality. "Are the blooms beautiful?" *Blooms* meant bombs.

"The blooms will be out soon."

The homemade bombs were also Madino's doing. On Saturday, she and Caaliyah drove into Wisconsin to buy fireworks. Using the propellant gleaned from breaking the rockets apart, the two girls managed to cobble together three homemade bombs, each the size of a small loaf of bread. Aya had been very clear with Madino that the bombs were there to scare people, not hurt anyone. Madino just grinned at her.

"You are such an ingenious girl," Imaan said, the tone of her voice making her sound very pleased. Aya blushed. The heat of the sun felt like Imaan's love raining down on her from heaven.

Imaan's tone turned insistent. "Have you studied the location?"

"Oh yes, our jobs give us easy access and I've laid out a way to make sure our demonstration will be a success. All I need is the message and the time."

"I will send the message by email, my dear," Imaan said.

"And when?" she asked.

"July Fourth. Your American Independence Day will have a new meaning after this year. Start the protest at noon, Minneapolis time."

Aya laughed out loud, causing a runner, all churning legs and scowling face, to look her way when he passed by. The day was almost here, the day when she would prove her worth to her idol.

"Are you okay, my child?"

"I'm just so happy, Imaan, to be doing my part. Like you said, we must claim our rights to be part of the West. We were born into these societies. We are people, too."

"You are a gem, Ayana."

"Imaan, I am yours."

After she ended the call with Imaan, Aya cradled the phone in her lap. Her senses felt stretched in all directions, alive, in touch with everything around her. Very soon, she would complete her mission, show her worth to the most important woman in the world. Everything was coming together. Finally.

Her fingers probed her forearm, searching for that patch of rough skin. On the weekend they'd borrowed the van, the Muslim-American Women's Studies Club had done more than just drive north to buy fireworks and shoot guns. They also did something that would bond them together forever—no matter what happened.

Glancing around to make sure she was still alone, Aya pulled back the sleeve of her shirt. With her finger, she traced the outline of the flame tattooed on her forearm.

"I am yours, Imaan," she whispered. "I am a Soldier of God."

CHAPTER 44

Reza Sanjabi's foot tapped a rapid tattoo on the floor as he waited in front of his videoconference terminal for the expected call. Although Donald was the one who had asked for this call to update him on the hunt for Roshed, Reza had a plane to catch. He frowned at his watch. It was nearly eleven PM on a Sunday night in the US. What could be so important?

The telephone icon blinked, indicating a secure incoming call. He answered and waited for the screen to clear. Don's face, when it appeared, looked haggard and his friend had clearly put on weight. A Diet Coke can showed in the lower right of the screen.

Reza offered a broad smile for the camera. His friend must suspect nothing. "Donald, good evening."

"Reza, I decided to have a call during your working hours for a change."

He laughed for Don's sake. "You look very tired, my friend. Are you well?"

Don grimaced. "Between you and me, I feel like shit, but evil never sleeps, am I right?"

"It appears there may be less evil in Somalia, thanks to your special operations forces, Donald. President Rouhani sends his belated regards to your President for striking a blow against Daesh in such a public fashion."

Don's grimace grew deeper. "Well, you can tell him thank you, but the public part was not intentional. Sometimes a free press can be a burden."

"So the young al-Shabab fighter really was an American?"

"Yeah, he really was an American. Tough to believe, but true."

"To be young again, eh, Donald?"

Reza thought of his own youthful exploits, his enlistment in the Iranian army at the tender age of seventeen, the fierce battles of the Iran–Iraq War, and coming to the attention of a rising political star named Hassan Rouhani. Sometimes the rashness of youth worked out for the best.

He realized Donald was speaking. "Pardon?"

"I'm sorry about changing the time of our call this month. With the Independence Day holiday here in the US, my travel schedule is a mess. Still, I wanted to make sure we caught each other up on the hunt for Roshed."

Reza's smile froze in place. "Has there been a development?"

"Unfortunately not, I'm afraid." Don fiddled with the Diet Coke can as he offered up a brief summary of his outreach to the world intelligence agencies. The net result of the brief was nothing new.

"Our best guess," Don concluded, "is that he is somewhere in East Africa, working on a plan to disrupt the allied bases in

Djibouti, but we've scoured every known source and come up empty-handed."

"I agree, Roshed is a tricky bastard—but I believe you are looking in the wrong place, Donald."

Don squinted at the camera. "You have new information, don't you, Reza?"

Reza inclined his head. "Perhaps. Your lead from French intelligence about the sighting in West Africa, I checked into it. Our man in Ghana reported a similar sighting—no photo, but the description was good enough that I had him fly to Tehran for a consultation. His source was able to pick out a modified photo of Roshed from a lineup."

"That's fantastic! When? Where exactly?"

Reza spoke cautiously. This was the tricky part, lying to Donald. A man who had risked his own career for Reza's sake. Not an outright lie, Reza told himself, more of a blurring of the truth.

"Accra, Ghana." That part was true. "Some weeks ago. The trail is cold by now." That was the falsity. In fact, his man had just reported another sighting a few days ago, and this one was backed up by photographic evidence.

Donald's face fell. "Well, at least we know where he was. Any idea what he was doing there? Why Ghana?"

Why indeed? Did it matter? The only thing that really mattered to Reza was a bullet in Rafiq Roshed's head.

"No idea, Donald. Perhaps in transit to East Africa to coordinate an attack in Djibouti?"

"Maybe." Don pursed his lips. "Well, my congratulations to your asset in Ghana, that's really fine work. If he surfaces again, let's nail the bastard."

"I agree, Donald, let's nail the bastard. Good night."

He stared at the dark screen for a long time. He owed his life to Donald Riley and he'd just lied to him. Reza's eye strayed to the photo on the corner of his desk, to the smiling face of a young Hassan Rouhani. Sometimes deception was necessary, even among friends. Perhaps he should brief Rouhani before he left Tehran . . .

No, these kinds of decisions were best kept at arm's length. By rights, taking out Roshed belonged to Donald and the Americans as much—maybe more—than the Islamic Republic of Iran. After all, the man had tried to detonate a nuclear bomb on US soil. But allowing Donald in at this point would raise too many complications.

If the Americans got to Roshed first, they would try to capture him, take him alive, put him on trial. The man knew too much, held too many secrets that were better off in an unmarked grave.

Would the Americans risk a public trial? Probably not. But there was always that famed American free press. What if they found out about the capture, dug into Roshed's background, and began to connect the dots? The trail would lead back to Iran, and more importantly to President Rouhani. Under the glare of world opinion, how would Iran fare?

No, the risk was too great. Rafiq Roshed needed to be put down like a rabid dog—with a bullet to the brain. His eyes locked on the photo of himself and Rouhani from so many years ago. This was not a job to be delegated.

"Sir?" His secretary appeared in the doorway. "Your limo is waiting downstairs and I've confirmed your flight to Libreville. Your bags are in the car."

CHAPTER 45

Helsinki, Finland
04 July 2017 – 1400 local

Chantal shut down the chat room software and let the automatic shredder program remove all traces of her conversation with her contact in London.

She felt a rise of pride in what she had accomplished. For so long, she sang in front of crowds of people about feelings of isolation and disaffection, of being the outsider in society. Her music connected with those audiences, but those words had no effect on the larger society, the society that made the rules under which they all had to live.

Victor changed all that for her. He showed her that proud Muslims who'd grown up in Western countries did not need to hide in the shadows, afraid of what their neighbors thought of them. They needed to stand up and be counted, make the world take notice of them as people. After today, the world would be on notice that Muslims in the West were here to claim their rights as citizens of the West.

She still worried about someone getting hurt in the demonstrations. There would be violence—of that she was sure—but only enough so that they were taken seriously. Victor had made her see that, too. Their protests needed time to get their message out, to start a worldwide revolution on social media and across the news media. Time enough to make ordinary people stop and think about the way Muslims were treated in their society. So they would threaten violence, not actually use it.

As Victor had told her so many times, this was about social justice, about taking back what was already theirs. "Without the threat of force," he'd said, "they will not listen to you. They will not take you seriously. To make an omelet, you need to break some eggs."

So there were guns, and there were explosives—not lethal, but bombs nonetheless—and some people might be hurt, or even killed. But that was the price of social change; Chantal believed that now. Victor had shown her the way.

Victor . . . how she longed to be with him now. Chantal found that when she was separated from her lover for too long, what he'd taught her started to unravel in her mind. He was like a drug that she needed to keep taking to stay on the true course.

And what a drug it was! She closed her eyes for a moment and let a shiver of anticipation course through her body at the thought of their next meeting. No more separation after this. He would be hers, and she his, every day for the rest of their lives.

She was lucky, she knew that, to find the love of her life on the first try. How many women in this world could say that? It was as if Allah himself had read her mind and put every single feature she needed into that man. When she gave thanks to Allah, that's what she thanked him for—Victor, the love of her life.

JIHADI APPRENTICE

The clatter of a busboy clearing the next table brought her back to reality. By this time tomorrow, she would be on her way back to her lover, but for now there was business to complete. Chantal called up the email on her computer for one final read through.

> *Our actions today declare our rights as citizens of this country. We were born here, we live here, we work here, we pray here, but we are not part of your society. You denigrate our religion, you spy on our men, you shame our women—and all for what? It is time for the West to recognize that Muslims are people, and deserving of their rights as human beings in your society. #muslimsmatter*

She had written and rewritten this statement that would be read by their hostages and blasted all over social media. It seemed odd to her that Victor, who had been deeply involved in all aspects of the campaign, had approved the wording of the message the first time. At the same time, it had filled her with a glow of pride that she was so in tune with her lover that she could capture his message on the very first draft.

She addressed the email to her main contacts in Minneapolis, London, and Berlin. They would be in charge of making sure the message was deployed at their demonstration.

Chantal said a silent prayer as her finger hovered over the enter button on the keyboard. This was the final piece of the puzzle, the last contact she would have with any of these people. She thought of young Ayana in Minneapolis and hoped the girl would come through this ordeal safely.

She touched the key; the message disappeared from her screen.

The final act was to destroy her computer. Victor had given

her a program to erase all of the information from her hard drive, then she was supposed to drop it into a river to ensure any data was unrecoverable.

Chantal toyed with the idea of calling Victor one last time. He had insisted on radio silence in these last days, but now that she was part of the Helsinki demonstration, surely she deserved one last conversation with her lover before she went into harm's way. Victor had arranged for her to get away safely before the police arrived, but there was always a chance things could go wrong . . .

She called up Skype on her computer. This would be just a quick chat between lovers, nothing more. She scrolled through her contacts. Victor's name was gone. She entered his Skype handle into the search bar and nothing came back.

Chantal fished her mobile phone out of her bag and dialed Victor's latest number—he changed his mobile every few days, but always gave her the number. The number had been disconnected.

There was one other way. Victor had given her an emergency number where he could always be reached, but that was for true emergencies. Life-or-death decisions. He'd stressed that again and again when he made her memorize it.

Chantal started the shredder program on her computer and slipped her mobile back into her bag.

Tomorrow, then, my love. I'll be with you tomorrow.

CHAPTER 46

Shaafici Mosque, Minneapolis, Minnesota
04 July 2017 — 0700 local

The mosque was mostly empty after morning prayers on this holiday. Aya had barely slept last night and was up with the first light of the Minnesota summer dawn. She moved as if in a dream. Every action of her day, from selecting her outfit to the way the early morning sunlight made a pattern on her bedspread, seemed preordained, part of a larger pattern.

Independence Day. A fitting symbol for what she and her sisters were about to do. Their actions, their voices would make the lives of Muslim women living in Western countries so much better. Their protest would wake up the world from its consumer-induced slumber. People would see with new vision how she, a Muslim woman, had been treated all her life, and change their ways. They were going to make a difference.

She slipped earbuds into her ears as she prepared to leave the mosque. The sound of Imaan's voice filled her head. She'd listened to this album hundreds of times, but still the first few words of *Rise Up!* made her shiver.

Imaan had picked her. Out of all the girls in the world, Imaan had picked her! Even now, months later, the idea that she'd been chosen to embark on this wonderful journey with her idol still made her giddy with joy.

Behind the music, she heard the sounds of the few other worshippers preparing to leave, but ignored them, preferring her own thoughts to any idle conversation. A hand pressed her shoulder and she jumped. Imam Nabil smiled down at her.

"I didn't mean to startle you, Ayana. I called your name, but I think your music was a bit loud."

Aya stripped out the earbuds, aware of the loud music spilling out into the nearly empty foyer. She lowered her head. "I'm sorry, imam. I was daydreaming."

"A fine summer day for dreaming, I agree." He folded his hands. "May I speak with you for a moment, Ayana? Privately. A cup of tea, perhaps?"

The handgun in Aya's bag suddenly seemed heavier than it had only a moment ago. "I—I need to get to work . . ."

The imam checked his watch. "It's still early. Surely you have time for a cup of tea. I need your assistance with a matter of some importance."

Aya did her best not to let her eyes slide to the door. "Well, okay. But I only have a few minutes, imam."

"Wonderful." The older man led her back through the empty mosque to his office. Between prayer sessions, they turned off the air conditioning in the main building, and the still humidity of the Minnesota summer seemed to close around her.

The imam unlocked the door to his office and stepped aside to allow her to enter. She sat down quickly, tucking her bag under the chair and wrapping the strap around the chair leg so it stayed upright. Imam Nabil busied himself with the tea-making.

She'd always liked this office, the way the imam had decorated it. The rest of the mosque was ugly, just a converted warehouse, but this room . . . this room, the imam had made his own. Aya scanned the titles of the books and dug her feet into the thick carpet. The scent of cardamom filled the space and her stomach growled. The imam placed a cup of tea in front of her and offered her the sugar bowl.

Aya shook head. "No, thank you."

"You used to take two lumps, Ayana—sometimes three, if I wasn't looking."

She eyed the sugar bowl. "I've changed, imam."

"So you have, young lady." Nabil settled into his chair, peering at her over the top of his eyeglasses. "Do you keep in touch with Hodan?"

Aya's finger clenched the teacup handle and the amber liquid trembled. "She is my friend. I know her . . . well."

"Her mother came to see me this week. She's worried about her daughter."

Aya forced herself to take a sip of tea. It did need sugar. "How so? I haven't noticed anything wrong."

Imam Nabil's eyes seemed to cut through her. "Her mother says she's become very devout, moody, and not sleeping well. I asked Zacharia if he—"

"You talked to my brother?" The teacup clanked down and a little bit slopped into the saucer.

"Her mother told me she had a crush on him. I thought maybe he would have some insight into Hodan's behavior. Your brother is worried about you, you know. For the same reasons."

Aya stayed very still. "He said that?"

"In so many words, yes. Ayana, I know being a Muslim teenager in America has challenges. If you need to talk with someone—"

"Challenges? That's what you call my life? We live in a country where we are hated for our religion, where politicians say we are the enemy. I am a citizen, I was born here, so why do I have to listen to men call me names? Why do they tell me to 'go home' when this *is* my home?" She was on her feet now, pointing her finger at the imam who had pushed himself back in his chair. "You apologize for them. You preach forgiveness for their ignorance. But that way has yielded nothing. It is time we change the conversation, time we stand up for our rights as citizens and demand that we be treated with respect." Her whole body was shaking, her face burned with anger. She balled up her hands into fists and still she wanted to scream.

"I need to go." Aya spun on her heel and threw open the door. She ran across the empty prayer room, the air even warmer now. The hairline of her headscarf was damp with sweat. She had just reached the front door when she realized she'd left her purse in the imam's office.

Oh, no.

Aya tore back through the prayer hall, skidding into the open door of Imam Nabil's office.

The old man crouched next to the chair where she'd been sitting. The strap of her bag that she'd carefully wrapped around the chair leg was unwound and her bag had tipped over, spilling the contents onto the floor.

The imam turned the gun over in his hand. He looked up at her, his eyes wide and white behind his glasses. "Ayana, what is the meaning of this?"

She launched at him, her fingernails seeking his face, her own lips curled into a rigid mask of rage. And she was screaming. "It's mine!"

The force of her assault knocked the imam off-balance and he sprawled onto the floor. Aya raked his face, then her fingers scrabbled for the gun. He held on, pressing the weapon against his body.

Aya touched metal and wormed her fingers under his. She felt the barrel, the rough checkering of the hand grip, the curve of the trigger guard, and then her finger found the trigger.

The sound of the gunshot, even muffled by the imam's body, was deafening in the small space. Her ears rang. The older man's hands relaxed and she snatched the weapon away. His white shirt was a pool of red, dark red, almost black, and a heavy smell filled the air.

Aya raked her belongings back into her bag and stood. She wasn't shaking now. All was calm, her thoughts felt clearer than they ever had in her life.

"Ayana, please," he wheezed. The imam held out his hand.

Aya closed the door to his office. She checked her watch. If she hurried she could still catch the eight-thirty light-rail to the Mall of America.

CHAPTER 47

Brendan flipped the bacon with a fork. After making breakfast nearly every morning for the last six weeks, he'd gotten pretty good at making bacon just the way Liz liked it: crispy, but not burned. Experience had taught him there were only a few seconds between the two.

The last few months at home had gone fast, but this place still felt like Liz's apartment. His previous experience with a live-in girlfriend had been more about the girlfriend and less about the living. The short-lived experiment had left him with an empty bank account and a ruined credit rating. He chalked Amy up as a bitter life lesson.

This time was different. Liz was the girl he was going to marry; he could not afford to screw this up. More than anything, he wanted this to work. Hence the breakfast every morning. He figured the best way to stay in Liz's life was to be useful.

Except it didn't seem to be working. Their first few weeks had been a sex fest, all giggles and lovey-dovey stuff. Then the reality of making a life together seemed to intrude. And then there was her job. She was busier than he'd thought possible, receiving calls at every hour of the day or night, always on the run. When he tried to talk to her about it, she told him about the sign that hung in the FBI Field Office: *The bad guys only need to be successful once. We need to be successful every single day.*

During the first weeks of his return, they'd talked about the wedding and even started to discuss a venue, but that had petered out under the strain of her job. In the back of his mind was the devastating thought that maybe she loved her job more than she loved him.

Pull your head out of your ass, McHugh. Nobody loves a loser.

He'd fix that today. They'd spend the Fourth of July holiday together doing whatever she wanted to do and then cap off the day by watching fireworks from the balcony.

He turned his attention back to breakfast. Coffee: check. Eggs: check. Bacon: check. The toaster popped up. "Liz, do you want jam on your toast?"

No answer. He heard the toilet flush and water running in the sink.

"Lizzie?" he said louder. "Jam on your toast?"

Liz emerged from the bedroom looking flushed. She was dressed in jeans and a polo shirt. "No need to yell," she snapped.

"Sorry. I made you breakfast."

"Oh, thanks." Liz's phone rang and she walked into the living room to take the call while Brendan rummaged in the refrigerator for the jam.

He looked up when he heard the sound of their apartment door closing. Liz's coffee was gone and so was she.

Brendan gritted his teeth. He was really trying here, but right now it felt like a one-way street.

♨

Minneapolis, Minnesota
04 July 2017 — 0900 local

Liz pulled into the parking lot of the CVS down the street and launched out of the car, just as the store was opening. The kid at the counter looked up as she bulled her way through the door and rushed past him.

"Can I help you?" he called after her. Liz ignored him.

She turned into the women's aisle, passing quickly by the tampons and sanitary napkins, suddenly slowing in front of a display of pregnancy tests. She took a shaky breath and pulled one off the shelf that showed a picture of a young woman smiling with unrestrained joy.

Three minutes and forty-five seconds later, it was official: she was pregnant.

Liz slumped over the sink in the CVS bathroom, unsure how to feel. Excited? Concerned? Instead of any of those, she just felt empty. Then she remembered Brendan, how he'd made her breakfast and she just ran out the door without even saying goodbye. How would he take the news?

She slipped her phone out of her purse and started to dial his number when another call came in from Agent Kamen.

"Soroush," she said into the phone.

"Liz, we've got some action on Zacharia Ismail. He was in

the mosque then left in a serious hurry. It looks like something's going on."

"Where's he headed?"

"Not sure. Definitely not back home."

"You stay on Zacharia. Have Adams meet me at the mosque in fifteen minutes."

"Okay, boss."

Her stomach twisted as she straightened up. Since she'd already thrown up this morning, there was nothing in there except a few sips of coffee. She paid for the opened pregnancy test kit while avoiding the eyes of the kid behind the checkout counter.

She took a deep breath to still her nausea as she turned out of the parking lot into traffic. She'd almost pulled the surveillance team off Zacharia last Friday. Trask had questioned whether it was worth paying two teams of agents over the holiday to work a suspect that so far had yielded nothing.

Her phone rang again. Adams this time.

"I'm five minutes out," she said. "What's up?"

"There's a Minneapolis PD cruiser and an ambulance outside the mosque. They're responding to a 911 call."

She stepped on the gas. "Where did the call originate from?"

"Inside the mosque."

She skidded her car to a stop behind the police cruiser and raced up the steps. The cop outside the door raised his hand, but dropped it when she flashed her FBI badge. Liz didn't bother to take off her shoes, but ran through the prayer room to Nabby's office.

Two paramedics were just lifting a gurney up to waist-height as she came around the corner. One of them held up an IV bag as they pushed Nabby's body past. Her friend's face was the color of wax and she could see his shirt was stained deep red beneath the compresses the paramedics had put on his chest. The Minneapolis cop next to the door shook his head slowly.

"Dude's in rough shape," he said.

She showed her badge to him. "Can I go in? I won't touch anything. I—I know him; he's a friend."

The cop shrugged and stepped aside.

The rug in front of Nabby's desk was stained with blood and his glasses lay on the ground. Liz resisted the urge to pick them up.

Nabby, who did this to you?

She swallowed hard. The heavy smell of blood in the room tickled her heightened sense of nausea.

"From the way the body was lying, it looks like there was a struggle for a weapon and he got the short end of the stick," the cop said from the doorway. "One shot in the abdomen, angled up into the chest. Poor bastard never stood a chance."

"Did you find a weapon?"

"Nope. It's a wonder he was still alive after losing all that blood. The 911 call came from that desk phone, by the way. I'm thinking there was a fight over a gun—accidental shooting, you know—then the shooter felt bad and called it in."

Liz nodded. She stepped back into the hall, feeling as if she might heave any moment now. "We've got a suspect for you," she said. "Zacharia Ismail. I've got a team on him now. We'll pick him up—"

Her phone buzzed. Liz looked at it and cursed.

We lost him, the text read.

Minneapolis, Minnesota
04 July 2017 — 0910 local

Aya watched the city of Minneapolis slip by outside her window. The light-rail car was packed with people heading to the Mall of America for the concert, but she'd managed to secure a spot by the window. The seat next to her stayed empty for the entire ride. Her ghostly reflection in the glass appeared calm, as if she was looking at herself from afar.

She'd killed a man—a holy man, no less. She should be raging and crying and begging forgiveness from Allah . . . but all was calm in her heart. Imaan had spoken the truth: in a battle for her rights as a human being, there would be casualties. Imam Nabil was only the first.

"You are Soldiers of God," she'd said. "You must be willing to risk everything for your cause."

Everything felt and looked sharper now, as if the struggle with the imam had heightened her senses. Aya looked around at the occupants of the car. Couples in shorts and T-shirts leaning together, people hunched over their phones, a group of twenty-somethings dressed in superhero costumes for a sci-fi convention, and a gaggle of teenage girls huddled together. Their eyes raked over Aya's *hijab* and dark robes.

Aya didn't blush or feel self-conscious about her dress. She had a sudden urge to stand up and shout at them. *Do you know what I've done today? I killed a man.*

Instead, she let their gazes pass through her. *I am a Soldier of God. I feel no pain. Shame cannot touch me. You will see me as I am.*

Her phone buzzed, a text from Madino.

Where ru?

Aya hid a smile. Always the impatient one. The light-rail was just pulling into the Minneapolis–St. Paul airport station.

B rt there. 5 mins.

She met the rest of the girls in the parking lot next to the MOA light-rail station. Caaliyah had driven her parents' minivan down to the mall. The ancient air conditioner was barely keeping up with the nervous energy of six young women. Aya squeezed into the car and pulled the door shut behind her. The eyes that met hers were frightened and the air rank with sweat. She peeled back her sleeve, showing the tattoo of the flame on her forearm. Words came to her lips unbidden:

"We are strong Muslim women."

They stared at her.

"Say it with me!" she said sharply. "We are strong Muslim women."

"We are strong Muslim women," they whispered back.

"Louder!"

"We are strong Muslim women." It was louder this time. Aya noted a few self-conscious smiles, but less fear in their eyes.

"We are citizens of the United States."

The response came back more forcefully. More confident.

"We are soldiers of God. We demand our rights."

They shouted back at her so loudly that her ears rang. Aya looked at each girl. Madino and Caaliyah twisted around in the front seats, their eyes gleaming with excitement—and something darker. Yasmin and Leylo looked scared but determined, fake smiles on their faces. Aya knew she could count on them. And Hodan, delicate Hodan, who still had a crush on Aya's brother after all these years. Hodan looked on the verge of tears. Aya gripped her friend's hand.

"Our goal today is to be heard," she said finally. "Too long, the Christian America has demonized and ignored us. To them, we're either evil or not relevant. That ends today." The girls were nodding now.

"Today, our voices will be heard. We will make them listen to us." Aya pulled the handgun from her bag. She could still smell the acrid scent from the recent firing. "These are tools. Tools to make them take us seriously. When the police show up—and they will—we will surrender peacefully. By that time, we will have flooded social media with our message. You all have the message?"

The girls nodded. A few held up slips of paper where they had copied down the words from Imaan's email.

"Good," Aya said. "We go at noon."

CHAPTER 48

For Chantal Deveraux, prayer had always been a ritual, something she was supposed to do. Comforting words and familiar
actions that offered a sense of stillness, but lacking in meaning.
She said the words and knelt when she was supposed to, but
Chantal was always the same person before and after she said
her prayers.

This afternoon was different. This afternoon, maybe for the
first time in her life, Chantal Deveraux prayed.

And not the timeworn phrases of the Qu'ran, but a real conversation between her and her Maker.

Allah, deliver me safely from this trial . . .

She believed in their cause of rights for Muslims in the Western
countries, but now that she was about to enter the field of battle,
the strategy sounded hollow to her. Victor called it "pseudo-vio-
lence." Using guns to get people's attention, a show of force to

keep their focus on the cause. No one was supposed to get hurt; the guns were only there as a way to ensure they had people's attention.

She lifted the 9mm Beretta from her purse, a gift from Victor. The black steel gleamed in the late afternoon sunlight. It really was a deadly beautiful thing. She weighed it in her hand, aiming down the gunsights using two hands like Victor had taught her. He had insisted she learn to use it and even she had to admit, the feeling of shooting a weapon accurately was empowering, even intoxicating. Victor had caught her practicing quick-draw maneuvers in front of the mirror and laughed at her.

Chantal put the weapon back in her purse. The Finnish demonstration would come off without a hitch, she felt sure of it, but Victor still insisted she stay. *Once the team has a sufficient number of people corralled in the stores, you can leave,* he told her. She wanted to argue with him, but he turned cold when she resisted him. Chantal ended up agreeing to stay.

Her stomach fluttered at the thought of setting off an explosive or using her gun to threaten people. Yes, she was only herding them into a store so they could make statements on social media, but they wouldn't know that. They would be afraid, deathly afraid.

I should leave now. Good luck, but there's been a change in plans. Proceed without me. She could be back on Victor's yacht by tomorrow afternoon if she left now. She rubbed her shaking, sweaty hands down her thighs. It would be so easy.

No. If for any reason the Helsinki demonstration failed, she would be to blame.

Chantal knelt for one last prayer, letting the words flow through her, still her fears, settle the hammering of her heart.

Allah, deliver me safely from this trial . . .

Resolved now, she got to her feet and picked up her bag off

the bed. A change of underwear, a few cosmetics, cash, and her handgun—it was all she had left in Helsinki. Everything else had been shipped out of the country with her band yesterday to a gig in Tunisia—a performance she would never do. Even her passport and credit cards were gone. The contact she was to meet in the parking garage of the Kamppi Mall would have a new identity, credit cards, everything she'd need to start her new life with Victor.

Chantal took a cloth and wiped down all the surfaces she might have touched in the room since it was last cleaned.

Then she shouldered her small bag and stepped into the beautiful Helsinki evening.

Minneapolis, Minnesota
04 July 2017 — 1100 local

The ambulance with Nabby was gone by the time Liz got back outside. She slid behind the wheel of her car and put her phone on speaker to call the office, trying to ignore the sourness in her stomach.

"Listen up, people," she said, "this is a Minneapolis PD case, but we need to help them find Zacharia Ismail. Pull footage from every camera anywhere near Cedar Riverside and figure out where the hell he disappeared to." Liz took a breath. To her own ears, her voice sounded like a hysterical rookie. *Pull yourself together, Liz.*

"Solange, can you play the 911 call for me?" she said to the technician on the phone.

"Standby, Agent Soroush."

A woman's voice came from the car speakers: "911, what's your emergency?"

"I need an ambulance at the Shaafici Mosque. The imam has been shot. I put a bandage on the wound. Please hurry!" Liz recognized Zacharia's voice from the other surveillance tapes. He sounded panicky, but concerned for the imam. Maybe the shooting was an accident?

"Sir, I am dispatching police and paramedics to your location. Please stay on the line."

No answer.

"Sir, are you there?"

Nothing.

"So he shoots the imam, but then calls the paramedics and runs away?" Liz said. "The scene indicated a struggle, so maybe it was an accident?"

"Found him!" the technician on the phone called out. "I have him ducking through a fence and hailing a cab on South Sixth Street . . . and I can get a cab number from the video. Let me call it in and get a destination. Standby."

Liz put her car into gear. Law enforcement had a special number they could call to get dispatch information on taxis as quickly as possible. "Okay, good work. I'm headed back to the office—"

"The cab let him out at Karmel Mall," the technician interrupted.

Liz paused at a stop sign before pulling into traffic. "Pass that tip on to Minneapolis PD. He's probably changed cars, but keep them in the loop anyway. I'll see you in fifteen."

Karmel Mall—why would Zacharia go there? Liz burped, leaving a burning sour taste in the back of her throat. She really should try to eat something; maybe that would settle her stomach.

She pulled into a McDonald's drive-thru and ordered a breakfast sandwich, still thinking about Zacharia. Why would he go to Karmel? Then it hit her—his mother. She had a coffee shop in Karmel. Zacharia went to find his mother.

At the fast-food service window, Liz took one whiff of the much-anticipated sandwich and swallowed down a sudden surge of nausea. Tossing the bag onto the passenger seat, she pulled into traffic.

The smells of the Somali coffee shop had a soothing effect on her stomach. Based on her current experience, Liz was beginning to think that being pregnant was like being punched in the stomach over and over, just a dull ache that never went away. The shop was deserted except for a pair of older men at a corner table deeply involved in a game of checkers. Liz approached the older woman behind the counter. There was no mistaking her as Zacharia's mother; her son had the same open face and straight nose as this woman.

Liz slipped her ID out of her hip pocket. "Good morning, my name is—"

"I know who you are, Agent Soroush. What do you want?"

Liz scanned the shop again. Was it possible Zacharia was still here?

"I'm looking for your son."

"He's not here and I'm busy." The woman fussed behind the counter, avoiding Liz's eyes.

"Have you seen him this morning?"

Silence.

"Is that a yes, ma'am?"

The older woman wet her lips. "He was here about an hour ago. He didn't do anything wrong."

"Imam Nabil was shot this morning." The woman flinched, but stayed silent. "We'd like to talk to him about that."

"He didn't do it. You keep harassing him, but he's a good boy." Her eyes started to fill with tears and she wiped at them with a dishcloth.

"Imam Nabil is seriously injured, ma'am. Your son was the one who called 911."

"He didn't do it. He went to the imam's office and found him like that."

"Why did he come here?"

"I don't know. He was looking for his sister, but she's at work. At the Mall."

"Ma'am, I need you to tell me where your son is. This is serious." Liz studied the older woman's face. She was holding something back.

"I don't have anything else to say to you, Agent."

Liz stepped back into the steamy heat of the Minnesota summer morning. When she unlocked the car, the smell of the fast-food bag cooking on the passenger's seat made her gag. She tossed the bag into a nearby trashcan and turned the fan on the highest setting to clear out the smell. She thought about going back into the shop for a tea, but she could see Zacharia's mother watching her through the window.

Liz dialed the office for one of the tech specialists. "Hey, run a phone check on the Somaliland Coffee House at the Karmel Mall. Any outgoing calls in the last hour. I'll wait." The operator came back on the line after a minute to report that only one number had been dialed. Liz recognized it as the Ismail home number.

She slid behind the wheel and dialed her surveillance team. "Adams, check out the home address for Zacharia. I'm going to drive down to the Mall of America to talk to the sister."

"Roger that, boss."

Liz put the car in gear and pulled into traffic—with the windows down.

CHAPTER 49

Hodan fingered the handgun in the makeshift holster under her robes. The cold metal of the weapon felt clammy against her skin. She hated the thought of carrying a gun, but at the same time she couldn't stop touching it.

When she and all the girls entered the employee's entrance at the Mall of America, Aya led them. Her friend was unafraid as she walked past Adam, the security guard. As Aya scanned her ID card, she even joked with him about having to work on July Fourth. Adam smiled back at her. Aya made it look easy, just like another day at work.

Madino and Caaliyah, with the bombs hidden in their soft-sided lunch bags, had carried the explosives through the employee checkpoint. Those two seemed to be enjoying the excitement of what they were about to do, but Hodan was terrified. She refused to touch the bomb, making Madino place it in the bottom of her cleaning cart.

"Can we rely on you?" Madino asked her, the bigger girl's eyes narrowing to slits. "The timer's already set. All you need to do is put the cart next to the statue and walk away. That's it." She grabbed Hodan's arm. Madino's fingers pinched her flesh. "Can you do it?" Madino hissed.

Hodan nodded, afraid to do anything else. She wheeled the cart into the elevator and pressed the button for the first floor.

She could hear the thump of the bass and the screams of fans even before the elevator doors opened. The open rotunda was filled with teenagers, most of them a few years younger than her, bouncing and waving their hands in the air as they mouthed the lyrics. Up on the stage, an elfin singer barely older than her audience bobbed her head as she sang into a wraparound microphone. Hodan recognized the tune from the radio.

She navigated her cart around the edges of the crowd, angling toward the tall statue of SpongeBob SquarePants that stood at the entrance to the indoor amusement park. Her cart grazed the arm of a tall white girl who whirled on her. "Hey, watch where you're going!"

"I'm sorry." Hodan automatically ducked her head. The other girl huffed at her and turned back to the concert.

Hodan parked her cart in front of SpongeBob, suddenly angry with herself. Why had she apologized? She wasn't really sorry; the girl had backed up into her cart. She hadn't done anything wrong. This was exactly the kind of thing that Aya was talking about.

Jeremy, who worked as a plainclothes officer in the behavioral detection unit, waved to her from across the rotunda. The BDU officers were the first line of defense in mall security. If they saw someone acting suspicious, the BDU officers were supposed to approach them and strike up a conversation. If needed, they could detain the person or call for security. She waved back. Hodan and Jeremy often worked the same shifts and she was pretty sure he liked her.

She checked her phone. 1151. Nine minutes to go.

I m in place, she texted.

Her pulse hammered when she thought about what she was about to do. At noon exactly, the explosive in her cart now parked next to SpongeBob would go off, along with one outside the police station upstairs. The explosives were just the guts of fireworks in a duct-taped package with a timer on them. They weren't aiming to kill anyone, just scare them. The sounds would drive people into the stores that lined the hallway, where Mall protocol required the store owners to shut their security doors and shelter everyone in place.

Barnes and Noble and the aquarium were their targets. Leylo and Yasmin worked in the bookstore, Caaliyah and Madino in the aquarium. That's where they'd stage their demonstrations. Hodan was supposed to meet Aya downstairs in the mall control room.

Hodan moved away from the cart. She slipped her hand around the grip of the handgun, loosening it in the makeshift holster. When the moment came, she wanted to be ready. She slipped it out and held it against her belly, still under her robes. The gun was heavier than it looked and her hand was sweating.

"Sucks that we have to work today, huh, Hodan?" She whirled around to face Jeremy. His eyes were at exactly the same level as hers and they were blue, very blue.

"I, uh, uh," she stammered. Jeremy was very close to her and he'd raised his voice to be heard over the music. Hodan swallowed hard and tried to poke the muzzle of the handgun back into the holster.

She missed. The weapon slipped out of her sweaty grasp, clattering to the tile floor between her and Jeremy.

His gaze dropped to his feet. When he looked up, his very blue eyes were wide. "Hodan?" he whispered, a tinge of panic in his tone.

She needed to get away now. Aya was waiting for her. She needed to be on time. Aya was waiting.

Hodan turned, but Jeremy had her arm now. She twisted in his grasp.

"Hodan?" he said again.

Behind him, the bomb next to SpongeBob exploded.

Jeremy let go of her arm.

Kamppi Center Mall, Helsinki, Finland
04 July 2017 — 1955 local

They'd broken up into groups of two to enter the mall. Chantal had chosen Bashir as her partner. He was the one member of the group who might get trigger-happy and start shooting civilians. She'd told them again and again: Their mission was to make the Western governments listen by using the threat of violence. Violence itself was the last option.

Chantal peeked at the Rolex on her wrist. Five minutes to go. Her heart fluttered. It was almost over. All she needed to do was get this started then get out before the police arrived. Back to Victor.

She took Bashir's arm as they strolled into the large circular atrium. Even at this hour, the mall was crowded. These Finns loved their summertime with its few hours of darkness. It was as if they were storing up daylight for the long winter ahead. They had to stop as an older couple cut them off. She felt her escort's arm tighten with impatience and she gave him a gentle squeeze. They positioned themselves against a pillar opposite the Dressman store where they would corral their captive audience— and Chantal would escape. She eyed the exit to the parking garage on the opposite side of the atrium. When the explosive charge in the garbage can went off, she would help Bashir herd as many people as she could into the store, then slip away.

Would they feel betrayed? Would they give her up under questioning? Probably, but it wouldn't matter. Victor would take care of all that—new identities, plastic surgery, and a life of luxury aboard his fabulous yacht. No one would ever find them.

In the open rotunda, a line of high school boys occupied the railing of the second floor above them. They called down to a group of girls in front of Chantal, who giggled and waved back. She wondered what Ayana was feeling right now. Excitement? Fear? Probably—

"We're being watched," Bashir hissed.

Chantal stiffened, but forced herself to smile and move closer to her partner. "Where?"

"Ten o'clock . . . and three, also. They know we're here!"

A tall, well-built man in his late twenties was pretending to look at his phone, but his gaze slid from the phone every few seconds to rest on them. His gaze met hers and Chantal knew Bashir was right.

"Get down." Bashir pushed her to the floor and whipped out the machine gun pistol from under his jacket. As Chantal looked up, two shots hit Bashir in the chest, spinning him around. The weapon, Bashir's finger still clamped around the trigger, swung wide, spraying bullets everywhere. One of the high school girls went down hard, bleeding from the neck. There was a split second of pregnant silence as the crowd absorbed the sound of gunshots, then pandemonium broke out as everyone rushed away as fast as they could.

On her hands and knees, Chantal scrambled to the parking garage exit. A running woman kicked her in the face, and she crawled over a body in the melee. A rough hand gripped her shoulder and flipped her onto her back. It was the man with the phone from across the hall, and he held a gun in her face.

"I've got you," he said in Finnish. "Police." He kneeled on her chest.

An explosion went off behind him and he whipped his head around. Chantal ripped her own weapon from the holster under her left armpit. The black Beretta felt light and deadly in her hands. She fired once, twice, three times into the policeman's chest. His mouth was open as if he was trying to say something and his body sagged on top of her.

Chantal's ears rang from the explosion and the gunshots, making the chaotic scene around her very quiet. Bits of dust and trash floated through the air.

But she was alive. She heaved the Finnish policeman's body off her own. Then Chantal staggered down the steps into the parking garage.

CHAPTER 50

Liz parked her car in a handicapped spot outside the east entrance of the Mall of America and slipped a tag over the rearview mirror to identify her vehicle as belonging to a law enforcement official. She'd make this a quick trip. The Bloomington police department had an office just inside the mall east entrance. A quick stop in there to let them know she was onsite, then visit mall security and have them call in Zacharia's sister for a chat.

Her phone buzzed. Brendan. She hesitated then sent it to voicemail. Explaining her bizarre behavior this morning was not something she wanted to get into right now and there was no way she was going to tell her fiancé that she was pregnant over the phone. A quick chat with Zacharia's sister, then she'd let the Minneapolis PD handle it from there.

She smiled to herself. Then, she'd tell Brendan—and she'd do it right.

Her stomach growled and Liz had a sudden desire for a soft pretzel with spicy mustard. Maybe she'd get one of those while she was here, too. Her mobile buzzed again. It was Trask this time.

"Tom, what's up?" she said.

"Liz, we just got notification that there's a terrorist attack in progress at the Mall of America." Trask's voice was rushed. "Here's the crazy thing—it came in as a tweet."

"I'm at the mall right now and it looks quiet." She quickened her pace as she walked through the first set of automatic doors. She could see the police department office. "I'll check in with Bloomington PD and—"

The blast shattered the doors in front of her, showering her with glass. Liz fell to the ground, dropping her phone. She clawed for the mobile and checked the screen. Her fingers shook as she redialed Trask.

"It's real," she croaked into the receiver. She could hear gunshots coming from inside the mall and a body lay on the floor inside the east entrance. "Bomb just went off, I can hear gunshots. I'm going in."

Liz used the wall to lever herself to her feet. Nothing broken; a few cuts and plenty of bruises, but she was okay. The interior set of glass doors had protected her from the brunt of the blast. She staggered through the opening, weapon drawn. Bits of trash and what looked like toilet paper floated in the air. Outside the police office stood the remains of a janitor's cart. The source of the explosion.

The body of a black man lay facedown in her path. She dropped to her knees and felt for a pulse. The man was alive. She carefully rolled him onto his back and then sat back in surprise. It was Zacharia Ismail. The bomb was less than twenty feet away. Did he plant the bomb and set it off accidentally?

He stirred and mumbled.

"Zacharia, can you hear me?"

He whispered something. Liz put her ear closer to his lips.

"Allah," he said.

"Allah?" she repeated. A flush of anger made her want to punch the kid in the face. It was definitely him. Liz holstered her weapon and pulled out her handcuffs. "Zacharia Ismail, you are under arrest for—"

Zacharia shook his head violently. "Not Allah," he said through a deep red gash in his dark lips. His right eye was nearly swelled shut, but the look in his good eye made her stop.

"A-ya-na," he said, his words slurring. "Sister."

Liz looked around. "Your sister did this?"

Zacharia nodded.

"And the imam." Liz sat back on her heels. "Ayana shot the imam, and you found him. That's why you called 911 and ran. You figured out what she was doing and you were trying to stop her." It all snapped into place. That's why all the signs pointed to Zachariah but surveillance had yielded nothing.

Right family, wrong kid.

"Shit." Liz thumbed her mobile for Trask's number. He answered immediately. "I found Zacharia outside the Bloomington PD office. It's his sister—we were looking at the wrong person all along." Her gaze traveled to the shattered police office, then back to the young man. "He was coming here to stop her." Gunshots rang out from deep inside the mall. "I'm hearing gunshots inside."

"Liz, initial reports indicate multiple bombs, as many as two, maybe four, at different locations. We've got all available local law enforcement en route to lock down the mall and clear it."

The Mall of America was a massive multi-acre, multi-story

affair. Clearing it would take hours and dozens, maybe hundreds, of officers.

"I'm going in for a look around," she said.

"Be careful, Liz. We have no idea what or who we're dealing with here."

"Yeah. Tom?" She thought about telling Trask to let Brendan know she loved him and was carrying his baby. Then she dismissed the idea. Was she starring in a Lifetime movie?

"Liz? Are you there?"

"Nothing." She ended the call and turned to Zacharia. "I'm going to find your sister. Find Ayana. Okay?"

Zacharia was looking past her at the stairwell behind her, his eyes wide.

"Ayana," he said.

🔥

Kamppi Mall, Helsinki, Finland
04 July 2017 — 2010 local

Chantal staggered into the underground parking garage. The rows of shiny cars were still and silent, as if the carnage upstairs had never happened. Her rapid footsteps echoed on the cement floor as she hurried past the parked vehicles.

Go to the northeast corner of the lowest level. She was all turned around now. Which way was northeast?

Chantal forced herself to stop and draw a deep breath. She'd come down the stairs, the south stairs. Northeast was to her right. She ran through the last section of parking lot. One more turn, then a door.

The door was locked.

She smashed her hip against the crash bar again and again. It couldn't be locked. This was where Victor had said to meet her contact. This was how she had to escape.

She pressed her forehead against the cool metal of the door. *Think!* The police knew about the demonstration before it happened. Had they discovered her contact as well?

She needed to get out of here. Now.

Chantal ran for the automobile entrance. The ramp was steep and winding; her breath came in labored gasps and her heart hammered in her chest. She needed to get away. She needed to get back to Victor. They'd failed. *She* had failed. Victor would be disappointed in her, but he loved her and that was all that mattered.

Chantal could hear the noises on the surface street up ahead of her now. She stopped. The gun! She needed to get rid of her gun or they would know. She stripped off her jacket and wriggled out of the shoulder holster. Gun and holster went over the wall of the parking ramp. She started forward again, then stopped.

What if they knew what she looked like? The police would arrest her and . . .

Chantal ran her hand along the concrete wall. She needed to disguise herself. Swallowing hard, she reared her head back and smashed it against the corner of the wall. The cut in her scalp bled freely. Chantal rubbed her fingers in the blood and smeared it on her face.

Good enough. Chantal pressed her jacket against the side of her face and staggered up the last turn of the ramp.

"Help me!" she cried in Finnish. "I'm hurt!"

A police officer caught her as she collapsed in his arms. She kept her body limp, her face down.

"I've got you. You're alright," he said. He was strong, like Victor. He lifted her up and she buried her face in his broad chest, crying. "It's okay," he said. She bounced lightly in his arms as he jogged her away from the mall.

"I've got an injured woman here," he said, slowing.

"Put her over there," said another voice. "I'll get to her when I can."

Chantal felt herself being lowered to the ground. "You'll be okay. They'll be with you in a minute." She kept her face averted, her eyes in slits.

"Kiitos," she said in Finnish. "Thank you."

When the police officer's tread faded away, she opened her eyes. A team of two paramedics was working on a group of a dozen injured. There was a girl, no more than twenty years old, with a gunshot wound in her shoulder. Her face was bone-white and she shook like a leaf. Chantal got to her feet.

"Please, sit down. I'll be with you in a minute," one of the paramedics said.

Chantal used the wall to help her to her feet. Her head rang, and her right eye was sticky from the smeared blood. She pointed at the corner of the building. "I'm going to be sick," she said.

The paramedic shrugged. Chantal rounded the corner and started running.

She slowed at the end of the block, then made her way at a fast walk to the Hakaniemi metro station. In a public restroom, she cleaned the blood off her face. The wound in her scalp had stopped bleeding under a congealed mess of hair and blood. She poked at the tender flesh, wondering if she would have a scar.

The next eastbound train arrived quickly and Chantal boarded. She took a seat in the corner where she could keep her injury shielded from prying eyes. She needed to get away from Helsinki and contact Victor. Victor would know what to do.

Chantal got off the Metro at the last stop, Vuosaari. She paused on the street, forcing herself to think.

First things first: a disguise. She spied a convenience store across the street. Using her limited Finnish, she bought a mobile phone, a floppy hat, and a pair of sunglasses. Her Finnish was passable, but not good enough to support more than a casual conversation.

Chantal went back to the Metro station and found an out-of-the-way bench. The sun was low on the horizon, but they still had hours of daylight left. This time of year Finland never got completely dark.

She powered up the phone and dialed the emergency number Victor had given her.

It rang once, twice, three times, then four. Chantal's heart sank. Her head throbbed with every heartbeat—she should have picked up some Advil at the convenience store.

"Hello?"

Victor's voice, deep, resonant, comforting, sounded in her ear.

Chantal started to cry.

"Victor, it's me. I'm alive."

CHAPTER 51

No one was supposed to get hurt.

The thought looped in Aya's mind as she squinted at the black and white pictures on the computer screen. It was hard to believe that only minutes ago this entire area had been filled with dancing teenagers, shoppers, and parents who'd been dragged to the Mall of America on their holiday.

Now it was empty, except for bits of trash—and four bodies.

Her phone buzzed. It was Leylo in the bookstore. *Security doors closed,* read the text.

The computer screen was divided into quarters. She leaned closer to see the image of the exterior of the bookstore; she could see movement inside the store. Aya turned to the mall security cop she'd zip-tied to the chair. His nametag said JASON. "How do I make this picture bigger?"

Jason's lips twitched. He looked only a few years older than Aya. This was probably Jason's first job out of school and he was probably wondering if he should resist her request. She picked up the handgun on the desk next to her and pointed it at him.

"Please," she said.

"Double-click on the image, then you can use the joystick to move the camera and zoom in," the young man said sullenly. The other guard, a woman named Mabel, rattled her chair to show her displeasure. Aya had gagged her when she wouldn't stop talking.

It had been remarkably easy to take over the control room at the Mall of America. Over the past months, she'd made a point of hanging around and getting to know the people who worked there. Every day she emptied the waste baskets and made some idle talk with whoever was on duty. When Aya knocked on the door, the security team on duty buzzed her into the control room without a second thought.

That was five minutes to noon.

When the explosions went off, the guards reached for the phone—and Aya reached for her weapon. With Hodan's help, they had Jason and Mabel tied up in no time. More importantly, now they could see anywhere in the mall using the network of high-end cameras.

Aya zoomed in on one of the bodies on the floor of the rotunda. No one was supposed to get hurt. The bombs were supposed to scare people, not hurt them. Madino made the bombs; she was responsible for this.

No. I am responsible for this.

She shifted to the camera outside the Sea Life Aquarium. The security curtain was down and no one stirred in the foyer.

"Leylo says they have twenty-six people in the bookstore. Caaliyah has thirty-two in the aquarium. They're talking to them now." Hodan tapped at her phone. "I'm not seeing anything on Twitter yet. No sign of the hashtag."

Aya nodded, still studying the screens. "It's still early. All the protests are set to start at the same time, remember? Tell them to start with the statements as soon as possible." She scanned the mall entrances one by one, all of which had been locked down as part of the security protocol. No sign of any police officers. Yet. She had no idea how much time they had before the police showed up. Fifteen minutes? An hour?

Her gaze snagged on movement in one of the screens, the upstairs hallway where they'd placed the second bomb. She flinched. Another body lay on the ground, only a few feet from the wreckage of the Bloomington police office.

As she watched, someone—a woman—ran in from outside and bent over the prone form. Aya double-clicked on the image and leaned toward the screen. She toggled the camera and zoomed in on the two people. The woman had her back to the camera, but the man on the ground turned his face in her direction.

Aya's heart skipped. It was Zacharia.

Hodan gasped beside her. "That's your brother, Aya."

The camera's image was sharp, showing her brother's face as bruised and bloody. He was saying something to the woman, but she didn't seem to understand. She leaned down so her ear was close to Zacharia's lips, twisting her face toward the camera. Aya bit her lip so hard she tasted blood.

It was the FBI agent, Elizabeth Soroush.

❁

Liz froze.

"Don't move," a voice said from behind her. A girl's voice, but firm. She heard no trace of nervousness.

She raised her hands. "Don't do anything stupid, Ayana. I'm not wearing body armor. If you shoot me, you'll be killing a federal agent."

"Give me your gun."

"I was just helping your brother, Ayana. We both want to help Zacharia, right?"

"Your gun. Now."

The girl's voice was as hard as the stone floor beneath Liz's knees. She pulled out her weapon and laid it down next to her. "Your brother could die, Ayana." *Keep using her name. Keep talking about her brother.* "He could have internal injuries—he could be bleeding inside right now."

"Shut up. Push your gun toward me."

Liz's Sig Sauer made a scraping sound as it slid over the floor. "The police will be here soon, Ayana. A lot of people—your friends—are going to get hurt if we don't stop this now."

"No one was supposed to get hurt," the girl replied with unexpected sharpness. "Kneel over there, keep your hands on your head."

Liz watched as Ayana knelt down next to her brother. She placed a hand on his forehead.

"Zacharia?" she said. "Can you hear me?"

Her brother stirred, but didn't open his eyes.

Ayana's face took on a hard look and she pointed her weapon at Liz. "Why was he here? Why are you here?"

Liz swallowed. The safety was off on the Beretta. "I was coming to the mall to talk to you. I thought Zacharia shot Imam Nabil and I was looking for him. I wanted to see if you knew where I could find your brother." She saw Ayana flinch when she mentioned Nabby's name. "But he didn't shoot the imam, did he, Ayana? You did."

The muzzle of the gun wavered. "It was an accident. I didn't mean to kill him." The girl's voice had lost the surety of before. She sounded hollow, resigned. Liz considered rushing her for the weapon. Too risky.

"He saw the gun in my bag and we fought over it," Ayana said in a rush. She looked down at her brother. "It just went off. I didn't mean to kill him. I didn't mean to kill anyone." The muzzle dropped a few degrees. "We just wanted people all over the world to wake up, to see how they are treating their own citizens. London, Helsinki, Berlin, and us—we're all one movement. We're the Soldiers of God."

Liz cursed to herself. How could she have been so stupid? The signs were there the whole time, but she'd been so focused on Zacharia that she missed Ayana completely.

"I want you to listen to me very carefully, Ayana," Liz said, keeping her voice as calm and steady as she could. "The imam is not dead. You didn't kill him, I swear it." The girl's eyes narrowed and the muzzle came back up. "But if we don't get help for Zacharia, he could die. I've seen it happen."

Liz paused, watching the emotions play across the girl's face. Ayana took one hand off the gun and stroked her brother's cheek.

"Put the gun down," Liz said. "This doesn't have to end like the Xcel Energy Center. Faruq hurt people and they shot him. Is that what you want to happen? Think about your friends."

"It's not like that!" Ayana was crying now. "We aren't here to hurt anyone, just to scare them a little. Imaan says we need to shake them up to make them listen."

"Imaan? The singer?"

Ayana nodded.

"What does she have to do with this, Ayana?"

Ayana hung her head but stayed silent.

"This was Imaan's idea? She tricked you into doing this?"

"No!" Ayana said in a sharp tone. "She didn't trick me. She didn't make us do anything that—"

"Who warned the police before the attack started?" Liz interrupted. "Was that Imaan's doing also?"

"What do you mean?" Ayana stared at her. The handgun was still pointed in Liz's direction, but angled down at the floor now. The girl wiped her nose with the back of her hand.

"We got a warning on Twitter before the attack started. It called your demonstration a terrorist attack. Who sent it?"

"You're lying." The muzzle rose up from the floor. Liz's breath caught in her throat.

"You have a phone," Liz said. "Check it out for yourself."

Ayana's free hand disappeared under her shawl and reappeared holding her mobile. After a few seconds of one-handed typing, she let out a gasp. "It was sent twenty minutes before noon. No one knew what we were planning—"

"Except Imaan?" Liz asked.

"No!" Ayana got to her feet. The aim on the handgun swung wide. "She would not do that to us, to *me*. I'm her little flower. We're her Soldiers of God." Now the girl was crying so hard she had difficulty catching her breath. Liz shifted her weight to the balls of her feet. If Ayana came just a few steps closer, she would try to take her down.

"Think, Ayana," Liz said in a hard tone. "You're a smart girl. If it wasn't Imaan, then who was it? She set you up—you and all your friends. In a few minutes, the police will come through that door and more people are going to get hurt. Is that what you want?"

Zacharia stirred—finally. "Listen to her, Aya," he said through broken lips. "Listen."

Ayana's convulsive crying slowed to labored breathing. The gun she had trained on Liz wavered and the muzzle slowly angled down as if being dragged down by gravity.

"We can fix this, Ayana," Liz said in a fierce tone. "Together, you and me."

Slowly, the girl knelt down and laid her gun down on the floor. "Help me," she said.

Liz got to her feet.

CHAPTER 52

Leylo scrolled through her Twitter feed. She frowned. The hashtag should be trending by now, but her search on Twitter yielded nothing.

"You," she called to a blonde girl in shorts and a T-shirt. She positioned her against a bookshelf and handed her the slip of paper with the manifesto printed on it. "Read this." She turned to the rest of the people kneeling on the ground. "The rest of you, get out your mobile phones and record her. Then I want you to post it to all your social media sites."

The group of people, mostly teenagers, did as they were told. An older woman stared over Leylo's shoulder at a silent TV screen. Yasmin prodded her with her toe. "You, too. Get out your phone."

The woman pointed up at the muted TV screen over the information desk. A reporter was stationed with a Mall of America sign over one shoulder and the Radisson Blu Hotel rising in the background. The banner read "Terror in the Heartland."

Terror? Yasmin was searching behind the desk for a TV remote to turn up the volume. She finally gave up and climbed on top of the desk to do it manually.

". . . the police say they first learned of the terrorist attack from a tweet sent to the FBI at 11:43AM. It read: 'The Mall of America will come under attack by terrorists at noon.' Police then say that at exactly noon, a series of explosions happened inside the mall. We are getting word that similar attacks happened simultaneously in London, Berlin, and in Helsinki, Finland. Authorities are saying the attacks in the other countries have all been stopped and the terrorists killed. No word on what these groups are after."

Leylo and Yasmin exchanged glances. Yasmin's eyes were wide and her dark face ashen. Someone had told the police about their demonstration before it happened—and called them terrorists. The demonstrators in all the other cities were killed?

The people in the bookstore were all looking at them. A few of them had their phones pointed toward the girls.

"Keep reading!" Leylo shouted, waving her gun at the blonde girl. "Get this posted now!"

Her phone rang. The caller ID said AYA. She swiped the screen. "Aya? What is going on? They are calling us terrorists on television."

"It's over, Leylo. We've been betrayed. Open the gates, let the people go, and wait for the police."

"Aya?"

"It's over, Leylo." Aya's voice was firm. "I'm calling Caaliyah in the aquarium now —"

The sound of a gunshot boomed through the empty mall. It came from the direction of the aquarium.

Mall of America, Minnesota
04 July 2017 — 1230 local

In spite of herself, Liz was impressed with the level of organizational control that Ayana displayed over her operation. She'd single-handedly managed to take down a major private security operation with a few of her teenage friends. She might look unassuming, but Liz—and everyone else—had clearly underestimated the girl.

When Ayana led Liz into the MOA command center, the other Somali girl in the room jumped to her feet.

"Aya, do you know what they are saying about us on TV? They're saying—"

Ayana held up her hand to silence her friend, then she hugged her. "It's over, Hodan. This has all been a mistake. We have to make sure no one else gets hurt." She waved at the security guards. "Let them go, and give your weapon to this woman."

Liz stepped forward and flashed her badge at the security guards. "FBI Special Agent Elizabeth Soroush." She nodded at the older woman, who was rubbing her wrists where the zip-ties had cut into her flesh. "Get on the phone with the local PD. Let them know that there's a wounded man on the second floor east entrance. We're working with the demonstrators now to defuse this situation peacefully."

Liz turned to Ayana. "How do we get in touch with your people?"

Ayana slipped her mobile phone out from under her robes and thumbed her way to a number. She frowned. "No answer from Caaliyah," she said to the other girl. "You try her, Hodan." The second girl produced a mobile phone and started texting.

"We have two girls in the Barnes and Noble bookstore and two in the aquarium," Ayana said to Liz. "They have hostages in each. Our plan was to have the hostages make statements, post them to social media, then let them go." Her tone was wistful, as if she was a little girl reluctantly telling a parent what she'd done wrong. "Caaliyah and Madino, the ones in the aquarium, they're sisters—and very dedicated. I will need to convince them that giving up now is the right thing to do."

Ayana dialed another number and spoke in Somali. Liz couldn't understand what she was saying but it seemed sincere, so she let it pass without comment. Ayana's gaze strayed to the other girl, who shook her head. The look on her face told Liz she was worried.

Ayana's call was coming to an end. She wore a sad smile and she spoke tenderly to the person on the other end of the line.

The sound of a gunshot boomed from somewhere deep inside the building.

"Can you tell me where that came from?" Liz asked the security guard sitting in front of the video screens. He shook his head nervously, looking like he was about to wet himself. Liz turned back to Ayana. The girl's face had drained of color.

"Leylo said she thinks it came from the aquarium," she whispered.

Liz clenched her fists, trying to think. The Mall of America was a huge installation, one that would take law enforcement hours to clear in a measured manner. But an active shooter changed everything. Every second she delayed put those hostages in greater danger. "How do we get in there?"

The female security guard stood up. "I can take you in the back way, through the water processing plant."

The guard led Liz and Ayana through the bowels of the Mall of America at a fast trot. She stopped in front of a set of double doors. Liz peered through the narrow windows to see a three-story room filled with pipes and tanks. The yellow sign on the door said "Hearing Protection Required."

"It's noisy in there," the guard said, still red and puffing from the run. "Follow this aisle about twenty yards in, then take the stairs to the second level. You can access the aquarium from there." She held a keycard over the pad next to the door. "You ready?"

Liz held up a hand. "I'm ready, Mabel. You two are staying here."

"No argument from me, lady," the security guard said. "They don't pay me enough to get shot at."

"I'm going with you," Ayana said. "I started this, it's my fault. Caaliyah and Madino are my friends. I can talk to them. Please, you need me."

Liz studied the girl's face. Some color had returned to her cheeks and her jaw was set. The girl was willing and they were wasting time. She wished again for body armor—for both of them.

"Alright, but stay behind me." The whining noise of the pump room machinery was so loud they couldn't even hear the door close behind them. Liz ran flat out along the corridor of steel grating until she reached the stairs, then took them two at a time to a steel door. Ayana caught up with her, completely out of breath. Liz mimed that she was going to open the door; Ayana nodded.

They stepped into a dim alcove. A long curved glass passageway stretched out to their left, a hundred feet long and completely exposed. Overhead, a school of fish flitted by, followed by a white-bellied shark that had to be at least twelve feet long. The other direction led back out to the lobby. Liz's ears still rang from the noise of the pump room, but she could hear Ayana's heavy breathing beside her. Liz gestured toward the entrance. "We'll go out and raise the security gate. Then see if—"

A gunshot rang out from down the long glass-covered hallway. A few seconds later, there was a deeper boom—a shotgun, Liz decided.

Ayana started running down the glass tunnel. The long shape of the shark passed over her head.

Liz cursed, then ran after her.

CHAPTER 53

Caaliyah stared at her mobile phone. The text from Hodan read: *Aya says to let everyone go. The FBI is here.*

Let everyone go? They hadn't sent out a single post yet, not even a tweet, and they were just giving up? She shot a look at Madino, who was strutting in front of their hostages, brandishing her sawed-off shotgun. Her sister was not going to like this at all.

They'd gathered their captives in the snack bar area, pushing the tables and chairs to one side of the space to make room for everyone to sit on the floor. The aquarium was big enough that there were probably other people hiding in different places, but the sisters decided it was best to stay together.

"Madino," she called. Her sister stopped her pacing and joined Caaliyah next to the snack bar sales counter. She handed her the phone.

Madino's lips compressed as she read the text, making the scar on her chin pucker. "No," she said, handing the phone back.

"What do you mean no?" Caaliyah hissed, aware that the people sitting on the floor were watching them. "Aya said to let them go. We have to do what she says."

Madino glared at her. "Give me your gun," she said, putting her shotgun on the counter. Caaliyah handed her the weapon, a heavy black Beretta 9mm. Madino waved it at their hostages. "Listen! You will do what we say." She pointed the gun at the ceiling and pulled the trigger.

The sound in the small space made Caaliyah's ears ring. She could hear the people screaming, but it seemed like they were very far away. Madino flipped the safety on and handed the handgun back to her sister. Caaliyah's hand was so sweaty the heavy gun almost slipped out of her grasp.

Madino gripped her by the back of the neck, pulling her close. "We are not leaving until we do what we said we were going to do." She turned back to the hostages. "Get out your phones. Now!"

Caaliyah grabbed at her sister's arm. "But what do I tell Aya?"

Madino ignored her. Instead, she pulled a terrified girl from the crowd and handed her the slip of paper with their manifesto printed on it. She ordered the other people to record her reading.

Minutes ticked by and Madino became more frustrated. The first girl was so frightened that she could barely speak above a whisper. Then the lighting in the snack bar was too dim to support some of the people recording and they had to move to a better lighted area.

Caaliyah's phone buzzed again as Hodan tried to call her. She sent it to voicemail. Another text showed up. She deleted it. She watched with growing concern as her sister seemed to be enjoying her role as amateur movie maker, stopping the recording and making adjustments before telling the people with phones to start their recordings over.

Caaliyah pls answer me!!! Hodan's texts were getting frantic. Maybe she'd better give her an update after all. She looked up from the phone to call to her sister and the words died in her throat.

In the brief second she had looked away, a burly man dressed in T-shirt and jeans had snatched up a chair and was bringing it down on Madino. The metal on her sister's head made a dull slapping sound. Madino dropped to the floor.

"No!" Caaliyah screamed, bringing the Beretta to bear. She aimed it at the man and pulled the trigger.

Nothing happened. She pulled it again before realizing that she'd forgotten to turn off the safety. But it was too late.

Someone tackled her from behind. The gun flew out of her hand when she hit the floor. Her face smacked into the tile, and she felt warm blood gush from her nose. She rolled onto her back just in time to see a woman pick up her gun and flip off the safety with her free hand. She was an older woman, with bushy brown hair and glasses. Caaliyah could see a dark spot on the woman's jeans where she'd peed herself.

She pointed the gun at Caaliyah and pulled the trigger.

A force like an enormous fist punched her in the chest. She felt all the breath leave her lungs and a curious numbness seized her torso. Her mouth gaped open and shut, but no breath came in. She was going to suffocate—

A blaze of smoke and fire enveloped the woman who'd shot her. One minute she was there, then she was gone from Caaliyah's sight.

Madino's face appeared over her. She was crying, tears dripping off her round cheeks, running over the scar on her chin. All around her, people were running away, but her sister stayed by her side.

"Caaliyah," she was saying, over and over. "Caaliyah." She could see her sister's lips move, but the sound was so very far away.

Her vision narrowed until all she saw was Madino's face above her. She felt like she was breathing underwater now. Caaliyah could feel the water bubble in her chest.

She blinked heavily. So sleepy. Madino's face grew darker, her features less distinct and the light behind her sister's head so bright. Too bright . . .

Caaliyah closed her eyes.

🔥

Mall of America, Minnesota
04 July 2017 — 1245 local

Liz raced down the glass tunnel, her weapon in hand, expecting to hear another gunshot any second.

Aya was far ahead of her. What had possessed her to bring a civilian kid into this kind of tactical situation? Overhead, fish wandered by in the azure-blue water, not noticing or caring what these people were doing to themselves on the other side of the glass.

The tunnel ended up ahead and Liz slowed. She peeked around the corner, then stepped into the space.

It looked like a cafe area, but all the chairs and tables were pushed to one side of the room. The body of a middle-aged woman lay in front of her, skewed at a crazy angle. It looked like she'd taken a close-range shotgun blast to the left side. Liz knelt and felt for a pulse.

Nothing.

A few strides away, a Somali girl lay flat on her back. Her eyes were closed and her front was soaked with blood. Liz didn't bother feeling for a pulse; she was most definitely deceased.

The place was deserted and there were no weapons in sight. Assuming both of the Somali girls had been armed, that meant there were two guns in the aquarium. Liz surveyed the room. One doorway said EXIT, the other SHARK TANK. She heard yelling from the latter.

"Shark tank it is," she muttered, wishing for the tenth time that she had body armor.

The curving hallway was dim and carpeted. Liz crept down the passage toward the voices. She could make out three distinct people: Ayana's calm tones, a loud, near-hysterical voice of another woman, and what sounded like a man weeping.

"There will be no more killing today, Madino," said Ayana.

Liz stepped into the circular space. A huge sheet of glass filled the wall in front of her, revealing a series of slim, deadly-looking sharks gliding through the blue water. In front of the glass, a man in jeans and a T-shirt was on his knees, his face chalk-white and his breathing labored. He held his hands up as if that was going to shield him from the sawed-off shotgun that was pointed at his head.

"No more, Madino," said Ayana. Using both hands, she trained a 9mm Beretta on the girl with the shotgun. Even from across the room, Liz could see the bright red dot on Ayana's weapon, indicating the safety was off. "Put it down. This is all my fault. No one else is going to get hurt today." Her voice was flat, without intonation.

"Please," whispered the man. He had his eyes clenched shut.

"Caaliyah's dead, Ayana," Madino said in a hoarse voice.

"She's dead because of him." She poked the man in the head with the muzzle of her weapon, eliciting a soft shriek. Then she started to cry. "All we were doing was trying to make people see us for who we are . . . and now Caaliyah's dead." The shotgun muzzle wavered.

Liz spoke: "Madino, my name is Liz. I'm with the FBI. You need to put the gun down. Now." The man started to move away, and Madino poked him again. "Sir!" Liz said sharply. "Stay where you are! Madino, put the gun down."

Ayana moved a step closer to her friend. "Madino, this is all my fault." Liz could hear the tears in Ayana's voice. "You need to put the gun down now or I will shoot you."

The girl was blocking the line of fire between Liz and Madino. "Ayana," Liz said. "I'll handle this. Get out of the way." She side-stepped for a better angle.

Ayana stepped closer to Madino, blocking Liz's shot again. Liz cursed under her breath.

Madino's face hardened. "You," she spat at Ayana. "You give up too easy. Did you really think a few tweets were going to change the world?" Her eyes slid over Ayana's shoulder to rest on Liz. "You want to make a statement, Ayana? Try this one."

Liz saw the muzzle of the shotgun swing in her direction, but Ayana was quicker, using her body to block Madino's shot. Liz dove to the floor to try for a better angle just as the shotgun discharged. The weapon sounded like a cannon in the enclosed space. Liz was dimly aware of Ayana's body flying backwards from the force of the blast.

Liz hit Madino with two shots center mass. Madino dropped the shotgun, then crumpled to the floor. In the tank behind her, the sharks scattered.

Ayana was dead, her battered body propped against the far

wall, but Liz held her hand anyway. The sleeve of the girl's shirt had ridden up her forearm and Liz peeled the material back to show the full tattoo. The mark of the Soldiers of God. Ayana's face was still, her eyes staring at the endlessly circling sharks.

"I could've stopped you," Liz said. "It was all right in front of my face the whole time, but I was too dense to see it."

Liz gently closed the girl's eyes. Her own vision was getting blurry.

"I'm sorry, Ayana. I let you down."

CHAPTER 54

The new computer had cost her five hundred euros, more than half of the cash Chantal had brought with her. She settled herself in the booth of a coffee shop with a clear view of the door.

The call to the emergency number had saved her life. Victor's voice washed over her like a waterfall. She was in his hands now and he knew exactly what to do.

"Get a bus ticket that takes you east, away from Helsinki. Buy a computer and contact me via the chat room in three hours."

The bus to Porvoo was the first bus that went east.

"Find a place to stay the night," Victor told her. "I'll work on getting you out of the country."

"They knew we were coming, Victor. They knew who we were." She bit her lip to hold back the tears. "They're all dead—the entire Helsinki cell."

Silence.

"Victor?"

"All that matters now is that you're safe. Contact me in three hours."

Then he was gone.

After she bought the computer, Chantal checked into the Old Town Bed and Breakfast Ida-Maria, an out-of-the-way private hotel that wouldn't require a credit card. Another hundred and fifty euros gone.

The B&B was mostly empty in midweek and she told the woman behind the counter that she was waiting for her boyfriend to join her. Yes, a bath would be lovely. No, she hadn't heard anything about the shooting in Helsinki at the Kamppi Mall.

Chantal tended to the cut on her scalp—she probably needed stitches, but there was no way she'd chance a hospital—and tried to take a nap. But sleep would not come. She fretted that if she fell asleep she might not wake up in time for her call with Victor . . . and then she'd be alone.

She turned on the TV, searching for an English-language news channel. BBC was running the story of the London attacks nonstop, alternating news updates with expert commentary. The entire London cell had been taken down before the demonstration even started. The same story in Berlin. All dead. She waited for an update on Helsinki and Minneapolis but the commentators seemed more concerned about the riots that had broken out in both cities to protest the killing of Muslim citizens.

The clock on her mobile said 2215 when she left her room to wander the streets of Porvoo.

And now she was here, in this coffee shop, waiting until the little clock in the bottom corner of her computer screen told her she could talk to Victor again. At precisely 2330, she went through the Tor access procedures and logged into the chat room. The timer in the upper right corner of the black screen read 2:00.

Two minutes, that's all the time they had.

Victor went straight to business.

You will meet this man outside the train station at 0600. He flashed up a picture of a man with high cheekbones and thinning blond hair parted in the center of his scalp.

He will have new ID and will get you to St Petersburg.

Chantal's fear evaporated into a laugh of nervous joy. This nightmare would soon be at an end. Victor would make it all right again.

Thank you. We'll be together soon, she typed. There were only a few seconds left on the counter.

No answer.

I love you, she typed.

The counter ran to zero. The computer exited the chat room screen and started an automatic shredder program to erase any trace of their meeting.

Mossad Headquarters, Tel Aviv, Israel
06 July 2017 — 0400 local

Moshi Levin was the Mossad duty officer on the graveyard shift. He yawned and scratched his beard. The first few hours of the shift were always busy—that was when the Americans were still awake—but it usually calmed down after that. He checked his watch. Another hour or so and the day shift would start filtering in.

Tonight had been busy, what with the fallout from the coordinated attacks in London, Helsinki, Berlin, and Minneapolis. For a man who had grown up with the threat of suicide bombers and crazy Iraqi dictators lobbing missiles at his country, those attacks seemed comparatively tame.

As duty officer, his job was to answer the phones, check the message traffic, and be Johnny-on-the-spot for any emergent issues. Most nights it was deadly dull.

At 0412, his computer pinged telling him he had an incoming email. Moshi turned the email pinger on at night when things got slow so that he wouldn't miss any messages. It also kept him awake. He dropped the paperback novel he was reading in his lap and twisted in his chair so he could face the computer without taking his feet off the desk.

The email had no subject line and an unnamed attachment. He snorted. Spam. How was it possible that one of the most advanced spy agencies in the world still got spam in their inbox? He positioned the cursor over the delete icon, then hesitated. He *was* supposed to verify all emails.

He quarantined the attachment and ran the agency virus scan on it. It came back clean.

Moshi opened the attachment and his feet hit the floor. The document had a headshot of a stunning black woman and a travel itinerary for one Safira Mustonen. At the top of the page was a single word: Helsinki.

With his free hand, Moshi reached for the desk phone.

CHAPTER 55

Minneapolis, Minnesota
07 July 2017 — 0530 local

Brendan let his girlfriend sleep. After the week she'd had, Liz needed her sleep.

He laced up his running shoes and set off around Lake Calhoun. As it did every morning, his bad knee creaked and groaned, but once he got the joint moving he was able to keep up a respectable pace. It was one of those muggy Minnesota mornings that reminded him of his childhood. The new sun lit up wisps of fog that clung to the glass-still lake like smoke. The early runners were out, some nodding as they puffed by, but most lost in their own early morning meditations.

The only thing that would make this day better would be if he had a dog. A friend he could count on. But to have a pet, they'd need to move out of Liz's apartment. Brendan let his thoughts wander as his feet moved. That might not be a terrible idea . . . in fact, maybe that's exactly what they needed—more space. His transfer back to Minneapolis with the CIA had seemed ideal at first, but more and more he wondered where they were headed as a couple. He was proud of her, but Liz's mind was so occupied with work that half the time he felt like he was intruding on her life.

Brendan chided himself. *Your girlfriend just stopped a terrorist attack on the Mall of America and you're whining about not having enough quality time with her.*

The nonstop news cycle called it a terrorist attack in America's heartland, but Liz told a different story. A group of Somali teenagers—all girls—who'd been duped into starting a demonstration that someone, somewhere, tried to turn into a bloodbath. In Berlin, London, and Helsinki, all the demonstrators had been killed before anything even started. It was only in Minneapolis that most of the protesters survived.

Liz hadn't even been home until yesterday afternoon, two days after the attack. Brendan had taken her a fresh set of clothes on Wednesday morning and came away alarmed. Liz looked terrible. Haggard and pale, Liz had given him a kiss on the cheek and said she was still under the weather, but she'd be home as soon as she could.

Brendan had cooked a full dinner when she got home Wednesday night with all of her favorites: spaghetti carbonara, garlic bread, Caesar salad, and red wine. Liz had nibbled at the salad, had a few bites of pasta and ignored the wine altogether. Mostly she just wanted to tell him about the Somali girl, Ayana, and how brave she'd been in her final moments as she tried to make amends for what she'd done.

He let her talk. Eventually, the conversation petered out, leaving Liz looking sad and Brendan a little frustrated at her lack of appetite. Then she went to bed.

Liz was normally a light sleeper, but last night she'd been especially restless, calling out in her sleep and tossing back and forth.

Brendan picked up the pace and decided to take the long route around the adjoining Lake Harriet. The death of the Somali girl had hit Liz hard, he knew, but the discussion they needed to have about their relationship had been brewing for weeks. If they were going to build a life together, he needed more from Liz as his partner. She needed to spend a few less hours at work and a few more hours with him.

And a dog. They were going to get a dog, he decided. If that meant they had to move out of their one-bedroom apartment, then so be it.

Sweat darkened the front of his shirt as he passed the Lake Harriet Bandshell on his way back home. He powered up a small hill, focusing on the run instead of his relationship, letting the exercise cleanse his thoughts.

When he finally rounded the last curve, he slowed to a walk, enjoying the feel of his heart pounding in his chest. The brace around his knee was soaked with sweat, but the joint felt pretty good otherwise—better than it had felt in months.

Brendan sat on the grass and watched people walking their dogs around the lake. The serious early morning runners were slowly being replaced by the more casual walkers, the kind who walked with cups of coffee and mobile phones and dogs.

A chocolate Lab, Brendan decided. That's what we're going to get.

He heaved himself to his feet and walked across the street, casting a glance up to their apartment balcony, half-expecting Liz to be there. The balcony was empty.

Brendan took the stairs, taking his time. Their apartment was dark and still. He opened the blinds to let the sun in and made himself a coffee. He was still standing there, watching the activity around the lake, when Liz came into the kitchen.

"No breakfast this morning?" she said.

Brendan didn't turn around. "I would make it if I thought you'd eat it, but you don't seem to like my cooking."

"Just kidding, Bren. Chill out."

He whirled on her. She wore one of his old Naval Academy T-shirts that barely covered the tops of her thighs. She still looked thin and pale, but the gaze that met his was steady.

"We need to talk," she said.

"You're damn right we need to talk, and I want to go first."

Liz held up her palms. "Okay, tiger, you go first."

"I want a dog, Liz."

"Okay . . . you know that we can't—"

"I don't care," Brendan broke in. "I know we can't have a pet in this apartment, but I want a dog anyway. And if we have to move, then let's move. I think we need a place to call our own."

"Alright, let's do it."

Brendan frowned. He'd been ready with another argument. "You're okay with moving?"

Liz smiled. "Yeah, what the hell, let's move. It's a good idea."

"And another thing: I want you to stop working so much."

"I agree with that, too."

Brendan set his mug on the coffee table. "Are you screwing with me?"

Liz took a step closer. "Nope, I think you're one hundred percent right on both counts. Now we get to my conditions."

Brendan reached out and swiped a strand of hair out of Liz's eyes. "As long as I can get a chocolate Lab, you can do whatever you want."

"Fair enough," she replied. "I want to pick out the color of the nursery in our new house."

It was almost as if the gears in Brendan's brain started to slow down. His thoughts felt like they were surfacing through mud. "Nursery? That's . . . oh my God. Liz? Are you pregnant? *That's* what's been going on with you?"

She slid her arms around his sweaty torso, hugging him tight. Brendan felt his knees go weak as the enormity of her words swept over him. He pushed her back, gripping her by the shoulders.

"I don't know what to say."

"You could start by saying you want to be a father."

"Lizzie, of course I do! I'm just—" He bent to kiss her, but she put her fingers over his mouth.

"Not a good idea. I'm liable to throw up on you."

"Alrighty, then." He folded her back in his arms, kissing the top of her head. "Hey, I can still get a dog, right?"

CHAPTER 56

National Counterterrorism Center (NCTC), McLean, Virginia
07 July 2017 — 1400

Don Riley put the picture up on the shared screen so the assembled members on the secure video-teleconference could see it.

"This is Chantal Deveraux, a.k.a. Imaan, a folk singer of Somali descent and the only known link between the attacks in all four locations." The headshot showed a striking woman with fiery brown eyes, fine features, and skin the color of rich caramel. "Born in Somalia to a Somali mother and a Canadian diplomat father, she grew up in Toronto. At age seventeen she became a YouTube star and wrangled that fame into the persona of Imaan. Her music was the darling of lost causes all over the world but was especially popular in the Somali diaspora, which spread out around the world after that country collapsed in the late 1980s."

"And you think this singer is the mastermind behind all four attacks?" growled Admiral Daugherty. "She had the training to inspire four disparate groups of people to launch attacks on Western nations. Was she an ISIS agent?"

Don cleared his throat. "Sir, I believe the use of the word 'attack' might be overstating the situation. I believe they were intended to be demonstrations against the treatment of Muslims in the West."

Daugherty's tone was acid. "Demonstrations? Since when do people demonstrate with guns and bombs, Riley?"

"It's true that all four groups were armed, but handguns only and very little ammunition. In the case of the Minneapolis cell, these were all teenage girls, inspired by Imaan and led by a local girl. During their takeover of the Mall of America, they had ample opportunity to kill their hostages, but instead they were telling their hostages to read a statement and post it on social media."

"What about the other attacks?"

"Well, sir, here's the thing. We don't have any other survivors. All of the demonstrators—or attackers, if you prefer—were killed before they even got started. In each case, the police were tipped off in advance. It was a bloodbath."

The rest of the attendees were silent as Daugherty grilled Don. The admiral's eyebrows touched as his frown deepened. "So your theory is that this Deveraux woman recruited these demonstrators, then set them up to be slaughtered? Why?"

"The backlash from Muslim communities in the West has been very harsh, sir. If someone wanted to stir up tensions on both sides of the religious divide in the West, this is the way to do it. There's been almost continuous rioting in London and Berlin since the events and here we've seen a new rash of anti-Muslim rhetoric—"

"Thank you, Riley," the admiral said dryly, "I watch the news.

You don't need to remind me what I'm hearing in my own country. What can you tell me about who's behind this?"

"I don't know, sir." There was no shortage of terrorist organizations claiming responsibility, but none of them checked out. "I—I think we're dealing with a new group."

"Not Daesh? Not al-Qaeda?"

"No, sir, this feels . . . well, it feels personal. Why would you take out your own people before they were even able to do anything?"

"And you say this Deveraux woman led the Helsinki attack and then escaped?"

"Yes, sir," Don replied. "She's disappeared."

"Riley?"

"Yes, sir." Don steeled himself for what he knew was coming.

"I pay you to give me answers, not questions. Find her."

After the meeting ended, Don left the picture of Chantal Deveraux on his screen. "Where are you?" he whispered.

CHAPTER 57

Damascus, Syria
07 July 2017 — 1900 local

Who doesn't love a Finn? Chantal accepted the appropriately worn passport back from the Syrian customs official with a gracious smile.

"Enjoy your stay in Damascus," the customs officer said in English. His gaze flickered over her face, then swept down the front of her blouse, lingering on the enticing gap in the silk material.

"Shokran," she replied, slipping the passport into her Hermes purse. "Thank you."

Victor had outdone himself. Her alias, Safira Mustonen, was the adopted Somali daughter of a fabulously wealthy Finnish industrialist. Her persona dripped wealth, from the Dolce & Gabbana outfit to the Christian Louboutin shoes to the Coach hand luggage. In spite of the stress of being on the run, the trappings of wealth excited her more than she expected. This was a taste of her new life with Victor. A shiver of anticipation rippled over her and she felt a secret smile bend her lips.

"Ms. Mustonen?" A voice intruded. She walked past, lost in thought.

The voice followed her. "Ms. Mustonen? Madam?"

Mustonen, that was her! She spun on her heel to face a stocky young man with intense dark eyes and a close-cropped beard. "Yes?"

He held up a hand-lettered sign with her name printed on it. He made a nervous half-bow. "I am your driver," he said in broken English.

Chantal studied him. The man looked ill at ease in the black suit and he lacked the veneer of a service professional. She pointed past him at a black leather Coach handbag. "My bag." Then she turned and walked out the door.

The limo was a well-appointed Mercedes. The door made a satisfyingly expensive thump when it closed, shutting out the chaos of the Damascus airport. The driver's dark eyes—she should have asked him his name—appeared in the rearview mirror. "The drive to Beirut will take approximately two hours, but please allow time for the border crossing."

Chantal pulled a bottle of water from the holder. "Fine. Put up the divider, please. I wish to be alone."

With the divider up and the city of Damascus in deep twilight, Chantal felt like she was sealed in a capsule. The Syrian civil war had ended nearly six months ago, but it was a brokered peace and an uneasy one at that. Even with Bashar al-Assad in exile and UN peacekeeping troops in place, she still had a sense that violence was just under the surface. Chantal let her gaze wander over the shattered landscape that flew by her window. What exactly were they fighting for? Was there anything left?

It only got worse as they left Damascus proper and entered the countryside. Entire towns had been leveled, replaced by improvised shanties and tents with smoky campfires out front. Chantal saw precious little signs of rebuilding amidst the devastation.

But she was safe, here in her capsule, under Victor's protection. The nervous energy of the last few days began to trickle away. In hindsight, her trip had been surprisingly uneventful. The Finns really were the friends of the world. With the aid of her Finnish passport, obvious wealth, and airline tickets departing from St. Petersburg, they crossed from Finland into Russia with no trouble at all. After her flight from St. Petersburg to Moscow, she'd stayed overnight at the Moscow airport hotel—already booked by Victor, of course—then departed for Damascus the following afternoon.

Her heart sank as she'd watched the television coverage of the attacks from her hotel room in Moscow. In London and Berlin, all her people were killed before their protests even started. According to Al Jazeera, the Finns knew there was still a member of the Kamppi Mall attackers at large, but all they knew was that it was a dark-haired woman. The rest of her cell was dead. In Minneapolis, three girls were dead, the rest had surrendered. Chantal wondered if Ayana was among the living. She hoped so.

She alternated between weeping and ranting to herself about the betrayal. Their demonstration had turned into a bloodletting, sparking protests all over the west. Who had betrayed them?

A sharp rap on the window next to her head snapped her back to reality. She rolled down the window to reveal a Lebanese border officer. "Passport, please," he said in English.

It was full dark now and the floodlights of the border station cast harsh shadows all around the car. The officer accepted her passport, inspected it using a penlight, then handed it back and waved her through.

Who doesn't love a Finn?

After the devastation of Syria, the Lebanese countryside looked almost idyllic. Real buildings still standing, streetlamps lit, people eating and laughing in cafes. She was back in civilization. Chantal sat up in her seat, imagining she was in one of these tiny restaurants with Victor next to her. *Just one more day and we'll be together.* Where would he take her first? Someplace far away, she guessed. Maybe South America or Asia.

The Phoenician Hotel stood on a small hill outside Beirut, overlooking the Mediterranean Sea. As they passed through the wrought iron gate, the building reminded her of a Spanish castle. The doorman carried her bag from the limo to the marble front desk where the manager waited with her room key. He personally escorted her to the penthouse suite and threw open the sliding glass doors onto her own private patio. The Mediterranean Sea glittered in the light of a just-risen crescent moon.

"You grace us with your presence, Madam," the manager said in English.

Chantal gave him a generous tip and remained on the patio. She leaned on the balcony, dragging in a deep lungful of the sea air. Below her the city rolled out like a miniature setting: tiny car taillights winked in red, people the size of her pinky nail walked the streets singly or in pairs, squares of yellow lights in hundreds of tiny houses.

And she stood above it all. Free. Safe.

She spun away from the railing and did a pirouette in the dark. Soon her love would call and they would be together. This was the end of her journey to freedom.

Chantal's stomach growled and she realized she hadn't eaten since breakfast. She was in the mood for something sweet, something decadent. She called room service and ordered a chocolate mousse and a large brandy. Checking her watch, she almost squealed with excitement.

2130. Victor would call in thirty minutes! She slipped the new mobile phone out of her purse and made sure it was switched on.

Chantal stepped out of her blouse and skirt, then stripped off her bra and panties. She stood in front of the mirror, tracing the imprint the lace of her bra had left on her breasts. The breeze from the patio stiffened her nipples. She shivered at the sensation.

A knock at the door startled her. She pulled a silk robe from her luggage and shrugged into it. She hugged the thin material against her naked skin. "Who is it?"

"Room service."

Chantal flung open the door.

The man in the hallway was not dressed in the uniform of the Phoenician Hotel, and he did not carry a tray of brandy and chocolate mousse. But he did carry a pistol, and the end of the weapon was blunted by a long silencer.

The muzzle swung up until it seemed like she should be able to see all the way down the barrel. There was noise like someone punching a pillow and the sight left her right eye.

Chantal was falling backwards. Her face was warm. Her body must have bounced off the tile, but she didn't feel any pain. The man stepped into the room, letting the door shut behind him. He stood over her.

Chantal tried to form the words. "Victor is coming," she tried to say. "Victor." But her mouth seemed to be disconnected from her brain.

The end of the gun moved again. This time it pointed at her chest. It spat twice in quick succession.

Chantal Deveraux's world went dark.

CHAPTER 58

Somewhere on the coast in Equatorial Guinea
08 July 2017 — 2330 local

I have him. Finally.

Reza Sanjabi lowered the binoculars and allowed himself a satisfied grin. After nearly a year of false leads and cold trails, he had him in his sights. Rafiq Roshed, the man who had nearly started World War III, who put the entire Islamic Republic of Iran at risk of a nuclear strike, who put Reza's beloved Hassan Rouhani at risk.

He had him.

There were many things Reza *should* do right now. Back off and call in the Americans, for one. He weighed that option. The US could probably capture Rafiq alive and had the capability to render him to someplace where he'd never be found, but that would almost certainly mean he'd be lost to Reza.

He could call the five-man team he had stationed a hundred yards behind him. Maybe not as good as what the Americans

BRUNS & OLSON

could put up, but they were here and they would get the job done. That was the smart play, Reza decided.

And then there was the last option. Take him alone, mano a mano. After all, Reza had the element of surprise and his relationship to Rafiq had a certain personal edge to it.

Reza felt a stirring deep in his chest, a feeling he'd not felt in years. The need for blood.

In his special operations unit during the war, they'd called Reza a *djinni*. He had a knack for killing in those days—and a knack for staying alive. The Iran–Iraq War and its aftermath was a simpler time for Reza. The good guys were good and they deserved to live; the bad guys deserved to die—and that was his job. When he dispatched the bad guys that place deep in his chest felt at peace.

That was a lifetime ago, he told himself. You were a different man then, a younger man, a simpler man, a man who saw the world not in shades of gray, but in stark black and glaring white.

But *this* . . . this was personal. Rafiq had put at risk everything Reza held dear—his country, his mentor, his life. Tonight the *djinni* would make an encore appearance.

He keyed his radio. "Stay in position for twenty minutes or until I call," he said in Farsi.

"Yes, sir." The grudging tone suggested his man didn't agree with Reza's assessment of the tactical situation.

The jungle around him was alive with noise and Reza could hear the surf crashing in the distance, beyond the breakwater. He paused on the edge of the greenery, raising the binoculars one last time.

He surveyed the low-slung villa of brick and stucco. A light burned in the bedroom at one end of the house and a night-light in the kitchen on the opposite end of the property cast a dim glow in that window. In the center of the villa was a patio, his entry point. The surveillance team had reported all the house servants were off the property and accounted for. He swung the binocs to the left. A large oceangoing yacht was tied up to the pier. It seemed that Rafiq had managed to keep some of his Argentinean wealth after all.

Reza dropped the binocs to the ground and ran across the broad lawn to the patio. He was slightly winded by the time he flattened himself against the rough stucco wall. For a full three minutes, he listened for any sign that his approach was noticed.

Nothing.

The lock on the French door was an artifact of a less secure era, but he had a key from the villa staff all the same. He stepped inside and moved quickly against the inside wall so as not to provide a silhouette. Reza stilled his breath and listened.

The only sound was the ticking of a clock on the mantelpiece above a wide hearth.

On soft-soled shoes, he stole toward the bedroom at the back of the house. Reza froze when he heard a scraping noise from the kitchen behind him, exactly like the sound of a chair moving on a stone floor when someone stood up.

He switched directions, brought his weapon up, and pushed through the swinging door into the kitchen.

A dog was tied to a kitchen chair. It looked up at him and whined.

A tremendous punch in his right shoulder blade spun him around. His gun slipped out of his grasp and clattered to the stone floor. Reza gasped for breath; his legs lost their footing and he was on his back.

Rafiq Roshed stalked into the room, his weapon pointed at

Reza's head. A trickle of smoke wafted out of the suppressor on the end of the handgun.

The floor chilled Reza's skin except where his blood had warmed the stone. His shoulder was numb—for now. Rafiq kicked away Reza's gun and stripped him of his radio. "How long do we have?" he said with a wicked smile. "I know you have men out there. How long?"

Reza gritted his teeth. The pain was starting to kick in. His only chance was to keep Rafiq talking until his backup arrived . . . fifteen minutes more? Ten minutes?

"You," he said through clenched teeth.

Rafiq laughed and stepped over Reza's body. He released the dog and fondled his ears for a moment before putting him outside. He winked at Reza. "He's a good watchdog."

Play for time.

"Do you know who I am?" Reza said.

Rafiq pulled a chair closer and looked down. "Reza Sanjabi, Director of Quds Force Special Intelligence Branch, lapdog of President Hassan Rouhani, and secret savior of the Islamic Republic of Iran. Do I have all that correct?"

Reza's vision wavered. "You killed Aban."

Rafiq's eyes narrowed to slits. "I did. Right under your nose, too." He laughed again. "I'm ashamed to admit I was related to that piece of shit. You knew I had help, right? It was an inside job."

Reza nodded.

Rafiq spun the chair around and straddled it. The gun hung loosely in his grip. "Holy man, ha! He died with a whore on his lap. Did you know that?" The silencer swung toward Reza's head.

"I have something you want," Reza said.

"What's that, Reza? May I call you Reza? What could you

possibly tell me that would convince me to let you live another second?" He squinted down the gun sights at Reza's head.

"I was there when Nadine died."

It might have been Reza's imagination, but he thought he saw the muzzle of the gun start to shake. Rafiq leaned over him and whispered, "You were there?"

Reza nodded. He was so sleepy. *Focus.* "I was there."

"Who killed her?"

Reza said nothing. Rafiq pushed the end of the silencer into Reza's shoulder. "Who? Who killed my wife?"

The pain was like a hot poker in his shoulder. Reza saw stars and hovered on the edge of consciousness. In his mind's eye, he saw Nadine's body, her nightgown splotched with red where the bullets had cut her down.

"Who?" The voice was insistent and the pain in his shoulder went off the charts.

Reza mumbled. The pain stopped and Rafiq's face appeared above him.

"Tell me and I'll let you live."

How much longer? To Reza, it seemed like he'd been on the floor for hours. Surely twenty minutes had passed by now.

He tried to spit at Rafiq, but his mouth was bone-dry. Reza willed his eyes to stay open.

"I saw Nadine die," Reza rasped.

"Who? Who did it?" Rafiq's face swam in and out of Reza's vision. The muzzle poked his shoulder again, but the pain seemed less now and the chill from the floor had seeped into his flesh. He struggled to keep his eyelids open.

Stay. Awake.

"Tell me!" Rafiq slashed him across the face with the handgun.

Reza heard the metal of the barrel connect with his teeth, but he felt no pain.

Reza had nothing left to give. He shook his head. He tried to snarl at Rafiq, to show one last act of defiance, but to his ears it sounded like air leaving a deflated balloon.

A flash of terrible anger crossed Rafiq's face. The blunt end of the suppressor hovered over Reza's chest and little puffs of fire and smoke spat at him. He counted them as his eyes closed.

One, two, three . . .

Rafiq Roshed held the empty weapon over Reza's bloody body. The muzzle wavered in his shaking hand.

Nadine . . .

He kicked the corpse. How dare he even mention her name?

His hands automatically ejected the empty clip from the Walther and inserted a fresh one. Then he exited the house and walked swiftly to the jetty. The captain was waiting.

"Get us underway. Now."

The three-man crew threw off lines as the big engines rumbled to life. Rafiq looked back at the jungle. The sound of his engines would surely bring in Reza's men. The deck tilted upward as the powerful yacht gained speed toward the breakwater.

The explosion ripped through the night sky behind him just as the ship hit the first swells of the open Atlantic Ocean. Rafiq smiled to himself. That would be the first booby-trap. He ticked off the seconds until the next explosion happened. The second blast was even bigger, designed to take out the men who tried to help their injured comrades. He nodded with satisfaction. That would keep the Iranians busy for a while.

For a long time, Rafiq watched the lights of the shore grow dimmer, then disappear altogether. He should have spent more time on Reza Sanjabi, found out a bit more about their search for him. His last informant claimed that the Iranians were working with the Americans to track him down. Hard to believe . . .

He gripped the railing until his knuckles turned white. But then Sanjabi had mentioned Nadine and all Rafiq could see was red. He took a deep breath and let it out slowly. The rage he'd felt as he killed the Iranian was gone, locked up again in that place in his mind where he kept his past life.

Rafiq pulled a briefcase from the floor and snapped it open on the table. He pulled out a passport and mobile phone, then strolled back onto the fantail.

He flipped open the passport, studying his photo. He tore it in half and dropped it into the ocean.

"Goodbye, Victor."

As he scrolled through the few photos on the phone, a faint smile bent his lips. She had certainly been a beautiful woman, he thought, already comfortable thinking of Chantal in the past tense.

Rafiq tossed the phone into the water.

THE END

Thanks for reading.

If you enjoyed this book, please tell your friends and leave a review on Amazon. As independent authors, we get our readers the old-fashioned way: one at a time via personal endorsements from other readers, like you.

If you'd like to find out more about the Two Navy Guys and their other books, visit www.davidbruns.com.

About the

David Bruns

David earned a Bachelors of Science in Honors English from the United States Naval Academy. That's not a typo. He's probably the only English major you'll ever meet who took multiple semesters of calculus, physics, chemistry, electrical engineering, naval architecture, and weapons systems just so he could read some Shakespeare. It was totally worth it.

He spent six years as a commissioned officer in the nuclear-powered submarine force chasing the Russians before leaving the Navy for corporate life in the mid-90s. For two decades, he schlepped his way around the globe as an itinerant executive in the high-tech sector, and even did a stint with a Silicon Valley startup.

David is the author of the sci-fi series *The Dream Guild Chronicles* and other works of speculative fiction. He and his family have visited over two dozen countries and almost all fifty states, but Minnesota is home.

Authors

J. R. Olson

Commander, US Navy (Retired)

Jon, a born and bred Minnesotan, graduated from the US Naval Academy in 1990 with a BS in History and a commission as an Ensign in the US Navy. His assignments during his twenty-one-year career included duty aboard aircraft carriers and amphibious ships; participation in numerous operations around the world, including Iraq, Somalia, Bosnia, and Afghanistan; and service to the Navy as a CIA-trained case officer. His final assignment before retirement was as the US Naval Attaché at the US Embassy in Helsinki, Finland. Jon earned an MA in National Security and Strategic Studies at the US Naval War College, as well as his Navy parachutist badge, logging thirty-five jumps during his career.

Jon and his wife, Melissa, reside in Webster, Minnesota on their five-acre hobby farm, where they care for their fruit trees and their six rescue dogs. He teaches courses on the US Intelligence Community at Carleton College and Metropolitan State University and has numerous philanthropic pursuits. Prior to his collaboration on *Weapons of Mass Deception*, Jon co-authored a screenplay on the Falklands War of 1982.

66253929R00193

Made in the USA
Columbia, SC
16 July 2019